Praise for *One Woman Three Men*

One Woman Three Men explores a different perspective on romance with an eye to blending philosophy, fiction, and real-world relationship concerns. Nothing is perfect or easy here, whether the goal is traditional or alternative in nature—but in the course of following the diary writer's life and revelations, readers gain a better sense of the sexual and psychological differences between men and women and the ideals and realities that can come between them . . .

A spicy, thought-provoking read steeped in entertaining moments and intriguing blends of psychological and philosophical inspection: a perfect romantic alternative to one-dimensional, singular novels about relationships.

—*D. Donovan, Senior Reviewer, Midwest Book Review*

One Woman Three Men

One Woman Three Men

A Novel About Modern Love and Sex

POULINE MIDDLETON

OVER AND ABOVE
PRESS

Editor: Rick Benzel
Cover and Book Design: Susan Shankin & Associates
Published by Over And Above Press
Over and Above Creative Group
Los Angeles, CA
overandabovecreative.com

All characters and plots in this book are a work of creative fiction.
Any resemblance to current or past persons and events is strictly coincidental.

First edition
Library of Congress Control Number: 2015920574
ISBN: 978-0-9890917-8-7
Printed at Bang Printing in the United States of America
10 9 8 7 6 5 4 3 2 1
Distributed by SCB Distributors

If you enjoyed reading this book, please share it
with others on Facebook, Twitter and other social media.
We'd also appreciate your review of it on Amazon or other book review websites.

CONTENTS

SATURDAY, APRIL 11 ᵀᴴ

Dear Diary

'VE BEEN A NICE, well-behaved Danish girl for years, believing that my good behavior would help create peace in 'Palesrael,' equal wages for men and women, and reduced poverty in Africa, while I waltzed into the Copenhagen sunset with my prince, till death do us part. Well, none of this has happened. They're still insisting that war is the way to peace, that women aren't good at negotiating and that's why we don't get equal wages, and that money must continue to flow to support dictatorial regimes even if they have no intention of reducing poverty.

And on a personal level my love life has been blown to pieces yet again, leaving me with no clue as to how to find that prince and move on.

My last love disaster happened right after New Year's . . . Thomas and I were walking on the beach and I was savoring the wind in my hair. He had just flown in from Barcelona where he had gone to sell a painting. I was certain he was on the verge of a big artistic breakthrough. He was painting more and more, using the new oils I had ordered from Milan, and they were helping him with the depth of color and nuances he'd been seeking.

He was not usually one for taking walks as soon as his plane touched ground, but on the way home, he parked at Amager Beach Park right outside the airport, saying he needed to get some fresh ocean air after the stuffy flight. I remember that as we started walking, I slipped my arm into the crook of his, but instead of pulling me closer to him like he usually did, he just kept walking, as if he was trying to get away from me. I reckoned he was tired, and I felt overwhelmed with love for him after what I thought was his grueling three-day trip away.

He was really the best thing that had happened in my life, ever since my divorce from Sebastian, another artistic type whom I was certain I could help. Sebastian and I had met at his band's concert in Berlin when I was 24 and I had been crazy about him. I felt drawn to his intensity both on- and off-stage. He was so sensitive that beautiful music actually raised the hairs on his sexy forearms! When I was seven, I had seen the same thing happen on my father's arms during a Bach organ concert. But while my father is an eccentric though astutely perceptive research scientist, Sebastian turned out to be a rather conventional bass player who spent all his time dreaming about his band's eventual fame, which never happened.

After the divorce, our daughter Mille (age 6 at the time) became my everything. Luckily I only had to be without her every other weekend, which was all that Sebastian could handle of her, the cad. Over time she got used to the arrangement. One morning she looked up at me and said, "Mom, you look tired." I glanced in the mirror, and saw that my kid was better at identifying how I felt than I was.

The next day I enrolled in a Goddess school that my girlfriend Rebecca had been raving about. I wanted to get away from a 'me' I no longer recognized. It took half a year of creating art with emotion, eating unknown foods with all of my senses, soothing my skin with wonderful fabrics from India while listening to other women's stories and sharing mine with them to reconnect with my Goddess self. Little by little, I felt my dreams, wishes and needs rise to the surface again, like a plant that had been submerged in heavy rain lifting itself upwards to the newly reappearing sunshine. Slowly, I regained my pride in being a woman.

Then I dated around for a while, until I met Thomas. He was so refreshing and, well, metrosexual, the first man like that I had ever met. As a struggling artist, he didn't feel threatened by my executive position, and we never fought about money or competed with each other. Mille loved Thomas, too; she even called him Daddy just three weeks after meeting him. The only exception to our smooth relationship were my books, which he felt were everywhere, taking over the house. He pointed this out to me at regular intervals with different levels of frustration in his voice.

Walking there on the beach with him, I was so grateful for our life and the fact that he was so sweet to my girl. But Thomas walked quickly, and I had to make an effort to keep up with him. I felt rushed but didn't pick up on what was coming. He led us toward the pier and turned right. I finally asked if he had had a good trip and managed to sell the painting.

"We need to talk," he said, as he continued walking straight ahead. The thought crossed my mind again that I would have liked to go to Barcelona with him, but Thomas and his French friend Jean-Paul have been going there together every January for years, and I didn't want to break their tradition.

"Something happened in Barcelona," he finally blurted out. He kept walking. "I'm sorry, Elizabeth."

I looked at him. He seldom called me by my full name rather than my nickname, Dixie. My whole body tensed; something was coming.

"I went there with a woman that I've been seeing the last six months. I meant to tell you about it, but it was difficult," he said.

What?!? Then his words, his implication, hit me like a baseball bat from behind. My arm fell from his and I slowed down. He kept walking, saying something I couldn't quite understand. I caught up with him and heard him repeating, "It wasn't supposed to happen like this, but she and I are getting serious, so I have to tell you about it. I'm really sorry."

I walked as if in a trance, my throat tightening. Everything around me seemed to freeze in time and I was unable to do anything to stop it. I blinked in slow motion until I couldn't open my eyes anymore, my tears starting to well up in the corners. The cold wind blew right through my clothing like a sieve. The only thing I could hear was its howl growing louder and louder.

Thomas stared straight ahead and strode directly into the wind as if he needed to get some place. Rage welled up inside me; I seized his arm, trying to make him stop. He tore his arm away, but the force of my grip surprised us both. He stopped and turned away from me. I wanted to scream, but instead I just stood there, glaring at the back of his head.

"She is also an artist," he murmured. "We have a lot in common."

"What do you mean?"

"Well, you know," he said.

"No I don't know," I screamed at him. "You need to come home and paint so you can be ready for a show!"

Tears were now streaming down my cheeks. Suddenly I was 12 years old again. It was early morning and the dim grey Danish winter light my mother loved was filtering through the windowpanes. I was supposed to be leaving for school, but if I left, I knew my mother would stay in bed all day and miss the sunlight that made her so happy. The inner urgency I knew so well made me set down my bag and enter her room. She was still in bed. Gently, I pulled her out of bed and helped her get dressed and brought her over to the studio. She slipped from my arms, landing on the floor with a thud. I lifted one of the unfinished canvasses that was leaning against the wall, pointed to a deep cerulean blue and praised her. She stared at me blankly. I set the painting on her easel and suggested she use it for inspiration, and then I gave her an encouraging smile for the umpteenth time and left for school with a knot the size of large melon in my stomach.

When I came home five hours later, I entered the house filled with anxiety and found her sprawled out on the studio floor, holding an empty bottle of vodka in one hand. The painting was torn to shreds, and she lay with her head resting on a bit of cerulean blue canvas. The sensation of distress I knew so well filled me. She was always on the verge of checking out, and I was convinced it was my responsibility to prevent her from doing it. I raced over to her and felt her wrist. Her pulse was weak but it was there.

"We need to talk," Thomas insisted again, bringing me back to the present.

My tears kept pouring out. This wasn't the Thomas I knew. My Thomas loved me more than anything on earth. I've been supportive. I've done everything I could to help him see life's possibilities instead of its obstacles. What the hell was he thinking, ruining everything like this? Who was this woman to make him do something so stupid? And why had he brought her to Barcelona and not me?

"Come Elizabeth," he said. We were standing next to the car, but I couldn't remember having walked there. I turned around and started heading back to the beach.

He followed me and shouted, "Come on, we're going home."

"Get out of here!!" I hollered. "You stupid shit!!!"

He ran back to the car, got in and sped out of sight.

I was stunned. I collapsed on the ground where I stood. Thinking about it now, I remember feeling the coldness of the sand, but I didn't notice it that day. I sobbed. Without intending to, my mind once again went back to my mother's studio on one of the many days I found her lying there. I immediately started to bring her back to bed before father got home, and I barely succeeded. When he asked me where Mom was, I told him that she'd gone to bed with a headache; he was furious and roared that her incessant illnesses had to stop. I sighed and made coffee and whipped cream to serve with cake, and by the time he had eaten, he had calmed down, somewhat. I put Stravinsky's *Le Sacre du Printemps* on the record player for him and went to my room. I believed I was doing the right thing to keep everything from falling apart. Just like I had done with Thomas. I supported, consoled, encouraged, praised and took care of the practicalities so he could make his true potential flourish.

It's been three months now since I last saw Thomas. I've cried and cried, I've talked to my best friends and a number of other people about his infidelity. It really hurt me that he had been seeing another woman for six months. Six months when I thought it was him and me together standing up to the world and then me finding out that I had been all alone. That hurt. I've also talked with people about love to try to understand where it goes wrong. Why in the world is it so difficult?

I'm 34 years old, my daughter lives mostly with me, I love my job helping entrepreneurs become successful, and I long to find a partner that I can have a deep loving relationship with. I want to be part of a relationship where we can both support and challenge each other in becoming our best selves. I want love to be an active partner in my life and not an adversary as has been the case so far. And I'm now prepared to do something different from what I've done before, since that obviously has not worked!

SUNDAY, APRIL 12TH

The Man of My Dreams and Me

I REALIZE THAT I need to move on. And since I don't have any more tears in me about Thomas, I'll try to leave it behind and look ahead. As a woman, I'm living in a golden age. There are so many possibilities for coupling, I can live exactly the way I wish to live—or so they say.

What am I dreaming of? Or should I ask: what is my mind dreaming of? It seems we're not always in agreement. I am so stuffed to the gills with stereotypes about love and a woman's role in it that I'm sick of it. Perhaps I should forget the silly romantic ideals Hollywood refreshes my memory with on a regular basis. Not because I believe those stories or find them of high quality or artistically impressive; but it's as if my mind does. Each and every time I meet a man, I expend quite a bit of energy on squeezing him into this same ideal romantic mold, and each and every time it leads to nothing but frustration, the rolling of eyes and long talks with my girlfriends about how different women and men are.

Then we display our respective cynicism at the 'man' talk itself, and we laugh at Bridget Jones and the absurd situations in which she draws attention to herself, because we recognize them in ourselves. But immediately afterwards, I'm vexed. What kind of idiot thinks like Bridget that meeting a man will ensure her eternal happiness? That's actually where the problems start—and if you ask me, she will not be happy choosing either of the two guys in the film—Colin Firth or Hugh Grant.

A relationship with Colin would rapidly devolve into an everyday routine of him working overtime and her begging for affection the minute he walks through the door. His mind is elsewhere and he can't understand what she wants. He wants some peace and quiet, and he's too tired to have sex.

If she chooses to settle down with Hugh, things would start to change after some very intense first months. He will fail to arrive on time to meet her; he can never give a clear answer as to where he has been; and he's always doing things that don't involve her and coming home reeking of cigarette smoke and perfume. And in bed he's predictable, almost boring.

Or am I just disillusioned?!? Whatever happened to Germaine Greer, Gloria Steinem, Erica Jong and Judith Butler? Or the Danish writer Susanne Brøgger who is known for promoting the open marriage? Why aren't their strong and sensual 'femininities' the ideals of my mind? Is my mind all wrong? What *is* love? Am I brainwashed? Should I just accept that men and women are fundamentally different and that most couples will never really succeed at deeply loving each other forever? And the romantic ideals my mind fabricates as soon as a potential man enters within a mile's radius—should I just accept that they're hopelessly unrealistic or maybe even immature? Maybe I should simply scrap romance and stick to having just an occasional physical relationship with a handsome man?

It sounds easy. But it feels empty. It isn't really enough for me. When I ask myself what I want, and I try to be as honest with myself as I can, the answer is always that I yearn for a *real* man. But at the same time that yearning infuriates me. What's a real man, anyway? A real man is someone who:

- is well-balanced
- knows himself
- loves sex as much as I do
- has good social skills
- has (enough) money
- is good-looking

- is funny
- is able to think for himself
- is able to commit himself
- knows how to listen
- can say no AND yes
- is romantic

I know this list might seem overwhelming to ask for, but I find it hard to make it any shorter. Should he not have a sense of humor? Or money? Or is it unimportant that he can listen to others? Or be romantic?

It's important that he wants to have sex with me, and not just any (or every) woman. And he should be willing to build a life with me.

What can I offer a man? Hard to say. The popular models for women's roles don't do it for me. At one end of the spectrum is the Florence Nightingale 'ideal' female model held by patriarchal society—a pretty, happy, service-minded woman who keeps house for her husband, raises well-mannered children, cooks delicious meals and basically runs a lovely, well-oiled household. The man wields the power and the woman yields to him, arranging herself and her private life according to what suits him. That means: sex when he wants it, and her spending evening after evening at home alone when his work or hobbies summon him. It means maintaining his social relationships to his parents, siblings and friends—so he can come and go as he pleases. He doesn't expect her to live out his sexual fantasies with him; either he hasn't got any fantasies to speak of, or else he lives them out with other women he meets here and there.

I understand men who want that kind of wife in their life. It's the perfect solution for an egoist who wants to fulfill his dreams and keep playing the field, though I fail to understand why a woman would want this for her life. It is not enough for me.

On the other end of the spectrum is the Lady Macbeth model. This woman has arranged a life for herself and her husband. She decides where their money goes, with whom they spend their time, what her husband does in his free moments; and if possible, she tells him how to do his work. I have met a number of board directors and CEO's who belong to this category where they need to ask their wife before they know what they think about an issue raised at a board meeting. Sexually, she's wearing the panties—and I imagine she keeps them on most of the time. Her man accepts the allotment of her energies and shuffles about on his own as much as he can.

I don't envy either of these women. But almost everyone I know lives a variation of one of these two models, and either the man or the woman inevitably suffers in silent frustration. I can see why.

That's not for me. I long for a love where my partner and I are equals, yet we also have an intimate place for us to experiment with the power shifting back and forth between us both in terms of sex, finances and other important matters. Our individual and joint development as people are a key part of a good relationship when I look ahead. It hasn't been when I look back, so I really must approach this in a different manner.

My girlfriend Karen says there's no such thing as an equal relationship where both parties have their say. One will always be dominant; sometimes it's the woman and sometimes it's the man. It's very possible that she is right, and relationships have been like that for many decades, but that's not how I want my life to be. I want a fair, equal relationship with fun and varied sex where we are both strong individuals who nurture each other and urge personal development.

12:30 A.M.

CAN'T SLEEP. I FEEL like an animal in a burrow that has strayed from all of the other animals. There is no one to nuzzle my fur or forage for food with me.

What must I do to find a little love? What do other people do? How the hell do they know what to do??

TUESDAY, APRIL 14TH

One Woman Seeking Three Men

I REALLY DON'T FEEL like going back to my previous love experiences and this morning when I woke up, I wondered if I couldn't just live without a man or a steady relationship. I mean, what purpose does a man serve in my life?

I sat up in my bed and grabbed a sheet of paper where I made a short list of things to use a man for. I thought I would find maybe three to four things and then I could just decide to live without him. What a relief if that was the case. But before I knew it, the list got long.

I need a man:

1. To talk with about work, both his and mine
2. To laugh together
3. To make love (often)
4. To assist me in making the appliances and equipment in the house work
5. To tell me about important historical events when I want to know more
6. To discuss politics with
7. To paint the kitchen and the rest of the house with me
8. To remind me that it really doesn't matter what other people think of me
9. To give me a massage from head to toe
10. For pure unconditional love
11. To travel the world with—or just spend a long weekend in New York
12. To discuss books with
13. To pay the restaurant check without asking me to share the bill
14. To feel desired
15. To kiss
16. To flirt with
17. To mow the lawn
18. To cook with me and share delicious food
19. To provide good practical advice on many matters
20. To buy what's on the grocery list
21. To go to the DIY store and come home with the right stuff
22. For grilling food
23. To play with
24. To think and dream big together and make ambitious life plans for us
25. To open jars of jam or pickles that I can never open
26. To cuddle on cold Copenhagen nights (and even those few warm ones)

Well, a list with 26 points probably means that I cannot live without a man in my life. And judging from my list it cannot just be any man.

But wait a minute . . . when I sort these 26 points into different categories, some of them can be grouped together. Then I end up with the following three main areas for a man in my life:

A. I enjoy having good talks about work, politics, practical matters, life, love and so on
B. Sex, caressing and cuddling are important to me
C. Practical matters of all kinds must be solved without quarreling

I got up and took a bath. It felt good to be concrete about my specific needs. As I rinsed myself off in the shower, I had an idea. Not just any idea, but a real brainstorm!

I'll scrap the traditional boyfriend hunt and instead of looking for one man, I'll look for three men to meet my needs: one to talk with, one to have sex with and one to help me with practical things.

This way, I can improve my skills at dealing with men in three different areas of my life and try to have my different needs fulfilled by different men. And each of the men will have a need of their choice satisfied. As long as I'm open about telling them what I'm looking for, they'll know the preconditions. Most of the time, things go wrong because people's expectations of each other are too high and often not properly defined. With this three-men model, everybody delivers only what they have to. It's a win-win situation, as they say in the business world.

Is this totally preposterous? Maybe. But what else can I do? And what do I have to lose? I've decided I want to try a different approach, and this is different. I guess I can post a profile on a dating site and see what happens. How can I create a profile that makes sense?

Seeking three men . . .

Hmmm . . . some say that men only want sex. Maybe I should write that one first to attract attention?

~~~~~~~~~~~~~~~~~~~~~~~~~~~~

In my excitement, I called my friend Karen and told her about my idea to get her feedback. She was quite shocked about the idea, and warned me about getting a bad reputation. When I didn't want to enter into that discussion, she claimed that I'll never find a man to do just the practical stuff. Men just don't feel like doing that kind of thing without getting something (i.e., sex) in return. She always has to ask her boyfriend a minimum of five times before he finally mows the lawn. But then again, she could be wrong. I know quite a few men who like to do manual tasks, and with my solution they will get a cooked meal and beer in return and be exempt from all other expectations.

As for the conversationalist, I don't think I'll have any problem finding one. Most men who like to talk actually love talking about themselves. Maybe I should be more specific: a man to talk with who also likes to listen. On the other hand, that might make me seem like someone who never stops talking, and that's not true. Or maybe it's that men who are good conversationalists just talk a lot because they're hoping for sex? I guess I can gauge a guy in terms of how much he likes books. I love books in all their forms and they have always played an important role in life for me.

Thomas was always irritated about my many books. He said there were too many books everywhere. But when I find a beautiful or interesting book, I need to buy it, as then I always have a book for a rainy day or if I get sick and need to lie in bed for a while. What was his problem about books anyway? Some women buy a lot of shoes, I buy a lot of books. Anyway, Thomas is gone so I don't have to worry about it anymore. I just have to make sure that I find a man for whom my many books don't pose a challenge.

~~~~~~~~~~~~~~~~~~~~~~~~~~~~

Unlike Karen, my other dear friend Rebecca thinks it's a brilliant idea to look online for three men. She's got a colorful bouquet of internet dating stories of her own, as she is very active and outgoing. She has attachment issues and they manifest in a tendency to either attract men who want her too much, or men who don't call her back after having had sex with her. The first time she posted a profile online, she got 250 messages within three days! She found it completely overwhelming. Basically she was looking for a man with a passion for life; someone to explore the world with. She ended up choosing one of them, a good-looking fellow who had written an original response. They made a date for a phone call, and on a Monday evening around 10 p.m., after exchanging a few words, she asked him what his goal in life was.

Whoa, talk about jumping the gun. Needless to say, he was rather taken aback, and didn't give her an answer she was satisfied with. I tried to tell her that you have to meet men in the real world first to experience how the chemistry is. If it's good, you need to meet again. Then *maybe* on the third date, after some mutual trust and interest have been established, she can ask him about his mission in life. "It can't be an immediate test of the guy," said the specialist in broken relationships (me).

<hr />

My three-men plan puts me in a great mood! It gives me a chance to approach this love game more playfully than I usually would. And it's interesting to feel that I am sitting in the driver's seat, knowing that I'm the one in charge—kind of like the princess in the Hans Christian Andersen's tale *Jack the Dullard* where she is presented with one elegant well-meaning suitor after the other and each time says "No good, next" until the shabby but witty and ingenious Jack the Dullard conquers them all and wins her heart. I could be a nice version of her, thinking that if a man isn't good at one thing, he probably has talents in one of the other areas. And at the same time, I'm free to say no any time to any of them.

Ok, I started writing my dating profile. Here's how it reads:

Looking for three men . . .

I may be a romantic movie specialist, but frankly, I don't feel that romance provides a feasible model for relationships. It irks me that I keep coming back to these films, and that I keep watching them over and over with my daughter. It has to stop. So I've come up with a formula of my own. It's called 1W3M—I'm looking for three different men for one woman to meet each of the following needs:

1. A rational, philosophical man for conversation.

I'm the Executive Director of a large association for entrepreneurs and their startup businesses, and I have a twelve-year-old daughter who lives with me part-time. I like intellectual challenges, so I need a man to talk with about everyday issues, politics, philosophy, my books, which I collect because I love books, and I want to talk about life in general.

Advantage: We can be honest.

2. An attractive man for sex on a regular basis.

That means 3-4 times a week, or whatever we're up for. He should be curious and ready to explore both his own and my secret passions, but most importantly, he's spontaneous and he enjoys sex with me.

Advantage: We can have great sex often and explore our passions.

3. A do-it-yourself guy to do handiwork for me.

I live in an old townhouse and need help maintaining it, such as fixing a leak in the roof, repainting, hanging lamps, making room for my book collection, mowing the lawn, or just hanging out on the sofa with a good film on a rainy Sunday. I'll serve cold beer, warm meals, hot coffee and fresh cake in return.

Advantage: Mutual fulfillment of practical needs and the occasional cozy Sunday.

When I look in the mirror, I see a 34-year-old, 5'7" almost natural blonde; well-built, womanly, educated, interested in politics. She's environmentally conscious and erotically intrepid—and she watches way too many romantic films.

Well, my profile's online now. I'm really excited about it. And nervous; and full of a number of vague expectations. I sense both fear of being ridiculed as well as a sense of complete victory of having finally solved the riddle of love. As if!

Luckily I'll be attending a workshop tomorrow, so I'll discipline myself not to check for replies until the evening. Don't want to get ahead of myself.

WEDNESDAY, APRIL 15TH

Wonder If There Are any Answers...

HAVE A FEELING I will be quite disappointed if no one answers. Will probably take it personally, even though they have no idea who I am.

Karen thinks I'm out of my mind. Three men! And if her lack of support isn't enough, she and her fiancé have invited me to a classic, perfect church wedding in June. I'll be there and so will Rebecca and her brother Oscar, my old childhood playmate. I hope that he won't be at my table . . . last summer he gave me seeds and seven pots to plant them in—"so I would think of him when they bloomed," he said. The pots and seeds are still in the garden shed. I don't exactly have a green thumb. The first time Oscar kissed me, I was 12 years old and we were playing mommy, daddy, and baby. We showed each other our parts, too. My lips tingled for the longest time after kissing him, and it was a revelation for me. Since then, Rebecca has guarded her brother like a lioness, but she can relax; he's too well-grounded and too quiet to be my type.

Okay, time to start checking for answers to my ad. Let's see if anyone was brave enough to try their luck at my new model . . . I mean, it won't be anything like the mountain of letters in *Sleepless in Seattle*. Just three replies, that's all I ask . . .

OMG—27 replies!!! Let's check them out.

1. I adore talking to women. In fact, I talk to women all of the time. I tell them all about my life, and my life is exciting, so you bet they listen. I work in machinery and I sell big contracts all over the world. And I can always, always talk to women. For example, I might tell them about the time I was in New Guinea . . .

Three pages of his New Guinea story and details about how great he is. And then, the pièce de résistance: *And if she hasn't gotten enough when we're done talking, I give her just what she needs. I tell you: they groan for it! Interested in meeting me?*

Phew, I'm groaning already! But I'll keep him in mind just in case I want to hear more about New Guinea.

2. 'Guaranteed Orgasm' has been my middle name since I was 17, writes Jens.

At the age of 17? Isn't the complexity of female sexuality slightly more than most 17-year olds can grasp? But I've got to hand it to him, it's a declaration of perseverance, and that's not to be scoffed at when it comes to giving a woman what she needs. Making love to a woman is a little like playing every instrument in an orchestra at the same time. If he knows how to carefully apply the right pressure needed to bring the c-flute to life, and he can switch easily between instruments, making a quick move to percussion when the tempo picks up, while circling in and out of the crisp tones of a Stradivarius violin and back to the c-flute and then the violin again until he brings it all to a climax with his baton while flattering me with loving words, well, chances are, he can create some beautiful music with me.

But perseverance without a finely-tuned pitch for one's partner can be so embarrassing. Good sex requires the recognition that the other is a special person and that an intimate meeting is precious, even if it is just for one night.

How old is this guy, anyway? 34 . . . hmm, 17 times two. Does that mean two orgasms, guaranteed? Alright then, I'll put him on the list for a potential #2 spot since he is so confident he can deliver. I'm 34 too, so age is not a problem.

3. You are out of your mind! I would never dream of responding to your egotistical profile where you want men to do everything for you ... Well, Einstein, you just responded, but fear not, no answer is headed your way since your profile fits my Delete button just fine.

4. I'm a first-rate handyman, and I'm really well hung. Now this one doesn't seem to understand that he only needs to fill one position. But maybe that's just how a man introduces himself when he wants to attract attention, hmm?

5.– 27. ... It's taken me an hour to read through all these. There are a number of answers from self-important men with stories of the women they've brought to their knees, women who've tasted their greatness and came crawling back for more . . . Jesus, such a turn-off. I wonder if I should ask them to provide references from their ex's? Hehe . . .

But I'm also surprised since there are a number of sweet answers as well. There just may be more nice men out there than I thought. I have now responded to 10 men who look interesting and asked them to choose one of the three roles. And so far Karen is right: No candidates volunteering only for the #3 caretaker position.

I've also made a bulletin board in my bedroom, where I've drawn three boxes saying the following: Philosopher, Lover, Handyman—and I put in the names of tonight's winners, though I'm not sure what I'll do with them yet. The remaining seven may qualify for a position in a box later depending on their answers.

PHILOSOPHER	LOVER	HANDYMAN
• New Guinea guy?	• Guaranteed Orgasm guy?	• Well-hung handyman?

FRIDAY, APRIL 17TH

Scrap My Inner Report Card

WHAT ARE THESE FEELINGS I get every time I meet a man I like? It's always the same: I want to surrender myself to him. What kind of instinct is that for a woman to have in this egalitarian 21st century? I thought I had agreed with myself to put that old patriarchal model to rest—but then comes my wildest fantasy and pushes me right back into it? I know, I know, I saw the film *Top Gun* five times. But still . . .

Where does that urge to surrender myself to a strong man come from? Some say it's evolutionary biology. I think there might be some truth to this. I remember longing for masculine strength as a ten-year old, well before my body began striving for sexual fulfillment. But the feeling cannot be only based on biology. Culture in our society also plays a key part. Generally speaking, culture and society give the service role to women and the executive role to men and a nuclear family model to fortify that distribution. That means that since I was born, I've largely met strong men and submissive women and anybody not fitting that pattern was a bit strange, I was told. The problem is that my body longs for a strong man, while my mind longs to be a strong woman.

Maybe this accounts for my problems once I get near a man: I start competing with him about who is the strongest, because one part of me wants to be strong like he is and then I give in to him because another part of me wants him to be strong. No wonder relationships are such challenging waters to sail.

Some women refuse to have the urge to surrender sexually to a man, but when you talk to women about their longings and fantasies, you can hear traces of it. I think it is important to accept that longing in order to understand my own dichotomy in terms of men.

It is also important to distinguish between the bedroom and the everyday world. In the everyday world, I expect to be treated like an equal in all manners such as pay, rights, and respect. In the bedroom, we close the door to all that and allow ourselves to live out biological impulses, only bringing along respect for each other's boundaries. Then again, sometimes it can be so hot to have a boundary challenged, even broken. So I guess the important thing in the modern bedroom is to be able to listen to and sense the context. Each intimate meeting happens between two people at a specific point in life. The outcome is influenced by how they are as people, how they feel at that specific moment, what went on before, what they think is all right to do, what their fantasies are, etc. In a confident setting, you can also play with the roles and switch who is in control and who takes the submissive one. It's my experience that most men have a need to let go of control once in a while, and be at the receiving end.

In order to arrive at such an egalitarian relationship, I'm aware that I have to clean out some of the cultural baggage in my mental system. When I was seven, I got my first report card and was very proud that I received 'Very Satisfactory' in every subject. Carrying it home with me in my bag, I felt the pride in having been evaluated positively. I should have kicked and screamed and tore it into pieces, because since then such a report card and others of its kind have dominated my life. Nice handwriting, nice behavior, nice manners, nice nice NICE! Obeying and being NICE seemed like the only important thing for a girl, and it turned out not to be worth anything at all.

But I didn't know it back then. So I constantly adhered to the boundaries and rules of good behavior. If I stuck to the rules, I deserved to be loved was the signal my dad, the school, and any other authority figure sent me. So I stuck to the rules and I evaluated others in the same way. What's right? What's wrong? What should I do? What's the highest grade you can get? I got hooked on being good and the praise that came with it.

My mom never got it. She always refused to be evaluated and I remember feeling sorry for her, for not knowing or playing the game.

When these questions and their answers became too much, I retreated to a secret place in my mind where I could ask questions like: Who decides what's right and what's wrong, and why? Who appointed the judge, anyway? And what are those grades good for? I finally decided that I wanted a life where there was room for Me and my priorities and feelings, which meant room for that secret place in my mind.

For years, I worked on creating space for my priorities and demanding self-respect for my emotions both in the real world and in the bedroom. But looking back now, I see that I never succeeded. I've spent years trying to act like a man to succeed at work and more years to become a woman again to feel whole. I believe it is the dichotomy that women face today. I know that I no longer want the patriarchal model, where a strong man sits on the top and decides everything. And with my new model, I'm trying to go beyond my own dreams and define my desires for a new life *on my conditions.* I'm done creating a space for a man and his emotions, wishes and dreams, silently expecting to get a 'Very Satisfactory' report card for my efforts to support him. I've had it dreaming that once he is fulfilled, he will turn and ask what I want so he can make space for me to live my emotions, wishes and dreams. Can I use my new model to find another way of living?

LATER

I'VE GOTTEN SOME MORE replies from guys. This is fun!

~~~~~~~~~~~~~~~~~

Benny writes: *I like your model and I'm for sex. I get really turned on by latex so if you are into that please respond and I'll prepare myself.*

Well, well now. Need to think about it. Haven't really considered latex one of my key sexual interests. It might be something I would be willing to try if the man I loved was really into it. But it is the sort of thing I need to be seduced into. Dealing with it like a point on a wish list is not really me, so no thank you, Benny, latex is a stretch for me.

~~~~~~~~~~~~~~~~~

I think you are funny wanting three men. I don't quite know if you are joking or not. But if you are not, I would like to apply for the sex position. But can we start by meeting and talking to see if we match? Kind regards, Jesper

Well of course we can, Jesper. I never imagined that we would just say hi and then start undressing and have sex! For me (and most women), sex is best if there is a build up towards it. So maybe we should just fix a date to meet and then see what happens? I wrote to him and he replied quickly.

Great! I'm away on a business trip right now but will get back to you with a date proposal next week. Kind regards, Jesper

~~~~~~~~~~~~~~~~~

Great model you have there. When can we meet? I want to start by talking, then if that seems fine, we can move to having sex and if both are good, I'm prepared to help you with some practical chores. Would you like to have coffee tomorrow afternoon? XX Erik

Well, a 3-in-1 who sounds reasonable at least. I emailed him back and agreed to a date for brunch tomorrow.

There were some other responses, but none really interesting. The Guaranteed Orgasm guy is not responding to my answer. And the well-hung handyman felt the need to send me a photo of his erect cock. I don't know who tells men that women love photos of cocks. Is it because men enjoy seeing photos of naked women and so they believe the reverse is true as well? I don't know any women who appreciate it except as an element in a very physical seduction process. It is certainly not the first or second thing to communicate to a possible date who is me!

PHILOSOPHER	LOVER	HANDYMAN
• New Guinea guy? • Erik	• Guaranteed Orgasm guy? • Jesper • Erik	• Erik

Baron von Trapp and the Millionaire

WHAT A WEIRD DAY! And completely different than planned!

It started out with brunch with Erik. He was nice, and I think he found me nice as well. But there was really not a whole lot of chemistry, so we won't be going any further. It's funny how someone can seem so attractive on paper and then be such a dud.

Then Mille got home from having an off-weekend breakfast with her dad Sebastian, and we spent two wonderful hours together playing chess. She beat me. She had a good time with Sebastian, so she must be alright spending time with him these days. Well, it was great to see her, and that was not the weird part. That happened after I had taken Mille to a birthday party for one of her classmates. Having driven her off, I joined my dad for a cup of coffee at a café, as agreed.

When I was a kid, my friends always made fun of me by saying that my father must have been a direct descendent of *Baron von Trapp* from *The Sound of Music* given the way he ordered everyone about in a home always filled with music. He didn't become less 'military' after the divorce, which is strange, because he was only conscripted for a year in the army like everyone else in Denmark.

Today it was like someone switched on a light glaring down on him, making me realize how much of an impact the patriarchal model has had on my life and how it has ruined my code of love. It commanded me to leave myself and my own dreams in the shadows, and instead make my 'beloved' the object of my efforts. All of a sudden, the source of my autopilot mechanism became crystal clear. It was almost too easy to finally see it. I was supposed to meet the Baron at a café—I thought it would be better than meeting him at his home—THINK AGAIN.

Baron von Trapp was sitting at a table strewn with papers. Some were balanced on a saucer while his coffee cup made rings on another pile of papers. Both of the two empty chairs were covered in papers. Regardless of where he is, he behaves as if he's in his own living room. As soon as I walked in, bang! I fell right into that energy which I know so well and which has always confused me: *longing and anger—an abysmal cocktail.* I wanted his attention, but I was left on stand-by while he fussed with his business, and when I got his attention I felt nervous about the verdict. Another dichotomy in my life!

He ordered me to have a seat. All of the chairs were full.

I attempted a greeting, but he burst out, "I've already written to them three times. Now I've had enough!"

As usual, my needs were unimportant. To break the familiar cycle, I left to order a double gin & tonic—even though his invitation was for coffee. After all, it was already five o'clock; time for my aperitif. When I got back to the table, he was reading and took no notice of my presence—and *surprise,* the chairs were still full of papers. I did my best to express irritation with not having a place to sit, but he didn't notice anything.

"Dad," I said.

He looked up, caught sight of me, looked irritated, then finally he cleared off a chair.

"The nerve," he began before I had even sat down. "Who do they think they are? Doubting the validity of my results! And instead they accept an article from that amateur, Johnsen. I won't stand for it!"

He went on and on. A vast incomprehension overtook me as I sought the answer to the question: why am I sitting here with him? Just as I've sat next to so many other men who have recounted the wrongs that have been done to them for hundreds upon hundreds of times. I couldn't come up

with an answer. I could only confirm that my own dreams and visions . . .
desires . . . needs . . . were being left unfulfilled. Looking at him again, I was
astonished at myself.

And this goes a long way back. As a child, I considered my father a
ticking time bomb. I detested it, and surprise! I married Sebastian, a ticking time bomb. Again, it was me on autopilot. Sebastian's rage against the
world could be activated—not unlike the Baron's—in a split-second. As
absurd as it may seem, that ticking communicated 'security' to something
deep inside of me. Sebastian's sulkiness and his innocent victim attitude
tricked me into wanting to help him. There are a lot of men like that, and I
seem to be constantly crossing paths with them.

Spending years with the Baron pre-conditioned me to focus on a man
and his needs, wants and frustrations, while maneuvering through a mine-
field littered with longing and repressed anger.

Sitting there at the café, I became aware that it is that precise pattern I'm
trying to break.

I interrupted the Baron's rant, saying: "Father, I put an ad on the internet looking for three men . . . one to talk with, one for sex and one to be my
handyman."

His clenched fist froze in the air before him.

"What did you do? Are you out of your mind?"

I took a big sip of my drink and looked at him. Clearly, he was about to
boil over, and then he did.

"Do you have any idea what you're doing? Society's family values are
already disintegrating. Everybody wants to live out their wildest dreams.
Who's supposed to do all of the work we need done to keep society working?
And who will care for the children when women like you are running around?"

I took another sip and looked at him. He didn't yield one inch.

"And why three men? Why the hell can't you find ONE man and hang
onto him? I need a son-in-law!"

The conversations at the tables around us fell silent. Who cares that I'm
the Executive Director of a successful company, or that I've given him an
amazing granddaughter—it's a son-in-law he needs! His tirade went on
without parallel. I felt that I had had it and stormed out of the café with him
yelling after me that I'd ruined everything and it was a pity since we were
having such a nice time!

Right outside the café, I literally ran into my ex-boyfriend, the million-aire Peter Nielsen, whom I had dated briefly after my divorce and before meeting Thomas. He lived in a knockout villa in Charlottenlund—the classy section north of Copenhagen where the houses are big, gardens are parks and even the dogs wear fur coats. We were together for about six months, and it seemed that my life was a dream. Except for his daughter, Tina, who was jealous of how much time I spent with her dad, and she resented having my daughter Mille in "her" house. In revenge, she stole my makeup and my underwear, and then she completely lost control when we suggested that Mille take over her old bedroom, which had been empty since she moved out. On weekends that Mille wasn't there, Tina insisted that Daddy take her out to dinner, to the theatre, to the movies . . . without me! Peter didn't say no to his 24-year-old daughter. The day I realized that Tina was a per-manent disrupter in our relationship and that Peter wasn't going to let his daughter grow up and live her own life, I left him.

Maybe it was fate running into Peter today. He embraced me, mostly because I collapsed into his arms since he was standing on the threshold of the café. Sensing that I was crying, he lifted my face in his hands and kissed me—first tenderly, but when he felt that I responded in kind, his kiss became lustful, which I also reciprocated. Then he grabbed my hand, led me to the Viking Brew bar, a classic jazz bar not far away, where he ordered me a double whisky and himself a pint. We sat down and raised our glasses, and he asked me what the matter was. I began sobbing again and explained through hiccups that it was my damn father.

He listened patiently to my complaints, and when my drink was empty he ordered me another one. When that one was finished—more quickly than usual—he reached out his hand and said, "Come with me." We got up and went around the corner to his car and onwards to his beautiful house in the fur clad suburb.

As soon as we got through the door, we began impatiently undressing each other. The spark was still there, and although I did my best between caresses and kisses to recall why we had broken up, I could not remember it. His daughter Tina had been a problem, but it wasn't just that. It wasn't until he stood naked before me that I remembered: our lovemaking had been rather impersonal and one-sided. Peter was the perfect name for him, as he had a rather large one. But he relished his own organ, and he gave his namesake more attention than he gave me. I felt that he kissed my sex and caressed my breasts so that I would spread my legs and let him hop on for a brief moment. That was enough for him, but not for me.

The café with my father, the G&T, the two double whiskies, Peter's kind listening at the Brew bar and my new model were spinning around in my body and head. I decided that I'd had enough of fake orgasms with Peter, like the famous scene from *When Harry Met Sally*. Either I'd leave, or he'd need to try something completely different to please me. I lay there enjoying his kisses on my breasts, but when he began moving his mouth away, I held his head firmly in place and said, "Yes, keep going!"

He stopped short for a moment, a bit bewildered, but then he continued kissing. I held his head down and let my moans show him when he was on the right track. He began moving his head lower, but I held his hair firmly, guiding his lips and mouth to my other breast. I could feel his arousal mounting, but I knew that his mind was not comfortable with the shift in power. When he tried to change position again, I resolutely followed his movement so that he tumbled onto his back and I sat straddling his naked body. He looked at me, astounded.

"It's fantastic to be with you again," I said.

"Yeah," he said, not quite knowing what to do.

Before he had time to get his bearings I said, "I'm glad to hear that. I could really use some compliments! Tell me. What do you find sexy about me?"

"Um, what?"

"Yeah, what?"

"Hmm . . . well, your boobs are ok."

"Ok? That's not exactly a compliment."

"No, but you know . . . "

"No, I don't know. What's so fantastic about my boobs?" I asked, and smiled at him.

"Uh, they're pretty. You have nice nipples."

"They're not pretty! They're beautiful, Peter, beautiful, because you've made them brim with lust!"

"Did I?"

"Yes. What else do you like about me?"

"Well, you've got a great ass."

"Exactly. And what makes it different than other women's asses?"

"Well . . . "

"Yes? Tell me."

"Well, you know, it's pretty."

"A lot of 'pretty' things, huh?"

"What's with you, Dixie? You're not usually like this . . . "

"You're absolutely right. We were together for six months and I never told you how impersonal your desire feels, or how invisible I felt in our relationship."

"Invisible? You're not invisible now!"

"Right. And what are you going to do about it?"

"My flag's at half-mast now, so it looks like you've missed your chance!" he said looking down.

"Oh, I can fix that. Come on, stand up."

He looked at me.

"Get up and stand next to the bed!" I ordered.

He got up reluctantly and stood next to the bed. I lay down on the edge and arranged my breasts so that one rested lightly on the other, curving gracefully. I spread my legs enough to give him a glimpse of my sex. Then I said:

"Your compliments control my hands. I'll start at my neck, because I think I have a beautiful neck."

I caressed my neck and throat with one hand, running a finger between my breasts and lightly touching the top of one breast. I watched him watching me with slightly spread lips, unsure if he should make a run for it yet at the same time drawn to what might await him.

"Where do you want to go?" I asked, smiling at him.

"Um . . . your breasts are lovely."

"Which is loveliest?"

"Uh . . . the right one."

Slowly, I led my hand down from my throat to between my breasts, opening my palm over my right breast. I stroked my nipple and gently massaged my breast, rubbing the summit until it stiffened and my breast became firm.

Peter's flag rose, and in the next half hour, his compliments and my hands aroused us both to a level of intensity neither of us had known in our months together.

That was my private, end-of-season dance for Baron von Trapp's nice girl, and the debut ball for the new Dixie, who will walk into the future to enjoy, seek fulfillment and define herself!

I've Got Mail

MY MOLECULES ARE STILL all aquiver after being with the millionaire. I had almost forgotten my new model with three men after that evening. And I had forgotten Thomas! When I think of taking him back, my longing for him shrinks. But I still miss him when I'm watching *The Late Night Show,* now with no commentary from Thomas to accompany it. And I miss all the art shows we went to that made me feel good to be part of our couple. And I miss a lot of other things that I refuse to remember just now.

Thomas still begs and begs me to meet him, but I am adamant. "I love you," he claims in email upon email. Love? . . . it seems more like we were two people with different roles. I supported, pushed, kissed, motivated, tempted, nudged, talked and did everything I could so he would be able to fulfill his dream of painting. Only I forgot to ask him if he was interested in fulfilling his own dream. And I forgot to ask myself, what was my dream? Is that love, or is that me being a total control freak? And him being a sissy?

Mille was so sad when he left us. Just peeked in at her. Mille—the apple of my eye. She's as fresh as dewdrops on a flower when she sleeps. I still check on her before I go to sleep, and the sight of her fills me with tenderness and love. There was some hefty adaptation to be done on my part when she arrived in my life. To suddenly have to be available for another person 24/7 took some getting used to, but she won me over so completely that I would burst in two if she disappeared.

She's been sleeping a lot lately, like teenagers do. Some experts say that it's necessary for them because their body is changing so much. Apparently it should say 'Closed for reconstruction' on their foreheads. When I was a teenager, the Baron used to say, "You can sleep when you're old." But now that the old man is old, he can't sleep, so I figure I'd better let my little girl get her rest now, while she's still young enough.

When Mille is around, Baron von Trapp goes into serious grandpa mode. Definitely different than when I was her age. Good thing he can tell a change of vibes is necessary—she sure as hell doesn't need to have that same autopilot I got instilled in her. I wish for her to celebrate her own talents, experience things, enjoy her femininity and find her strengths. The gods only know how hard it is to shield your child from dysfunctional autopilots, but I do my best to give her some perspective. I sing a little song for her when she is sad and I try to show her different aspects of life as often as I can to give her inspiration and different role models.

~~~~~~

I have received new responses to my profile. Among others, a candidate for the talking position:

Hi Elizabeth,

I'm contacting you as a potentially interested candidate for the currently available positions you have advertised. In descending order, my interest prioritized according to position is 1–3–2 or 3–1–2. Nevertheless, I do require additional information with respect to the terms of employment; and benefits.

You have furnished information regarding the salary for position 3. I assume that you consider the endeavors of position 2 comparable to a stipend. However, the salary conditions for position 1 remain unspecified. Additionally, I would like to know if your daughter is encompassed by the employment agreement, in which case I wish to inquire whether a separate bill may be submitted, though it may be surmised that her participation in conversation will decrease significantly after normal bedtime, for which a discount shall be offered. Regarding all three positions I kindly request you to provide the following information:

1. *Are the positions subject to the Employers and Salaried Employees Act? And how about vacation pay?*
2. *RE: The organizational chart of the enterprise, specifically: do personnel report directly to you, or to a managing director?*
3. *Number of working hours per week and their placement within the twenty-four-hour clock. Is there a trial period?*
4. *Are the necessary tools and uniforms available on the premises, or are they to be provided by employees?*

5. *Professional boundaries, conflicts, etc. For example: Imagine that you are engrossed in a heady discussion of Surrealist painters with 'position 1' in your bedroom while 'position 3' paints the window sashes from the inside and 'position 2' awaits in the nude completion of his task in the same room. How would you avoid a personal conflict of epic proportions as well as assume responsibility for the preservation of professional boundaries?*

Naturally, my intention is not to concentrate on potential pitfalls, but it is essential that I know whether you have already considered this or similar situations, or if you will react spontaneously, make excuses and laugh at your employees. Contingent upon your satisfactory responses to the above questions, you will receive my application in the very near future.

Best regards, Henrik

<hr>

Dear Henrik,

Thank you for your interest. Your high rating on the humor barometer has inspired me to reply promptly with the requested information and invite you to an interview tomorrow at 4:15 p.m. at a location of your choice.

Your prioritization of the positions 1–3–2 suits the profile I'm seeking ideally, as follows:

Position 1 may involve my daughter during the day, but she is with her father every other weekend. I see from your profile that you have children of your own, and I'm certain that we'll have things to talk about.

The position will ignore the Employers and Salaried Employees Act, since that offers security which is nothing more than illusory in the given situation. As for vacation pay, of course this will be respected to the greatest degree possible. Ideally, this would take the form of regular mini-getaways and business trips as an opportunity to spend a few days together in a new place.

All employees report directly to me, and the organizational chart is confidential. You'll be required to work extra hours since my life is seldom planned;-) Nonetheless, I would like to emphasize that I hope we'll enjoy each other so much that both of us will be inclined to spend our days together.

Additional appointments and the trial period depend on our chemistry.

With regards to professional boundaries, conflicts, etc., I must admit that there has been a certain unforeseen overlap: the men who've answered my ad insist on talking before sex! And after some consideration, I realize that this is probably a good idea—we all know that good talk makes good sex even better ;-) But that also means that the job descriptions get a bit muddy! After reading your hypothetical bedroom scenario, I must confess that you're perfectly right—it really can develop into a catastrophe!

At the same time, I just don't see a fixed relationship as a feasible construction anymore, and I need to try out a new model. I've decided to meet three candidates for position 1. The one who can communicate on my wavelength will go on to position 3. If we can manage to do some practical tasks without tearing each other's hair out—and without six months passing before we hang up a lamp or carry the heavy patio umbrella to the shed—the candidate will go on. He won't necessarily progress to position 2, but he and I can assess whether we want to go on to position 2 or not.

I hope you're still interested in the positions and can come to an interview tomorrow. I'm looking forward to hearing from you.

Best regards, Elizabeth

Funny guy, but gosh, his photo looks like a typical, dry intellectual who needs the tender loving hand of a stylist coach . . . or several. What the hell have intellectual men done with their macho-genes? Or with the mirror in their bathroom? Who told them looks and appearance don't matter?

Ah, he suggests that we meet tomorrow in Skovridderkroen which is that lovely seaside restaurant with the freshest fish north of the city by the beach. He wants us to meet in the parking area, and enter together so people in the restaurant won't be able to tell that we're on a blind date! This triggers my strange-man alarm that he can't tolerate looking like he's meeting me for the first time in front of some strangers who most likely won't even notice us.

Rebecca gave me a rule-of-thumb for first dates: let your suitor pick the location but tell him that you have time for just one drink. That will give you time to meet him and the possibility of leaving politely.

So my status today is as follows:

PHILOSOPHER	LOVER	HANDYMAN
• New Guinea guy? • Tom • Henrik applying for a job	• Guaranteed Orgasm guy? • Jesper • Tom • Peter the millionaire	• Tom

First Date Today!

I'M GOING ON THE first date with Henrik this evening at 6:15, and my romantic heart is soaring with curiosity! I'm trying to keep calm and stay realistic though, so I signed up for today's morning workshop event at House of Futures, which is a trend-spotting company telling us how the future is going to be. This will be relevant information for the entrepreneurs whom I provide support for in my job.

In the workshop, we heard that we're on the verge of creating a new gender movement where men and women will work together to shape the future and not be so much in opposition to each other anymore. I hope they're right. I feel like so many of us are struggling to extricate ourselves from old dreams, norms and ideals, and at the same time keeping the hamster wheel in motion from 9 to 5, taking care of everybody else and living with a creaking and fissured relationship model. It's a lot of ups and downs, swinging out of familiar models and dreams into unchartered territories and back again, maybe without even having found our own compass and being able to point the needle towards what's important for ourselves. Or else we have found it, but find ourselves all alone.

My own dreams are one of the greatest obstacles between myself and a good life. It's almost as if my dreams are from another time and space, and a mere humorous email from some unknown guy is enough to activate them. I'm already in the full throes of defining our romantic future together with Henrik who sent the job ad response and butterflies are starting to flutter wildly in my belly. Hopefully he's got things more under control than me so we can try out this three-men model! I mean, that's the point of all of this. He's interested in all three positions, but before we part ways he'll have to decide which function he wants to fill, assuming I want him to fill any.

This new model for men and women has already inspired me at work. I'm an Executive Director, which means I'm a success in terms of the system, but it all seems somewhat dull. I must admit that I'm not really satisfied. I want to work with innovation and change some of the things that don't work in our society. That's what I and a whole lot of other people have been doing with my company for the past ten years.

But it almost feels like we're still working on the same challenges as we were ten years ago. Many people are creating detailed studies about how to solve the problems of our society, but then the solutions are all filed away on the shelves. Pilot projects on new ways of solving problems are created by the droves. Even upon a positive evaluation, they, too, get filed on the shelf. A lot of passionate people work hard every day, but pointing out the need for fundamental organizational change is like punching a pillow.

Exactly like a relationship. *Don't rock the boat* seems to be some sort of unofficial motto of humanity today, even though so many people are frustrated by the way society is run and the resources being wasted. Or they are so busy trying to keep the wheels running that they succumb to stress. For me, the level of stress among people is another sign that society is not working properly.

And then there's a lot of talk about how society can't afford to lose the talent that women possess and that an effort must be made to bring more women into the workforce, especially at management levels in all capacities. But many people, both men and women, just aren't interested in a management career under the present conditions. Personally, I'd like to see more in-depth analyses of why that is and what needs to be done to fix it. Maybe we should introduce a 25-hour work week to distribute the amount of work among more people and thereby give everyone more free time to be creative while keeping the wheels moving?

I've tried to make a career for myself several times, but I find it hard to do in top-down organizations where independent thoughts and questions about the established way of doing things aren't welcome. The only way for me to succeed in my career has been to tone down my ambitions and accept sluggish bosses whose only interest is increasing their own paychecks, ignoring whether it is good or bad for the company in the long run. As long as I was loyal to them, I got promoted. Whenever I tried to suggest new ways of doing things or making an analysis of consequences of different possibilities, I was ignored. Seems like a rather unintelligent way of handling me and maximizing my potential.

The real challenge is that the alternatives for me and most people leave a lot to be desired. I could freelance. But then I'd spend a great deal of time on administration, and my professional expertise would suffer because I wouldn't have the cash flow or time to go to exciting, inspiring conferences or workshops, and I would not be hired for big projects that can make a difference. So I'd have to draw a lucky number to really make a big-scale difference as a freelancer. This is a problem if you, like me, really *want* to make a big difference.

I dream of a workplace where I can unlock my talents and ideas and help solve some of society's many problems in close cooperation with other people. There really are a lot of issues that can be solved, as long as we're ready to think outside the box—and outside traditional hierarchical structures. If you know of any organizations that fit the bill, and who are looking for talent, please let me know.

Ok, the lunch break is almost over and I need to focus on finishing some work so I can get to my date on time—wish me luck!

WEDNESDAY, APRIL 22ND

Mr. Managing Director

WELL, WELL, WELL, HAVE been on my first date with the candidate Henrik. We were supposed to meet in the parking area outside of the Skovridder-kroen restaurant north of Copenhagen by the sea. I got there five minutes late to be sure he was there already, so I didn't have to stand there staring at parked cars. But there was no man in sight and I felt my nervous batteries lighting up. Then a car pulled up. A shiny Audi. A man got out, stood next to the car and looked around. It was getting dark so I couldn't fully see him. I walked over and said, "Henrik?"

"No, sorry," he said.

Sorry is right, since he looked better than the photo of Henrik I had seen. I went back to my car wishing I had worn jeans so I could have leaned casually on the bumper instead of standing there in a dress and high heels. I was already a little annoyed at Henrik for making me feel stupid and I hadn't even met him yet. Out of the corner of my eye I saw a man jogging toward me. Hmm, a jogging date? Pretty weird, and not exactly my ideal, but ok, I'll give him a chance.

We exchanged greetings and went inside. He was decent-looking but not conspicuously so—clean-shaven head, dark eyes and a trim body. He got us a couple of beers and then he asked me to make him a promise: we had to meet more than once! He thinks it's unfair that you only get one chance on blind dates, since it's difficult for him to show who he really is in one go.

I told him that I'm no harsh judge—so I managed to answer his request without promising something I might not be able to deliver. The utterance itself made my hair stand on end, since he seemed too needy and a bit clumsy if he couldn't show himself in an hour. At least show enough for me to be curious for more. I tried to be constructive and told him how funny his application letter had been and how much I'd been looking forward to meeting him. Had he ever done any writing?

Nah, culture wasn't really his thing, he told me. But in my profile, he had seen that I'm interested in culture, so maybe I could teach him something. Aha, I thought, and I started feeling optimistic—but it was short-lived. It turned out that in return for culture he wanted to take me out in nature every day. He's got to be outside at least three hours a day or he gets restless. I told him that three hours of jogging weren't really a priority for me.

"I can teach you to be outdoors and move around," he repeated, demonstrating his substandard listening capacity for the second time in ten minutes. To make the hour pass quickly, I asked him about his management job. And that's where it all went wrong. It turned out he had had his own company five years ago—and *that* was his management position. But then he got tangled up in a lawsuit, went bankrupt and had to find work, but a year later he got sacked, three times in a row from different jobs. Well, it wasn't his fault, he said, but out he was. I tried to feign interest in his ideas for a new job, but it was proving difficult. There were just too many points of divergence from the profile I had read online to what I was sitting across from in real life . . . it seemed more like he had posted a description of the life he wished he was leading rather than the one he was.

He asked me about my work and I told him, and we talked about our children. Then I saw that the hour was up.

"Already? When do you want to meet again?" he asked. I told him I'd give him a call.

"You said you weren't a harsh judge. Do you want to see me again?"

"Yes, yes, of course," I said, even though I didn't mean it. I couldn't bear to tell him the truth. It felt like kicking a dying man.

"Then I'll wait for your call. I won't call you because I'll get disappointed if you don't answer my call," he said. "I think you're a really nice woman."

"Thanks. Listen, I've got to run," I said, giving him a quick hug. Then I made a dash for the door, away from a lonely man who hadn't really figured out how to make the best of his talents. I still wonder why he made such a profile, since it was only a matter of time until any date he had found out that he was no longer a managing director and that he had lost his sense of humor.

It was good to come home to an email from a nice guy, Michael. He writes—like so many others—that he's a three-in-one so he can meet all of my needs. I'm guessing he's a talker or a candidate for sex in my model.

Hi Elizabeth,

What you're looking for is a three-in-one. But does he exist? I'm looking for a three-in-one too: a woman with brains, body and soul. Conversation, intimacy and sex.

I've got a university degree, but I've always worked in private corporations. I'm insightful and expressive, and I like talking and listening. And I'm tough. I've always fought hard to achieve my goals, from becoming the Danish Formula 1 champion (in a prehistoric era), becoming executive manager (in a historic era) to becoming a good part-time father (very current). Today, I run my own consulting firm. I recently came out with a new and exciting IT product, and sales are going well. I'm happily divorced, but unhappily single (crooked smile), and I have a wonderful 12-year-old son who lives with me part-time. He's in secondary school just like Mille (nice).

The cards life has dealt me have make me pretty understanding when it comes to people. I'm looking for a woman who's both good-looking and feminine, sweet and warm, insightful and loving. She should enjoy erotic exploration, from tenderness to the outermost boundaries—but we can talk about that in more detail if and when we've met. I'll just say that it should be imaginative, sophisticated and exciting, send shivers up our spines and make us laugh with joy afterwards. But it should never be coarse or vulgar. I'm discerning. I want to be able to think about it the next day and feel happiness, pleasure and pride. Good erotic experiences give me fantastic fuel for the rest of my life—and it's not so much about quantity, but quality.

Can I match my own wishes? I have no skeletons in my closet. I'm ready for a committed relationship, complete with security and challenges. I'm not absorbed in physical appearances. One thing I've come to realize is that my next relationship should be a devoted one. Honest. Not a mentally distanced relationship with intellectual chit-chat, love-making and no emotional intimacy.

Of course, I'm not expecting fulfillment over a cup of coffee in some café, but that's my long-term goal for a relationship.

All in all: I'm interested in talking to you. Have I tempted you?

Best regards, Michael

A marvelous antithesis to Mr. Jogging Date! Michael's mention of soul-sex, pleasure and pride whet my appetite, and the butterflies are back fluttering in my stomach . . . Café The North Pole on Friday—it'll be interesting to see if he can tempt me for position one, two or three . . .

Must concentrate now and read all the material from work for tomorrow. Will spend most of the day getting ready for the next board of directors meeting. Once again, my colleague Horn is going crazy about some forms he claims the Ministry says everyone is supposed to fill out if they want to use the conference rooms. Will that man never retire??

THURSDAY, APRIL 23RD

Horn the Thorn and Svend, 52

TIM HORN IS LIKE an invisible thorn your finger keeps hurting on. He has been a nuisance for me at work for two years. And he continues to make trouble.

Our agency, funded by the Danish government, works with entrepreneurs to help them start new businesses and create jobs.

The entrepreneurs in our agency don't want more rules and regulations, but Horn approved the department's proposal that all entrepreneurs must fill out new forms in order to use the conference rooms. He claims that the head of our department in the Ministry called him personally and demanded it! I have a feeling Horn is the one to have contacted the department with the proposal for forms to give the impression that he's a big fish and in power. He's forgetting that he's only a board member and has no right to approve any proposals at all; I'm the only one who can do that. I spent most of the morning talking tactics with Chairman Carlsen. He says that Horn's probably working on the rest of the board to force me to approve the forms. Carlsen doesn't think he'll succeed, but you never know.

People like Horn really make me wonder. He claims to have what it takes, but he never leaves his desk to test his theories in the real world. I did some digging in the archives and asked around a bit, and it turns out that no one has ever seen or heard him present an original idea of his own. And no one has ever witnessed him make an idea come through. He was never an entrepreneur and it is a pity nobody tells him how his lack of experience influences his judgment. If he were truly passionate about making our agency a better place for the entrepreneurs, he'd spend time with them, talk to them and listen to their needs. But he doesn't. Instead he talks to members of the department, who never were entrepreneurs themselves either. Then Horn and the department people agree on what's best for the entrepreneurs—and right now, that's filling out forms just to book a conference room. They're supposed to fill in their company name, contact person, date and time and the room number—all of that is okay. But then they're supposed to supply all sorts of information about the people they're meeting with: contact person, official title and company name, telephone numbers and company tax ID number for everyone who participates in the meeting! Does Thorn imagine the entrepreneurs have secretaries employed to provide the government with such useless information?

And if I point out the inexpedience of any administrative process, I'm told that changes can't be made—that's just the way the system is. Have they forgotten entirely that *people* make systems—and can therefore also change them? Well, I guess I better listen to Carlsen and take it easy.

And in the middle of all this, my sister Amalie called from the other side of Denmark where she lives in Aalborg to rap my knuckles for being rude to our Dad. Something about a model and three men, she said, but I didn't bother to explain. Now he's upset, and she says that's unacceptable. He's still having a hard time since he divorced our mother five years ago. Ironically, our mother has started painting more, and is much happier since the divorce. But the Baron is pretending to be the victim . . . *after everything I did for her,* he fumes. Funny that Amalie can't see that Dad does everything he can to make her his ally.

And on a good note: I got another email. This internet dating is a lot of fun—it's got a different kick than flirting at parties. It's more clandestine, and you need to read closely to suck out all the information from between the lines. And wow, the things some men write about themselves. Hardly any men ask me what I'm like. Maybe they're just used to having to make more of an effort to sell their wares in the personals than women do. A lot of them ask for a reply, even if it's a rejection. I don't answer those. Frankly, there have been so many replies that I only have time to answer the ones that grab my attention, like this one:

Number 2 for sex—Svend 52—Independent. Has his own dental supply company. Separated for a year, wants sex, but prefers to have a chat first.

Yeah yeah, I guess we can manage a few sentences. He looks like a knockout in the photo—a wonderful, adult man.

Svend writes:

YOU:
- *are a 'naturally' attractive woman*
- *are just as comfortable in jeans as evening gowns*
- *can joke around and have a laugh*
- *have, like me, a good sense of humor and are capable of self-irony*
- *are well-mannered, but can break the rules*
- *give your partner room to maneuver*
- *are between 40 and 50*

ME. I:
- *am very humorous and sociable*
- *am well-trimmed (I keep up on maintenance) but not a sports fanatic*
- *enjoy cooking and collecting wine*
- *like having a nice home with both old and new things*
- *enjoy drinking champagne in bed in between the love-making*
- *am 100% monogamous*
- *still believe in a grandiose church wedding*
- *have an above-average libido*

Quite a mouthful? maybe, but I don't mind if you:
- *squeeze the toothpaste tube in the middle*
- *are occasionally bitchy in the morning, as long as the slate is clean before bedtime*
- *party all night with your girlfriends*
- *insist on painting the bedroom ivory*

Love, Svend

Made a date for a glass of wine with him on Saturday. Even if a grandiose church wedding isn't on my wish list, his above-average libido might be able to make me a little monogamous again.

Jesper, who was supposed to let me know a date for a meeting when he returned from his business trip wrote me that he had gotten back together with his ex-girlfriend so we couldn't meet after all. Maybe Guaranteed Orgasm has the same issue, since he has not responded. Well, he's off the list now. Too bad, since he did spur my curiosity. And Tom, the first 3-in-1 fellow has fallen off my list too. You win some, you lose some. But good thing I've got a date with the too-good-to-be-true, three-in-one Michael at Café the North Pole at 5 p.m. Friday.

PHILOSOPHER	LOVER	HANDYMAN
• Michael (possible 3-in-1?)	• Svend, 52	

Mail from a Journalist!

THAAANK YOU, NOW WE'RE shifting tracks . . . another day filled with adventure; is it fate or synchronicity? This morning I won a trip to the Allinge Retreat Center on the island Bornholm! This is a beautiful place with grey rock formations, white beaches and delicious marinated herring! I was driving to work, listening to a contest on the morning radio. I don't know why I called, but I did and now I won a week's stay at this workshop/retreat combo. It's supposed to be a marvelous place, where artists and scientists meet up and spend time going into depth on some important social or business topic that needs attention. I am a sucker for these intellectual retreats, and maybe there might be a guy there who's worth intellectualizing with.

Then just as I got to work, the phone rang. It was my friend Renate, who invited me to a party on their houseboat in one of the canals in Copenhagen. The party is on Saturday and I'm free so I said yes! You never know what interesting people might be at a house boat party. Being on the water seems to do something to free up our spirits, I've always found.

And then the coup de grâce: When I looked in my work inbox, there was an email from a real dream man, the type I used to focus on! Karen says it's a message from the universe to stop my experiment—after all, this email is finally presenting me with a man who has everything I'm dreaming of. I was taken aback at first because his mail was in my work inbox and not in the Gmail account I set up for internet dating. But that made it even more charming . . . extra points for ingenuity to this guy!

Dear Elizabeth, or should I say Dixie?

It wasn't hard to find you, since you revealed your nickname Dixie in your profile. My network is vast, and I happen to know a woman who knows you. You're as identifiable as someone whose name is Arkan Spartak. This is me—photo attached. As you can see on my website, I write books—the latest one should be a bestseller ;-) But most of the time I'm a reporter, and on Monday I'm off to Cuba for five days to do newspaper and radio correspondence. Do you want to meet for a cup of java before I depart?

Love, Arkan Spartak

Yes, yes, yes Arkan, right away, let's meet. Seems like he's super. He travels, he's cheeky, breaks the rules by finding me outside of the dating site—that turns me on. On his website, he writes that he's into documentaries and reports from abroad, in war zones or other hot spots. And he's good looking in a teddy bear way.

Given that I am busy both tonight and Saturday, I wrote to Arkan, *"How about drinks at The Brewery Sunday evening at 8 p.m.? Might be a good send-off for you for your trip."*

I sense a romantic-fantasy attack closing in and it makes me feel excited and somewhat shaken. Good thing my other plans for the weekend intervene, reminding me that I'm conducting an experiment and I have a date with too-good-to-be-true Michael at five p.m. and a house boat party on Saturday.

FRIDAY EVENING LATE

Talk or Sex?

I GOT TO THE bustling and cozy Café the North Pole at 5:15 p.m., or 5:20 p.m. to be precise. I don't like to be the first to arrive. I was filled with a good feeling of curious expectations since I had had a great day at work, and I was excited about meeting Michael. It seemed so promising.

Michael was standing at the bar right inside. He is tall and well-proportioned with beautiful blue eyes, thick, dark hair and great cheekbones. He was wearing well-fitting jeans and a dark polo shirt with a brown leather jacket. We smiled and said hello, and he pulled me toward him, kissing me on the mouth. That was a little hasty, but I figured he was nervous. Me, too.

We took a table upstairs and the conversation took off so smoothly that my nervousness vanished and excitement grew. We started talking about work—that was neutral territory, or should I say, could be neutral territory since it certainly hadn't been with Henrik. First Michael told me about his job, then I told him about mine. When I was finished he crossed his arms in front of him and said, "How on earth did *you* land that job?! Sounds fabulous!"

Apparently he was feeling provoked. What the hell kind of question was that? The man didn't even know me. Why didn't he assume I had gotten the job because I was highly educated and qualified? I told him that I was and he smiled and complimented me on landing it.

Besides that momentary lapse, our conversation was a hit. By the time I looked at the clock, an hour and half had already gone by; time flies when in nice company! And he seemed to be having a good time since he looked at me and said out of the blue: "Is this going to be a talk relationship, or are we going to have sex?"

I was surprised, but I didn't let it show. Told him that I found him attractive, because I did. "I'm attracted to you," he replied, "and I want to dress you."

Dress me? Isn't it about undressing me? Did he want to get me in a nurse's outfit? A little French maid? Was that his thing? Or a full leather suit? As puzzling as it was, I didn't want to ask him straight out. We weren't close enough yet, so how could I know if I wanted to play his sponge-bathing nurse or his nanny, if that's what he wanted?

As it turned out, he meant dress me in everyday clothes. In his opinion, I could look better and sexier than I did. But because I didn't know if I wanted to look sexy for him I had toned down my clothes—and he was clearly not pleased. He was looking for eye candy, he said.

Notwithstanding the fact that too-good-to-be-true Michael can't understand that I'm the boss, that he wants to dress me and not undress me and his kiss was too quick, we had a good time. But I'm not sure if we'll take it any further. So we probably won't.

BACK AT THE COMPUTER. Handyman ahoy! A no. 3 for handiwork, Lasse, 27 years old. A carpenter. Currently unemployed so he's got time to help me out which is good since one of my book cases is coming off the wall. It is only half in or half out, so I really need help.

Lasse seems like a nice fellow who's tired of eating pasta in his one-bedroom flat and wants to exchange services. His five-year-old son Martin lives with his mother in northern Jutland, far from Copenhagen, so Lasse sees his son here only whenever it fits with the mom's plans.

It sounds plausible, and it seems there's not a shadow of a chance that we'll end up in bed—he's bald and covered in tattoos! Who'd have thought I'd meet a man like that . . . but he's got nice eyes, and judging from his photo, there's nothing at all wrong with his biceps either . . . eye candy for mama.

We're going to meet next weekend. He'll come by with his toolbox and his son. I just tucked in Mille and she's looking forward to it, says she'll show Martin her old hiding place in the hollow tree. Nice that she's still a playful kid at heart.

PHILOSOPHER	LOVER	HANDYMAN
	• Svend, 52	• Lasse

SUNDAY, APRIL 26TH

What a House Boat Party!

LAST NIGHT I SAT on the deck of Renate and Ulrich's ultra-chic houseboat in the middle of Christianshavn's beautiful canal and felt so good. In the afternoon Renate and I had been shopping by motorboat! for the party. Full speed ahead through the canals, under bridges, bypassing the big tourist boats, we were looking good wearing a skimpy top, sunglasses and wind in our hair and feeling exactly as tough as we were. Luckily it was a warm and sunny day. First we went to the market, then we had a quick cup of coffee at a local cafe where she knew some people and then we did some shopping in a trendy clothes shop—it was unimaginably great and it made me feel like I was visiting another city far from home!

The party at the boat started at 8 p.m. where a lot of people I never met before talked, laughed and drank with each other. I sat in the stern and looked out over the water and the boats that sailed past and felt great. It was a relief to be alone. There were no ties to bind me . . . I simply felt pure joy at being on my own.

The hatch from the cabin underneath went up and a man with white hair stuck his head out.

"David! How are you?" shouted a couple of people greeting the new-comer in English.

"Hey," he greeted them and smiled broadly.

More people crowded around him to give him hugs and I thought, who is he?

I looked at him as he went around and talked to people and I began to guess. Was he an architect? An artist perhaps? Someone who even had an exhibition going on and that was why so many people were happy to see him? Or was he a rich guy with his own company? Or was he just a really nice unemployed guy with lots of friends? He was definitely a guy everybody wanted to be with.

I looked to see if someone followed him up the hatch. Nobody mounted. Either he had a lone night out or he was alone.

I turned around and saw that he was standing in front of me.

"Hi, I'm David, I'm from Belgium," he said.

"My name is Elisabeth and I'm from here," I answered.

"Oh, you're Renate's friend!"

"Well, yes."

"I'm Ulrich's best friend. And I've heard a lot about you."

"Well, now."

"Don't worry. I can see they were right."

"About what?" I asked.

"You are special."

"Aren't we all?"

"Where will you sleep tonight?" he asked, smiling at me. I was charmed by how quick he was and it aroused my interest. I smiled back and said, "In the cabin right below us."

"That is normally my cabin!"

"Then we'll just have to sleep together," I replied, and could see that it was not the answer he expected, but his smirk showed he definitely liked the idea. Funny how life can suddenly surprise you. I just sat there and felt so comfortable all alone, and then a man came to me on a silver platter. Well, let's see how he is, though, since I'm not quite sure what I'm up to with my three-men model and all.

My marriage was a prison for five years, and that is what they call a relationship. I will never go there again. The problem is that the things you do to get a good relationship are carved in stone so deeply that it's hard to avoid them. When I meet a man, I automatically begin to dream of romance and a nuclear family, even though I now feel it is not really what I want. I crave good sex, good conversation and practical things that are dealt with without fuss and quarrels. I have not experienced a relationship that gave me these three things, and therefore I'm not going there again. But this means I have to learn a new language for love. I need to find some new dreams to put into my personal kaleidoscope with my three-men model.

Actually, when I think about it, there have already been three men in my life. Sebastian, Thomas and the millionaire. But those are men who *were* in my life; i.e., past tense.

I suppose I could also count three men in my life in a different way: My father, my ex-husband and my future dream man. They all have something in common, which I cannot quite identify, but my challenge is to stop looking for the same commonalities in the future, as they have caused me many sorrows. My father's temper that I grew up with inculcated subconsciously in me that a real man is a guy with a temper. But as a child I hated this side of my father and feared his outbursts. I would do anything to avoid them and became a very obedient child. The revolt came much later and involved many years of living with the real me in hiding. Only in my mid-20s was I ready to come forward and own who I truly was—and take any blame for it, too.

But I have also come to realize that there is no blame. I am who I am. People have more respect for me now. I no longer want to meet temperamental men; they are so strenuous. So my dream man must have other characteristics. Or rather my three dream men . . .

A third way of counting is that there have been three men that I have had great sex with. These are not the same as the three men I've have had a lasting relationship with. Anyway none of those sex-based relationships lasted so it is time to try another method. Now there must be three men—simultaneously.

This I explained to David, when I sensed that he was about to move into a Venus and Mars talk, which I didn't bother to listen to. I've heard that argument so many times, and it just isn't enough.

"I would like to have three men in my life because I simply cannot imagine that one man can fulfill all three areas," I boasted to David watching him closely to see how he reacted.

"I can," he said.

Another three-in-one. "Oh, why are you so sure?" I replied, mostly to bait him and starting to feel the excitement at the prospect of succeeding.

"I love to talk, I'm good at sex, and I can pay somebody to do the practical stuff. So, in my view, one good man is enough."

"That's cheating," I said and smiled at his wit about how he'd fill the third role.

"Okay, listen up," he said, getting serious. "Why do you want different men to fulfill those three areas?"

"Because I need these different needs fulfilled and so far one man hasn't been able to do it."

"What about passion and intimacy?"

I thought a bit and said that I think those get covered under both sex and talking.

"Not necessarily," he said.

Aha, so he does have some experiences with women, I thought and it increased my sensation of excitement. At the same time, I felt a laziness in me not wanting to give up the positive position I had felt when sitting in the chair on the deck watching the world sail by.

I excused myself saying I was going to the restroom and went downstairs. There I found Renate. I asked her who David is and whether there is something I should know about him.

"Go for it," she said. "He's good in bed!"

"How do you know? Have you been with him?"

"No, but two of my friends say so. Just go have an affair with him, but don't expect more. He has wounded a couple of women who Ulrich and I know because he only has affairs."

"Okay, that's all I am interested in anyway," I said feeling my excitement about him and me rise. With an affair I could let things unfold at my own speed, and I could stop if I didn't feel like completing it. This was just the way of putting my needs in the center that I was looking for with my three-men model.

And with a guy who has charisma and is self-confident. They are normally the best in bed. He is not handsome or has a body like a model, but he radiates the energy of a man who knows what he wants. In my view, passion is physically-based, whereas intimacy grows with emotional sharing, and I'm only ready to take the passion trip with him.

An hour later, the party moved on to another level of energy and David asked if I would consider showing him Copenhagen by night. I nodded, and we left the houseboat and started walking along the darkened streets. He was holding my hand and stopped for a moment to try to kiss me, but I didn't feel like it. We had just talked about what happened between me and Thomas and suddenly I missed Thomas while still loathing him. It all of a sudden felt unimportant to have an affair with him. Like putting a small bandaid on a deep wound.

David must have felt that I was losing my interest in him. Instead of trying to take my hand again, he started asking about my job. He asked intelligent questions and was also interested in what I did in my spare time. And he didn't dominate the conversation or talk only about himself. He asked me about everything. I smiled and thought, he'll get tired of this at some point, but he didn't. I enjoyed his company and loosened up again a bit. When he finished cross-examining me, he went on to ask me questions about Copenhagen and I tried to answer as I best could. I showed him the canals and cafés, our historical buildings, and we walked to the Royal Hotel, which was designed by the famous Danish architect Arne Jacobsen, where we went to the top floor for cocktails at Alberto K. We sat by the window and had a beautiful view of Copenhagen by night. I felt pride in showing him a part of the Danish design legacy from the 1960s that is simple and beautiful and still holds.

When we left, we walked down Istedgade to the red light district of Copenhagen where the prostitutes hang out. Being surrounded by sexual signs and innuendos reignited my awareness of him as a man and me as a woman with the possibility of having an affair later if I wanted to. I asked myself whether I wanted to. Part of me did. I liked his energy and felt he would be there for me. Another part of me held back since he seemed quite eager about me, maybe a bit too eager. He told me about the famous red light district of Amsterdam where scantily-clad women sit in shop windows, and men can go window shopping for whatever woman they would like to buy for an hour or the entire night. He told in detail about the different things girls had offered him. My disgust factor rose, but at the same time I could feel the juices begin flowing in me because we were talking about sex. It was vulgar, seedy, yet arousing and brought the possibility of an affair up much more close and personal.

He looked at me, and I'm sure he registered the new change in my demeanor because when we left the red light district, he took my hand again. I let him hold it as we kept walking. Then he let his body touch mine every now and again, which felt nice too. A little later, when we stood looking out over one of the lakes, he placed himself behind me and hugged me. I leaned against him and enjoyed it. But at the same time, I felt that it was enough; he wanted me too much so I decided that I wasn't going to have an affair with him.

When we started walking again, he suddenly stopped and turned to me, pushing me gently but firmly against a wall. "There is one thing that must be clear between us. And that is that you must only kiss me if you feel like it. I do not want you to do anything other than what you feel like. And I count on you to follow that principle in all other areas of life as well."

At that moment I wanted to kiss him, so I did.

Then it went fast.

We kissed and caressed each other passionately as if we had been waiting anxiously to do it. He slid his hand into my pants, and I did the same to him. Right there in the middle of Copenhagen against a wall. It was hot and passionate, similar to some of the first sexual experiences in my life.

Between kisses, we agreed to try to find a hotel, but there was none nearby, and I wanted to get my travel bag, which was lying on the boat, so I could brush my teeth and change into something different the next morning. So we returned to the boat, and Renate met us when we came aboard.

"Hi," I said, sheepishly.

"Hello, hello. And what are you two up to?" she asked and smiled.

"We just need to pick up my bag," I said feeling both a bit embarrassed about the obvious affair I was about to have and not caring about it a bit.

"And then . . . ? "

"We'll find a hotel," David said.

"Oh no, you must sleep here."

"Well it seems like the front cabin is already taken," David said.

"Yes, but it's your cabin when you are here, David," she said and smiled, knowingly.

I hadn't mentioned to her that I had offered jokingly to sleep with David in that cabin when we first met.

She made some couple who had just gone into that cabin move to the living room couch.

"You don't need a double bed, they do!" Renate told the couple and laughed out loud, half-drunk as she was.

The cabin was very small with a very low ceiling, so David and I slept together in a space where none of us could stand upright. It made us giggle and David remarked that he hadn't thought about this when he said we were going to sleep here. I laughed, he kissed me and we quickly tore off our clothes and started to make love. It felt like everyone on the boat could hear and feel every movement we did, and every sound we made. But we did it. In fact, we did it to the max. We had wild and passionate sex for hours, and he showered me with compliments.

I thoroughly enjoyed my affair! It felt so good to just do exactly what I felt like, including deciding not to have it and then going ahead with it anyway. The love making was also uninhibited in a liberating way. Since he was living in Brussels I didn't have to think about which of the three roles I wanted him to fill.

This morning, we ate breakfast together with Renate and Ulrich and the other guests, and it was really nice. But I was a little surprised when we had to say goodbye, and David signaled for me to follow him outside. Out on the deck he leaned over and pushed me gently against the wall. He was definitely interested in more, as he told me how fantastic it was that we had met.

"I'll let you go only if you promise that we shall meet again," he said, looking into my eyes.

"Okay, okay," I said even though I really wasn't interested. This was a one-off thing and great as such.

"Let's meet in Paris—soon," he said.

I did not think it was necessary. We had had our affair. It was just sex like he normally has with other women and I felt no trace of guilt by doing it with him like this. It was a liberating sensation for me not to feel forced to consider his emotions. That was what he always did, and I enjoyed experiencing it, too. He insisted, so I said, "Alright."

LATE AFTERNOON

I MUST HAVE FALLEN asleep because I woke up when Arkan called me from the airport. His editor had called him and asked him to advance his trip, so he has to fly off to Cuba a day early and we can't meet. I wished him *bon voyage*, noting unwillingly that he was taking a little piece of my heart with him. How is that possible—I haven't even met him yet?!

MONDAY, APRIL 27TH

Oh, to be a Fly

AH, IT IS MARVELOUS to have the sun shining in on me as I'm sitting on the sofa in the late afternoon. I had a headache so I left work early, just in time to see the Nordic sun fading. Suddenly I remember that a sensation of comfort and care like this is the reason I subscribed to couple-dom in the first place: the idea that someone would be there for me when I'm old and grey and can't do anything for myself anymore other than sit in a sofa in the late afternoon sunshine. This always seemed to make sense to me, and it is one of the reasons people mention most often when advocating being part of a couple.

But then without our knowledge or consent, the twosome life somehow goes into retirement mode quite early on. It seems like there is less and less room for passion and curiosity as you form a couple with someone. Passion and curiosity are, in fact, considered dangerous enemies because they give you an explosive sense of being alive, which does not correspond well with the safe haven of couple-dom. But there is no guarantee that your loved one will be there when you grow old and are needy, so maybe it is too much to sacrifice passion and curiosity on the altar of security?

After this affair, I feel that everyone else can keep marriage for themselves; I'm going to recline on the sofa, enjoying my solo stupor in the sun.

Oh, what is *that* crawling there? A fly? Or a moth? It's too big to be a gnat . . . yes, it's a freaking fly! . . . oh, look, there's one more . . . it's unbelievable! The first one was just sitting there without lifting a wing and its partner comes ambling along and finds it! That can happen only to something with a tiny brain in our big big world. Why is it so easy for bugs, and so hard for humans? Yes, yes, they've got fewer needs than I do, but still. Aahhh, to be a fly . . .

TUESDAY, APRIL 28ᵀᴴ

Praise Yourself and Seek Ecstasy

THIS MORNING WAS A disaster. I was waiting for the train and my eye caught a bit of paper. It was a piece of that thin, delicate paper that street vendors use to wrap oranges, and it was hardly used. The wind set it dancing, and it landed on the train track just as the train pulled into the station. I could hear a brittle crackling through the noise of the train—and then the wind flicked a small corner of paper right into my eye. The flood gates opened as tears streamed down my cheeks. I had to wait for four trains to pass before I could move again.

When I arrived at the office, the first thing I heard was that my secretary's bike had been stolen and I started sobbing again! What is Copenhagen coming to? This used to be such a safe city to live in . . . one of the best cities in the world, inhabited by people who score highest on the happiness index. I certainly don't belong to that part of the population today! Maybe the bike was stolen by some forlorn woman who had just been shafted by a cheating boyfriend . . . Ugh, what an odd thought. I don't know where I got that from! I really don't want to become a man-hater!

Oh how this new romance model isn't simple . . . but it's hard to find the pause button now, I am really into it. But I can't put Mille on hold while I find myself and figure out this 3-man circus.

Just remembered: there are parent-teacher meetings today, I wonder if Sebastian will show up or if he'll text me some lame excuse or if he's forgotten it altogether. Am exhausted, everything is a MESS and there's a board of directors meeting tomorrow.

LATER

JUST TALKED TO KAREN and cried my eyes out; she's a good person to talk to when I feel like this. She makes time for me and she's so caring. We talked about Thomas. A couple of months have passed since I last saw him from behind the kitchen curtain.

He tried to let himself in, but I had already changed the locks. He rang the bell seven times. Seven. But I didn't open. He tried the door, which was locked. He held the bell in, ringing it again and again. The light was on, so he knew I was home. I saw him sit down on the porch. I went into the living room and put on a song I know he hates. Obstinate, he rang the bell again. Finally, he stomped down the garden walkway to the curb where his car was parked. When he got to the car I opened the door, music blaring, and I threw two bottles of his favorite aftershave out the door. They landed on the walkway and shattered. It made me feel good to do something forceful. I knew perfectly well the effect was only symbolic, but it helped me to be able to express my rage towards him for having cheated on me for six months.

Karen sent me an email to lift me out of my self-pity. It was a touching email, trying to make me feel better, in her own unique way. We've known each other since we were little, so I can tolerate the ruffles she puts both on her pillows and on life in general. But I have to share what she wrote; it is so simple, maybe even somewhat sappy and still true in some sense. It also reminds me of some of the things they taught us at the Goddess school where we went around each time we met, with each person bragging about something she had done. Apparently women are not very good at bragging.

Dear Elizabeth,

You need to start every day by praising yourself. Even before you've left the house, you've undoubtedly done something that deserves praise—maybe you've made coffee, set the table for breakfast, awoken your child with a tender kiss on the cheek, pampered yourself with a warm shower with some expensive, fragrant soap. Or maybe you've snuggled up close to one of your new men and abandoned yourself to one another in intense morning love-making.

Praise yourself by stopping for a moment and closing your eyes and imagining giving yourself a pat on the back and saying some words of praise. Then carry on with whatever you're doing.

Around lunchtime, it is time to praise yourself again. Maybe you rode your bicycle to work even though it was drizzling outside (oh, these Copenhagen mornings!). Or maybe you let a colleague tell you a ten-minute story she was dying to tell even though you were super busy. Stop, close your eyes and pat yourself on the back and praise yourself. Then carry on with whatever you're doing.

In the evening, when you're with family or friends or enjoying an evening in your own company, yes, it's time to praise yourself again. You might have gone for a run or made a healthy dinner for your family or just indulged them with a fast-food dinner, if that's what they prefer. Stop, close your eyes and pat your back and praise yourself. Then carry on with whatever you're doing.

When you're ready for bed, praise yourself again. When you've finished and your boyfriend initiates foreplay, remember that his lust is amplified because you're a wonderful person who has done her best at many things all day. You make passionate love for an hour if you're lucky, (for 5 or 10 minutes if you're not), then you enjoy a well-deserved night's sleep.

Elizabeth, this is the positive way of life, which encourages and creates love. You decide which energy you want to fill your life with. Each day we fill with negative energy holds us back from love. Each day we fill with positive energy brings us closer to love.

I hope you don't find this too sappy.
Much love, Karen

Yes, yes Karen, but you've already got a man who is a good father, two well-adjusted children and everything else and are soon to be married as you and your man are finally going to seal the deal after years of living together. But yes, I get it. Your sentiment is all right. And it can't hurt for me to try what you suggest. But it's a little hard to believe that self-praise and positive thinking will bring love back into my life. Hate myself for finding it hard!

Oops, there I am again with that negative energy. Going back and forth—is there something wrong with me, or is it with my 3-men model? Hopefully it's the model confusing me, but then I'm out of ideas again. And I have to take the blame. Damn!

It's no use sitting here whining, the winds are changing. Good for me, I'm standing up from the victim chair. Hanging onto my freedom of choice and enjoyment. The ancient Greeks said that humans go mad without ecstasy's purifying powers every now and then. We need to go out and get blown away, abandon ourselves, dance, drink, make love and forget who we are before we can reinvent ourselves . . . Hope the world is ready, because I am!

LATER

ODDLY ENOUGH, SEBASTIAN DID show up at the school and took part in the meetings with the teachers as a good dad full of praise and constructive suggestions. Wonder what is happening or rather when this harmonious phase will pass like they always do with him.

WEDNESDAY, APRIL 29TH

I'll Remember that Sheepish Look for a Long Time

JUST FINISHED A RATHER entertaining Board of Directors meeting. I had been so eager to find out if my strategy would succeed. Instead of acquiescing to Horn's requests, I had invited a representative from the Department so the Board could hear firsthand just why it is so 'critical,' according to Horn, for the entrepreneurs to fill out his stupid forms to use the conference rooms.

Chairman Carlsen and I started the day with a cup of coffee together and he inspired me to have stamina and be calm by reminding me that the majority of the Board is on my side. Nonetheless, I was nervous when I started the meeting and Horn strutted into the room like a cock on a VIP mission. He barely deigned look at Mr. Nielsen before I had introduced him. When he realized that the Department Head's personal assistant was there, Horn raised his nose even higher than usual, and he could hardly wait until we got to his item on the agenda: his beloved conference room reporting forms.

When we got to that point, I introduced the topic by explaining that we had heard rumors about more forms on the way for entrepreneurs who wanted an office in our agency. And one form in particular troubles us, I said, the one that entrepreneurs would have to fill out in order just to use a conference room. For each conference, they'd need to provide information about the length of time they met, with whom they met including the company's name, the people present and their job titles, and their company's tax ID number. That's an unreasonable amount of required information, and it doesn't help the entrepreneurs in any way. They fight a constant battle with time as it is—it's not easy to become a success in a new market.

Horn sat shaking his finger frantically to indicate that he had something to add to my speech. Unfortunately, the Chairman of the Board showed him mercy by first asking Mr. Nielsen if he could comment on the rumors. Mr. Nielsen thanked him and began to praise us—hehehe—for being one of Denmark's best-run entrepreneurial startup support agencies, and the only one with a waiting list of entrepreneurs seeking to join. Then he said that the Department had discussed introducing new forms like the ones I had described, but upon closer inspection, it had become 'absolutely' clear that our resources could be put to use more productively by performing a collective analysis of the documentation requirements for entrepreneurs overall—and to identify *how to reduce* the amount of reporting.

Horn nearly choked on his Danish pastry, and his once fervently waving hand became flustered and flapped strangely until finally, he stuck it in his pocket. I'll remember his sheepish expression with great pleasure the next time he tries his untimely interference—if he dares. What a joyous day it will be when he retires!

LATER

A Competition

FOR CENTURIES, WOMEN HAVE been struggling for male attention. I'm ready to turn the tables and be the one getting the attention. I think we need to turn the tables because the female and male roles that society has to offer nowadays are too simple and restrictive:

For women:
- Florence Nightingale = mother and caretaker
- Lady Macbeth = dominatrix
- Jennifer Aniston = trophy

For men:
- The Boss = father and authority
- The Lion from The Wizard of Oz = the henpecked man
- George Clooney = trophy

And we must choose between these roles. How limiting. Presently a lot of us are doing that and some are even stressing themselves out trying to play all three roles at the same time. What if we just decide to use this new model of mine, and fulfill different needs with different people? Or find a whole other new model? Or several new alternatives for love and romance? Whatever they are, they must be models where the intimate encounter is precious, because a fulfilling erotic, sexual life has a transforming capacity. You are more relaxed and happy, harmony reigns and you feel generous after having great intercourse. You become eager for more and want your whole life to be as good as that.

Just went online to check for emails—47 new ones! This is going exceptionally well! And some of them are really good, even if the pompous sexual manhood self-promotion percentage is staggering. It's so not a turn-on for me. I want lust, pleasure, soulfulness . . . and not just to get laid. Respect my brains, too, please, as it makes everything so much better.

The many identical replies indicate that intelligent, lustful women still haven't become a favorite cocktail in our society. Either you're smart and men respect you for it, or you're a horny girl who wants sex all the time and that does not generate respect. At the same time, I find that sexual life is still primarily defined by men, with their masculine expressions about setting up a goal, their images about preparing for the hunt and their desires when catching the prey.

I've read that when young people today go out and have sexual experiences, one or more of the parties involved are often under the influence of alcohol or drugs. This means that both parties don't develop a nuanced, poetic language and a nuanced range of physical sensations based on their sexual experiences. They just continue the stubborn male and female stereotypes leftover from the 1950's—where lustful men are virile and lustful women are cheap. There must be a better paradigm for women – and men, too.

I think it's time for a contest. There's myriad powerful, acceptable expressions for the sex-crazed attractive man: stallion, hunk, Casanova, Don Juan. I can't think of a single positive expression for a lustful woman. Just negative ones like slut, tart, man-eater, hussy, harlot, and these days, MILF and cougar.

Contest: Come up with the best positive name for a horny woman.
Prize: A medal that I design and a date with me ;-)

Must reschedule a date with the journalist, Arkan. He should be back from Cuba soon. And Svend, the dental supply guy; have to get back to him and fix a date, too. There are also some new good candidates for talk-dates among those 47 new replies . . . must follow up on it, but now I need to cook something for my Mille, who'll be home in 10 minutes . . . This is turning out to be a pretty time-consuming experiment!

LATER, IN THE EVENING

MILLE CAME HOME AND told me that her dad, Sebastian, has a new girl-friend! Instantly I felt like somebody had punched me in the stomach. And it only increased by hearing how excited Mille was about her.

"She's sooo nice, Mom!!! And she's a mega-good swimmer! Can I start taking swimming lessons from her? She says I can get really good at it, and she's a teacher at the place right down the street. Please, Mom?? She taught me how to swim underwater and I did it for almost a whole minute! She's been swimming with dolphins, isn't that amazing. Oh, and she says I can start on next Sunday afternoon at 10 a.m. . . oh please, can I Mom??"

A girlfriend??? What am I supposed to say to that? My heart stopped for a minute . . . with jealousy, UGH! I should be happy for my daughter . . . And it's fantastic if Sebastian has found a good girlfriend who cares for Mille as well.

It's actually lovely to hear Mille puttering around the house, not to mention the huge hug she gave me when I said yes to swimming lessons; now that's true love. And it's marvelous if she's found something she's passionate about . . . even if Sebastian's new girlfriend was her inspiration.

On the other hand, how on earth can that completely hopeless, choleric man find a nice woman when I have such difficulties in my love life? And why does that woman have to be so nice that I feel threatened as Mille's first preference? I'm sure she is an ugly, horrible bitch who is just out to steal my lovely daughter!!

Alright Dixie, calm down now! Jealousy has many faces. And I know that it can be a benefit of divorce that children get more adults in their life growing up and aren't stuck with just one pair of parents, but she's MY little girl . . . yes, um, rewind, Elizabeth. Rephrase: Mille is her own little girl and it's lovely that Sebastian has a nice new girlfriend. Must accept it. Done. Basta. For now! Must be a grown up mom who respects the new girlfriend of an ex-husband I don't even want back.

Rebecca just texted to invite Mille and me to her summer house this Friday night and I said yes.

SATURDAY, MAY 2ND

Shania Dixie Twain

WOKE UP EARLY AT Rebecca's summerhouse and went down to sit by the ocean. I love going to summerhouses because life at the beach in Denmark is much simpler. People often have quite small cabins where they do a lot of creative decorating and design. The outdoor patio is often made up as a living room and most of the time is spent here. Friends drop by, neighbors come for coffee and the Danish concept of *hygge* unfolds itself fully. The word means 'coziness' in its most literal sense, but it is more than that. It implies having a warm social ambiance, enjoying life's simple pleasures such as food and drink, talking and laughing together, wrapping a quilt around your legs when the light summer night falls around 11 p.m. this time of year, or taking a lazy stroll with friends by the sea. Nothing is urgent, no need to rush anything; just feel good and make the person next to you feel good, too.

As I sat there, my gaze wandered out over the sea to the horizon, and my heart began beating in time with the waves crashing gently on the shore. I felt an immense calm spreading over my body, and I could sense that my feelings about everything that had happened with Thomas were finally dissipating. Even if I wanted to, Thomas and I could never get back together again. It just wasn't okay that he had cheated on me for six months after I had been there for him and supported him and helped him get into a gallery. Sitting there on the beach, I realized that I now had to tie up the loose ends. I don't know why I let him keep his things in my house for so long—they needed to go NOW. The urgency of this decision made me decide that I had to leave Rebecca's house right after lunch, even though we had only been there one night.

As soon as Mille and I got home, she went over to the neighbor's and I put on Shania Twain's song, 'That don't impress me much,' rolled up my sleeves and emptied Thomas' chest of drawers and pushed, lifted and hauled it out the door into the garden, right in the middle of the lawn. I went back inside and came out with the drawers, which I put back in. With every step, I bid Thomas—and the dream of the two of us together—farewell.

I brought his clothes on hangers and laid them across the top of the chest. My heart ached at his smell still in his green spring jacket. I stomped back inside and began carrying out his canvases, both painted and unpainted, leaning them up against the sides of the chest. Tears began to stream down my cheeks. So many dreams . . . I forced my thoughts to go elsewhere, but I couldn't stop the tears.

I brought out a big wooden supply box and deposited it at the foot of the canvases. And next to that landed ten pairs of shoes, a full sports bag and a beautiful lamp with its thin white wooden lampshade that I knew was made by a very expensive Danish designer. I had to carry out his armchair, too. It weighed a ton, and the only reason I could carry it was that I was furious that something apparently had been missing in our relationship so he had to go elsewhere. But more than that, I was angry at myself that I hadn't let him know what I needed. Prodded by anger's poker, I maneuvered the armchair to its place alongside the chest of drawers. The sky darkened and I considered waiting a while before sending him a text so everything would be drenched by the time he got there. But reason got the best of me and I wrote him a text message: "All of your things are in the garden. If they're not gone by tomorrow, I'll set them on fire." Well, I thought that was reasonable enough!

It felt good to treat him like that. I wanted him out of my life, and that would only happen when his things disappeared. I know it was a rather drastic act of boldness on my part, and he had always hated my drastic side. Which only made it all the more appropriate.

I went back in the house and noticed all of his paints. I took the 15 tubes I had bought him from Milan and hurled them, one after the other, onto the pile. Then I threw the tablecloth he had gotten from his grandmother over everything, like a shroud. And the image of all of that love, lying there on a *lit de parade* hit me with a force I wasn't prepared for. The tears rose again, and I crumpled at the kitchen door. An hour later a moving van pulled up. I got up and brushed myself off. Two men I didn't know got out of the van and started carrying Thomas' things away. I drew the curtains and put on the Rolling Stones, whom Thomas didn't like, and turned it up loud while I cried.

SUNDAY, MAY 3ᴿᴰ

Do Emotions Belong in Respectable Circles?

THIS MORNING I WROTE some emails and planned a busy week. At 10, I'm going to the swimming pool with Mille, Sebastian and his new girlfriend. I'm nervous about it since meeting competition is quite unpredictable. Handyman Lasse is coming over at 2 p.m. with his son. He will be erasing all traces of Thomas in the garden and stabilizing my book case, I hope. And tomorrow night, some of my old friends from our university days are coming over for dinner.

I also need to set up a date with Svend, the dental supply guy, for drinks at the beautiful bar Quote in the center of the most affluent part of Copenhagen, Kongens Nytorv, close to the Queen's castle. I had thought about choosing Hotel d'Angleterre for a meeting place, which is also on that square. After its renovation, it really presents itself like the old jewel it always was. I love when old buildings are restored in a sensitive way so you still feel the ambience of its former days when famous artists sat there having intellectual discussions or playing beautiful music on the Steinway piano in the restaurant. But I decided on Quote, so we could sit outside and enjoy the view of the hotel's beautiful façade.

This coming week, Mille and I are also going to the movies to see Lone Scherfig's film, *An Education*, about how the life of a teenage girl in the 1960s is changed by the arrival of a handsome playboy who is twice her age. The film was nominated for an Oscar in three categories.

In an interview, the Danish director Scherfig calls her movie a *trivial* matter. I don't understand why, but movies and books about emotions with a woman in the main role are often labeled trivial or banal. This is repeated as if it is a statement of absolute truth, almost excusing people from thinking about anything banal for any amount of time. I think that excluding the banal from the realm of the respectable creates blind spots in our culture. Almost all emotions are banal, so we effectively exclude emotions from respectability. And because we detest the banal, we're bereft of appropriate words and descriptions for it. But then we don't improve our ability to deal with the increasing complexity of our relationships, break-ups and our waning and waxing desires. To tackle our hopes and dreams, we should be able to describe our emotions in detail and discuss them intelligently so we can be more and more precise in understanding how we feel. Emotions make life worth living. To take control of their complexity, one must master the banal.

I remember a period in my life when I didn't really know what I wanted to do. It gave me an unpleasant sensation of drifting about and I couldn't really act. Once I had identified a goal, it all changed. I was able to plan and start acting to reach that goal. Being able to describe in a precise manner how we want our emotional life to be enables us to start working at reaching that emotional state.

LATER

I'm Jealous and Not Proud of It!

HOW SEBASTIAN LANDED 'SWIM COACH' Marianne is beyond my comprehension . . . She is so nice and sweet and in some surprising way she has turned Mille onto swimming. It's kind of unfair, and it peeves me, even though I know I should be thankful. School is going well, luckily, and all of Mille's teachers sing her praises.

When Sebastian came over—with Marianne . . . and Mille threw herself around her neck . . . I felt like an intruder in my own home. Sebastian's head was clear, and so was his gaze. I was overwhelmed by a massive feeling of irritation about all of the times he had let me down, and I had a nearly uncontrollable need to start rattling at him, but I stood there, smiling and smiling. I feel like a deplorable human. I also don't trust Sebastian's supposed new lifestyle, as I know he'll suddenly hit the bottle and disappear for days on end . . . or maybe I'm just bitter because he's changed now, under Marianne's influence? Still don't think he's got a backbone.

We all left for the swim center. My nerves were more stable by then after having met the competition and actually feeling good in her company. We arrived early so we sat in the cafeteria and had a coffee. Marianne is amazed at Mille's talent for swimming, and she and I had a serious talk about the training. Mille is thrilled. It means swimming three times a week for an hour and physical training on land for three months, and later on, swimming five times a week and training on land twice. A pretty tough program for such a young girl, but it would be foolish to say no . . . even if I wanted to. Marianne says that Mille is one of the most talented young swimmers she's seen since she started her training at the National Training Center in the 1990s. She believes that with the right training, Mille can become a competitive swimmer . . . even Olympic material.

At one point, Mille and Sebastian left to deal with some practical stuff, leaving me alone with Marianne. She looked me straight in the eye and said that she'd like to have Mille live with them for a few months after Sebastian moves in with her! I was surprised since I had just met her, but at the same time, I liked her directness. There seemed to be no beating around the bush with her. The idea actually made me giddy—it was both scary and a good idea. Mille had already mentioned that she'd like to live with her father for a while, and with Marianne on the scene to be a substitute-mom, I believe it'll work. And then I'd have time for my experiment. But do I dare let go of Mille? And what does Sebastian have to say about it?

When Mille and I got home, I thought that I'd better talk to Sebastian alone . . . it's possible that he wouldn't think it's a good idea . . . and it would actually surprise me if he did. He refused to have Mille full-time in the past, even for a month. I can't grasp how some men just don't feel like being with their children . . . he was ecstatic about keeping the baby when I got pregnant, even though I was more inclined to have an abortion. He convinced me to keep it in the name of love; I was deaf to the alarms going off in my head about him. How naïve I was. And what a shock when he disappeared for weeks when I was four months pregnant—just about right after the date when it was still possible to have a legal abortion. Maybe I've never gotten over that. Felt trapped, deceived, betrayed. And right after Mille was born, he disappeared again. Damn, I can still feel the anger boiling up inside.

I never moved all of his things into the garden and set them on fire. I wonder if it's too late to do it with the cushions and the blanket of his that I still have?

A Handyman in My Birch Tree

LUCKILY LASSE AND HIS son came over at 2 p.m. and interrupted my train of thoughts. My new handyman was sexy, effective, and sweet, and his son was even sweeter.

The kids romped in the garden while Lasse climbed around in the birch tree trimming branches. He was nimble as a panther, self-confident, and alarmingly sexy. The smell of his fresh sweat filled the house when he came in from the garden, and I was certainly not immune to it until I caught his gaze with those deep blue eyes . . . pretty confusing. Must remember that the arrangement is based on handiwork and warm meals. And he's absolutely not my type! Though maybe I actually should have an affair with a guy who is not my type?

While Lasse erased the last traces of Thomas from the lawn, I put a few baked potatoes in the oven, made a nice green salad and grilled some burgers, which Lasse, Martin and Mille wolfed down. Two cold beers, and then Lasse went back to work while the children watched cartoons over a box of chocolates that Lasse had brought.

I was cleaning the kitchen after our meal and didn't hear the door open. I realized Lasse was there when I felt his hand on my hips and his kiss on the back of my neck. I was unprepared but my hands found his body by themselves and I leaned back and leaned in. He kissed me and I turned my head and kissed him and touched his member. It felt hard. My breathing intensified and so did his and before I knew it he had thrown me onto the kitchen table, put on a condom and we were at it. I enjoyed it thoroughly but took care to be as quiet as I could in order not to attract attention from the living room. We came together and then quickly brought our clothes in order. He grinned at me and went back into the garden. I smiled.

At eight o'clock, the two took off. By that time, my bookcase had been rescued before it fell to the floor, Mille's new computer was up and running, the birch tree was pruned, the lawn mowed, the gutters cleaned and the gutter that used to hang and bang into the side of the house when it was windy was repaired. It had been driving me mad since it dislodged in a storm in January. Martin's cheeks were red as apples with exhaustion and he had almost fallen asleep watching cartoons.

It was just as cozy a Sunday as I'd hoped it would be – and on top of that I had another affair, now with one of my handymen! I'm now lying here with a warm fuzzy feeling, buzzing with gratitude for a perfectly lovely time. So, looks like I've found one of my three men—ironically enough, first for the position I had thought would be most difficult to fill. I didn't promise him any sex for it. He just took what he wanted. Which was quite fine, since I enjoyed it. Wonder what will happen next time he comes . . . if he does.

MONDAY, MAY 4TH

The New Model

I HAD MY OLD university friends Erik, Kamilla and Kasper over for dinner tonight. We meet once a year for a bit of a reunion, and usually have a great time. We know each other so well—we did several projects together and wrote most of our group thesis together while we were studying. We called ourselves KEKE, because of the first letters in our names. We thought that made us pretty cool.

After the main course, I told them about my three-men plan. Kamilla thought it was exciting, brilliant, and very modern. I could see how interested she was when I listed the challenges that couples face and then I started talking about some of the dates I had had. But I was soon interrupted by Kasper, who said, "The premise is all wrong; where is the tenderness and love?"

"I think it's a cruel way to treat men," Erik said.

"It's not supposed to be cruel. I just think we need to articulate our needs differently than the standard two couple-model allows us to," I answered, in an attempt to defend myself. "There are so many people saying one thing and doing another. Take infidelity for instance; statistics says that 40% of all women and 60% of all men in a committed relationship have been unfaithful—well, I think that's because the relationship premises are all wrong."

"You just want men to fulfill your needs. Where is the love?" Kasper repeated.

"You can't look for love in the personals anyway," I answered. "We're all looking for love, and maybe we have a better chance of finding it when one or more of our other needs are fulfilled."

"I'm not so sure about that," Kamilla said. "It seems to me like love becomes insignificant if you start with needs."

"I just don't have the right words yet to explain it," I said trying to convince them. "I can't use the words available today to paint an accurate picture of love and all its nooks and crannies. The words I encounter around the concept are insufficient. The words we use only work in the center of the middle class' fortress of security. But for me, security is only one of the elements in a relationship. How about passion and curiosity for instance? They combine badly with security but that does not make them go away. The words we have to describe love in a relationship signify the creation of a solid, safe place, one that is ideal for children. That's important, of course, but what children need is not enough for grownups. We are maintaining an illusion! I've spent many years trying to silence the noise around love, relationships and twosomeness in my own head. That noise is made up of romantic expectations, imagined ideals, and unrealistic wishes. And in the twosomes I've been in, I've spent more energy on notions than on reality."

"I still think something is missing in your model," Kasper said.

"Yes, possibly," I responded, "but try to see it in the bigger picture of things. If we use my model, in ten years' time we'll be able to talk about love and deal with it in a completely different way. We'll be able to identify some of love's missing elements, and tell each other how each and every one of us wants to prioritize those elements. Presently, we can only be respected if we say yes to living in a monogamous relationship with the same person from high school till death do us part, as if life isn't a dynamic, changing thing. It becomes the only dream we are allowed to have. And yet the only thing we can be 100% sure of is that over a lifetime, things change and therefore love changes. We can either accept that living is a dynamic motion and let go of our immature longings for eternal bliss, or we can deny the changes and continue to try to control ourselves and the other person."

"I think you expect a lot from people," Kamilla said and she continued. "People need to be very conscious about themselves with your model and in control of their emotions—which they are not."

"Alright," I said and continued. "The paradox is that we pretend that something is working, namely our model of the ideal love, in spite of the fact that we constantly see its shortcomings in real life. What can you do, for instance, if:

A. you encounter somebody who spurs your curiosity, or
B. your preferred partner encounters somebody who spurs his or her curiosity?

"According to the romantic construction, it is a disaster. But from an existential perspective, that's actually where it becomes interesting. I believe that we have these images, words and tools to initiate love with another person, but I don't think that we have enough images, words and tools to bring love further than that with another person. But if we dissect love and divide it into its fundamental elements—which for me are talking and sharing, helping each other, and sex—we can understand each other better and make agreements about what we want from each other."

"What do you mean exactly, in concrete terms?" Kasper asked and looked at me.

"I believe that we'll have very different romantic relationships in ten years than we do now."

"How?" Kasper continued.

This gave me a chance to spell out my theory.

"I've made a list of the main elements of love that men and women exchange:

1. we talk to each other
2. we have sex
3. we take care of practicalities
4. we are loving and caring
5. we give each other security and have a good time together
6. we challenge each other
7. we have a child together

"Let's say that a relationship starts when two people meet, feel attracted to each other and give each other a #1 through #7 cocktail, and then she gets pregnant. Let's say both of them want parenthood, and a new chapter in their life begins where they now have to make a number of choices. When you have a child, you can't continue just like before. The need for a home becomes more tangible. You have less time to yourself. Most of your daily rhythms change, and so on. While the two people are creating their home, they can discuss which of the above are most important to them. Maybe she'll make a priority list, such as:

- we have a child together
- we give each other security and have a good time together
- we are loving and caring
- we take care of practicalities
- we talk to each other
- we have sex

"That means that the most important thing for her is having a child together, and security and caring and practicalities are also important. Talking and sex are also important, but not quite as important as the other things. Meanwhile, his list of priorities may go like this:

- we have sex
- we have a child together
- we have sex
- we take care of practicalities
- we have sex
- we challenge each other

"For him, the most important thing is that they have sex and that they have a child together, followed again by his need for sex. And he finds it important to challenge each other before cream-colored teddy-bear fur starts growing on everything. And then have sex.

"It's already clear that they both want the child. So my idea is this: What if they have the child together, and then have some of their other needs met elsewhere instead of spending years trying to get the other person to give something that they don't want to give and ending up with a divorce—which is hard on everyone involved.

"This way, women and men can create a solid, safe environment for their children. And when they've created their home, the man and woman decide which of the three roles the man will fulfill in their life together. So men can introduce themselves with: Hi, I'm a number three to Karin and Elizabeth's number two. And women can say: Henrik is my one and Peter is my two right now. And nobody needs to be ashamed," I explained with finality. "There, that's my take on modern love."

They laughed and I smiled. I actually meant it seriously.

"I think it sounds pretty cold and calculating," Kamilla said.

"But some couples already have arrangements like that now," Kasper agreed with me.

I could tell he had understood me, and he may even have experienced the same loss for words that I talked about to express what actually happens with couples today.

"I find that a lot of people have a hard time remaining within the narrow scope of a twosome," I said. "They can find parts of themselves, but they have a hard time finding themselves completely. That's why they go out looking for the rest of their needs. They're looking for passionate sex, better conversation, or a different type of social interaction, or maybe tenderness or excitement that they cannot get at home. The only thing people don't go out looking for is security," I added. "So let's make a model that ensures security and creates a safe haven for the children while also allowing grown up people to deal honestly with the rest of their needs inside or outside the security relationship.

"Nowadays, if people are dissatisfied with their relationship, they get a divorce and go out and find someone else to have a relationship with. Six months later they have a new partner, but maybe the same old frustrations exist and possibly another divorce follows. Haven't we seen this happen to many, many people . . . serial marriages?"

"But do you really think we can have security without love?" Kamilla asked.

"I think things become messy because we want security but we refuse to talk about the price we are willing to pay for it. In some way, we think that security, love and inspiring company can just mix and everything will be fine. But it doesn't work like that. Security deals with having a stable and decent place to live with nice furniture, etc. Love is a deep sensation of togetherness, desire and bliss with another person. An inspiring company is about searching for new ideas and challenges together to become wiser. These three areas are very different from each other and yet we try to stuff them into the same mold. Of course, it doesn't work!" I said.

"I know my list of three needs isn't the be-all-end-all answer, and some might ask where does love fit in? But I'm confident that love will find its place. That's actually what it's trying to do today, but it's having a hard time recognizing itself in the labels people give it."

"Fat bloody chance with your model," Erik said. "You talk as much as my wife!"

Hmm, I didn't know what he meant by that. Were he and his wife having trouble? "Anyway," I continued, "an awful lot of things need to fit before love can grow. And every time two people meet, there are nuances and details that need to work out. But when two people travel through life, they undergo changes, their needs change and their reciprocity changes. Our relationship model should be able to accommodate that. I don't feel that our narrow definition of a couple relationship can do that."

"Relationships between couples are fundamentally nothing more than a legal construct, created to ensure a high degree of conservatism in a patriarchal society," said Kasper. "Women are not supposed to be unfaithful because then men won't know if their children are really theirs, and there goes the order of succession. Patriarchal society is conservative and doesn't want people to relocate, or if they must, it should be motivated by a new job. Thirty years of home mortgage and the prospect of an expensive divorce are two elements that will pacify most people from splitting up."

"Yes," I agreed, "infidelity is a legal threat to patriarchy, more so than anything else. I just don't think that the conservative patriarchal institution of marriage is made for humans. I want relationships in which I can grow and bloom as the woman I am, and where my partner can do the same. If you look at how people are behaving these days, some of the most closely-knit traditions of love are already shifting. At some point, I'm sure the laws will catch up to behaviors as well."

"I sense that you will be at the forefront of that revolution," Kasper laughed.

"I just urge people to take themselves and their needs seriously even though society doesn't currently have a model to hold it. And you know what?"

They all looked at me.

"I propose that as many of us as possible should live with this three-partner model for a while to become aware of what is truly important in our love life and train our capacities to hold onto it."

They looked at me and we raised our glasses, but all we could agree to toast to was an improved love life for all.

One Text Message from Arkan and More from David

SEBASTIAN CALLED AND INVITED Mille to the swimming pool; surprisingly, he's venturing outside of 'his' weekends with her. I agreed on the condition that he would bring her home by 8 p.m. sharp since it was school day tomorrow. Sebastian promised he would.

He arrived to get her, and while Mille was packing her swimming bag, I seized the opportunity to talk to him about Marianne's idea to have Mille move in with them. Mille would love it, she told me yesterday. He agreed and went on to tell me that, in that case, he'd use the next couple of months' child payments to me to buy himself a new amplifier for the band! What a cad! I just nodded mutely and felt inwardly grateful that I wasn't Marianne, so I didn't have to clarify for him that *child* payments are meant to cover *child* expenses, not band expenses!

When Mille came out, her swimming bag slung over her shoulder, we told her the news. She was so thrilled that we agreed she could move on Saturday. A little sooner than I had imagined, but that's just how it is. And then there would be no more excuses: I'd have to get on with my three-men experiment. But of course I didn't tell Sebastian about it. Because even if the freedom that her moving to their place affords me is practical, it disconcerts me.

Is it really a good idea to send Mille to Sebastian's? Am I pushing her right into Marianne's arms? What if she likes Marianne better than me? I'd have an awfully hard time with that. Must try not to think about it because I know that I cannot offer her the same as Marianne can in terms of all the swimming.

At 8 p.m. Sebastian brought Mille home with an uncharacteristic punctuality.

Arkan texted at 11:15 p.m.: *Hey good looking, when's it my turn? Love Arkan*

Answered him at midnight: *As soon as you get back! Love Dixie*

I also keep getting texts from David: *Enjoying my memories of you. And fantasizing about the things we might do in the future. Longing for your eyes. Love David*

Keep fantasizing about possible future pleasures . . . you just might be able to interest me! I answered.

You can't always get what you want. Immediate satisfaction might make you lazy! David

I'm tired of not getting what I want so I don't have much patience! I wrote.

Remember the rule: The best satisfaction is postponed satisfaction. David

You are a pleasure expert! Have you ever considered writing a Pleasure Bible? I wrote.

Good idea! Will you help me do some research ;-)? David

The Limping Water Buffalo

TODAY'S THE DAY FOR my date with Svend, the dental supply guy. We're meeting for drinks at 5 p.m. And I called the The Allinge Retreat Centre—they have room for me starting next Sunday!

LATER THAT DAY

SVEND WITH HIS DENTAL supplies was a waste of time. I walked into Café Quote and within 30 seconds we both knew it wouldn't work. What to do? I tried to be a good sport. There's too much of a nice girl left in me. I was bored, and it was obvious that he was too. Interesting sensation to bore somebody and realize it while it takes place.

Then he mentioned that he collects weapons. Since I don't know anyone who owns a weapon, I decided to interview him.

Holland & Holland is one of the world's finest weapon manufacturers. They make firearms, including rifles that cost over 20,000 euros each. He had one of those. On top of that, he had twenty other fine weapons. The best hunt he'd ever been on was a week-long snipe hunt in England. He didn't manage to shoot any snipes, because they fly in a zigzag pattern

(. . . yaaaawn). And then there was the hunt for the South African water buffalo, which he had spotted before the local guides did.

"Get out of here!" I said, "Wow, that's impressive. Wasn't it dangerous?"

"Yes, but the thing wasn't exactly young."

"What does that mean?"

"Well, it had a bit of a limp."

"Okay, then it wasn't sooo dangerous."

It seemed to rile him that I suddenly didn't think it was very dangerous.

"Yes it was," he insisted. "If it attacked, we'd have been dead. They weigh over 250 pounds and they have killer tusks."

"What did the locals say?"

"Well, like I said, they hadn't seen it."

"Maybe because they didn't think it was worth it to shoot a limping, old water buffalo?"

"That's not true!" he pouted.

"Okay, okay, I wasn't there, what do I know," I said, thinking: am I right or am I right?!

We parted ways shortly afterwards, and I'm still snickering about him and his hobbling old water buffalo.

Who'd have thought it would be so hard to find someone on the internet to have sex with, especially with all of the new replies to my profile?

~~~~~~~~~~~~~~~~~~~~~~~~

Texted Arkan at 11:15 p.m.:

Hey Arkan, you're back tomorrow, right? How about drinks at The Standard Jazz Club, Saturday from 5 to 6 p.m.? Love Dixie

At 11:17 he answered: *Deal, Dixie! Love A*

At the same moment I received an email from Viggo who responded to my profile with an intriguing description of our first possible meeting:

Dear Dixie,

I want to meet you because I believe that I can give you what you are longing for. I am 40 years old, I have a good career in the telecom business and I know what I want in life. One of the most important things for me is a happily satisfied woman. Do you dare to meet me without knowing more, so I can be your next sex date? Viggo

Sure I dare! We are meeting tomorrow since I've decided it is best to quickly meet the men who respond, so I don't have time to build dream castles around them and me.

But I can see that this is harder than I thought. Still no one available for position #1.

PHILOSOPHER	LOVER	HANDYMAN
	• Arkan • David from Belgium • Viggo	• Lasse

FRIDAY, MAY 8TH

Oh No, Mr. Grey

THIS AFTERNOON MILLE AND I packed her stuff to prepare the move and listened to music and basically just spent some quality mother-daughter time together like we haven't done for a long time. Marianne can try to do be a surrogate mom, but she hasn't got a chance in the world of replacing me, I realized!

In the middle of it all, my mother arrived. I summoned her to look after Mille tonight while I'm meeting Viggo for a short date. My mom was serene and had a bottle of champagne under her arm. I hadn't seen her for a long time and was pleasantly surprised to see how good she looked—the divorce was the best thing that could have happened to her. And that wasn't all. The champagne was to celebrate that she has gotten a solo show at Gallery Jeppesen! The opening is on June 20, at 5 p.m. I can't remember the last time I saw my mother so happy. I suggested we go out and buy her some new clothes, and she's got a hairdresser's appointment next week. From her bedroom, Mille hollered that she wants to come along for the shopping, so that's the plan. Three generations shopping together.

I once made love to a musician boyfriend while listening to a radio program called "Two Generations Play It Again," where he and his father talked and challenged each other with different pieces of music. Making love to him while hearing him talk to his father was magnificent, like making love to him and everything that had made him what he was and his past and his future. Meta-sex, I guess you could call it. I can warmly recommend it.

Shortly afterwards though, he became past tense.

At 6 p.m. I left my mom and Mille in the house and went to the local bar where Viggo and I had agreed to meet.

Viggo was quite a charming, good-looking man who came to our date with a small suitcase. That should have made me suspicious.

He gave me a hug and held onto me tightly for ten seconds which felt like too long a time to hug somebody you don't know. That should have warned me as well. But he had already found us two places at the bar and ordered two glasses of champagne and some olives. We toasted. He looked at me with magnetized eyes that pulled me in, so I felt I had to let go of my hesitations. Final warning that I did not get.

After two glasses of champagne where he had been charming and entertaining about his work, my work and politics, he asked if I was ready to follow him for more. I looked at him and figured he was an intriguing type that I couldn't quite decipher. So I said yes.

He told me to put on my coat and close it all the way up. I did so, a bit puzzled. We went outside and he tied my scarf around my neck and held onto one end of it, so it resembled a leash. I just thought he was fooling around. He wasn't.

We went to an apartment nearby. I asked if it was his.

"Yes, I've rented it for six hours," he said.

"Oh," I said and understood that it was a love nest you could hire by the hour. It was a great apartment by one of the lakes in Copenhagen in the wealthy neighborhood of Frederiksberg.

After we had entered and were standing in front of the staircase to the apartment, he turned around to me and said, "I need to blindfold you."

I hesitated but said OK since the place seemed nice and I felt the sexual excitement inside me building up. It was also intriguing that he had gone through so much effort to plan things for us. I felt exhilarated by the fact that he had something in store for me.

He blindfolded me, we mounted the stairs and I could hear that he unlocked a door. We went in.

"Take off your panties," he commanded me.

I did and felt the excitement rise even more.

He grabbed my arms and before I knew it, he had tied them together behind my back with a piece of rope.

"I'm only interested in having safe sex," I said.

"Sure," he said.

Then I heard him make a sound with something in his hand. It sounded like a whip hitting his hand. Then a whip hit my thighs! And then again! Oh my god, I should have seen it coming.

"Ah!" I exclaimed.

"That's right! The more it hurts you, the more excited I get."

"Well, I don't really know if this is for me," I said more forcefully not quite knowing if it was exciting or too much.

"Do you know Christian Grey?" he said. "He knows how to handle a woman."

"From *50 Shades of Grey*? You gotta be joking. You read that book?" He didn't seem to pick up on my literary taunt.

"I bet you always wanted to surrender yourself to a strong man. Am I right?" he continued.

"Well . . . , I guess so."

"He is right here, right now ready to spank you till you come hard," he exclaimed with a pride I could not miss.

"Viggo, I don't really know . . . , " I said even though I didn't really feel safe anymore with him. He was not listening and I was too confused to know what to do.

"Bend over," he commanded.

I did as I was told, hoping in some contradictory way that he was right about my future excitement and fulfillment.

He got behind me and started slapping my buttocks. At first it felt erotic, but when he increased the force, it quickly got unpleasant.

I heard him unbuttoning his pants.

"No!" I yelled and tried to move away which was difficult since my hands were tied.

"Oh, yes," he said and tried to enter me. I could feel his member hard and stiff already seeking a way in.

"STOP!" I screamed and pushed him over with my shoulders.

I had caught him so off guard, he tripped over his pants that were hanging around his ankles and he fell to the floor.

I lowered my head sideways to my shoulder and succeeded in pushing off the blindfold. I looked at him and saw a wild man blinded by his own desire.

"You said you were ready for more. Come on, you sexy little slut."

I turned back and ran to the door. I heard him get up and hoped getting his pants back on would delay him. With my back towards the door, I succeeded in pushing the handle down to open it even though my hands were still tied behind my back. I ran down the steps.

When I arrived at the entrance door, I struggled with the rope and succeeded in liberating one hand. I used it to open the door and ran out to the street, untangling the rest of the rope from my other wrist. Then I took off towards the lake and ran along it as fast as I could. Once when I looked back I saw him standing by the water looking in my direction, waving his arms at me. At the end of the lake I hailed a cab and arrived home panting—and pantyless.

What a jerk! He really thought he was like Grey and had no idea that consensual sex means that you both give your consent to what is going to happen. It certainly doesn't mean that he gets to decide everything to get what he wants.

SATURDAY, MAY 9TH—LATE

What a Journalist

IT WAS TOUGH TO drop Mille off after the past few days of mother-daughter bliss, but she was ecstatic. And I was truly moved by Marianne's reception. I must admit I'm much more comfortable than I would have been if it were only Sebastian . . . but even he seemed relaxed. They're really making an effort. Mille even got her own little bedroom . . . yes, sometimes life surprises you. I bid them farewell, and was close to shedding tears when saying goodbye to my little girl.

I had thought of cancelling my date with Arkan after the horrible experience with Mr. Grey, worried that Arkan, too, might turn out that way. But then I would have given more importance to one bad experience than to being open to meeting a man with a lot of potential. Back on the horse again they say. Or should I say, back on a man again?

Arkan and I met at 5 p.m. at The Standard Jazz Club where we had glasses of wine instead of cocktails. He was not as drop-dead gorgeous as his picture suggested—it must be about ten years old—but we had a good laugh about it, and about so many other things. After asking me about myself, we talked about the series of articles he was doing on religion in Cuba after his trip there. It had opened his eyes to the fact that religion gives people hope, especially in the severest poverty. For many years, he had been a steadfast atheist, detested religion in every form—but that visit and interviews he did there showed him nuances he hadn't noticed before.

I was attracted to him, sitting there talking so intelligently. There's something fascinating about a man engaged in the battle between himself and the world. He's got personality, he's passionate about his work, alert, thoughtful—the kind of man I want to be with. And the kind of man whose woman I want to be. But then again, I had to ask myself, why can't my mind move on from that 1950's middle-class model of the one and only?? What happened to my three-men model?

Well, he didn't notice anything. I told him about the trip I won to The Allinge Retreat Centre and that I'd be going there on Sunday. Arkan said immediately that he'd come to The Centre, too! He had wanted to go there for quite some time and he was entitled to a room there through his membership in some journalist association. He had his iPad with him, so he went online right away and reserved a room for the coming Friday. Aaahhh, such marvelous spontaneity. There was already a lot of chemistry between us . . . his intensity almost blew me away, and then there's a sort of self-assured, kind of macho attitude he exuded that makes me juicy and weak in the knees.

We didn't get to discussing whether he was a 1, 2, or 3, probably because my mind already saw him as a 3-in-1 and was well on its way to making him my boyfriend! Which isn't all that odd, really, given the fact that he surprised me when he figured out how to bypass the contact channel I had established online and sent me an email directly to my work. He has an exciting job, and not only can he talk about it, it oozes drama and notoriety.

On top of that, I noticed that we can laugh together. Ah, the chimneys of my dream factory have already begun spewing smoke. Is he the man of my life? Does he love me? Is he fantastic in bed? Where are we going to live?

How many children might we have? When are we getting married? How does Elizabeth Spartak sound?

If I didn't know better, I'd think my mind had secretly been to some kind of romance-scientology course and was just waiting to transfer all of my money to a bank account in this guy's name?!

Luckily that did not happen since I was invited to a dinner at the Reserve later tonight so we ended our date with a delicious kiss and the excitement of seeing each other next weekend at the Retreat Centre.

VERY LATE SATURDAY NIGHT

A Trip to the Reserve

I ALWAYS HAVE MIXED emotions when visiting the Reserve, which I consider a club dedicated to the protection and preservation of the filthy rich. Their affluence with magnificent houses that are beautifully decorated and full of elegant furniture and art give a signal that here is the place where interesting discussions might flourish about how to run a well-functioning society. The beautiful music from the grand piano in the living room fills the rooms, and I imagine people sharing how they could use their 'surplus' to help the less fortunate. All of this potential fascinates me.

But the reality is that most often the filthy rich are egotistical individuals who struggle with finding a mission in life without seeing how their wealth allows them to help others and enable necessary societal changes.

This couple that I'm visiting tonight are friends of mine. I know the wife from way back when we attended the same business course. They know about my three-men project, since I had told her about my idea on the phone. She had not called to know more, and when I arrived they greeted me without mentioning it.

The dinner was with six couples and me. During the hors d'oeuvres, I started feeling like an outsider of sorts and grappled a bit with the feeling that everyone else seems able to figure out how to be part of a couple, except me. But when they brought the main course, the man next to me on the right began speaking to me in a low voice, asking such detailed questions that it was obvious he had heard about my model from others, and it intrigued him. Initially he tried for nonchalance—unconvincing, because we ended up talking about my model for forty-five minutes. Every so often, he glanced sideways at his wife to see how she felt about us being so deep in conversation as we were. And of course she felt threatened—because she is. I imagine they had some serious sex when they got home to straighten things out.

On my other side was a woman who is an icon of materialism in my view—always wearing the top brand names, great boots, makeup, the works. I had met her at other dinner parties and I had never gotten the impression of her waters being particularly deep, but apparently I had overlooked something. She asked me straight out how it could be that I was leading the life she had heard about. And while I tried to figure out what part of my model she's attracted to, she told me that she recently started playing the piano. She used to play when she was young—and now she has gotten to a point where she can hardly wait to get home and play every day. Her husband finds it bothersome, even if he loves music and used to play the guitar himself. She told him that she must practice every day, and he told her that he expects peace and quiet when he comes home to 'his castle.'

She looked me square in the eye and asked:

"How can I convince him that it would be better for us to live separately and see each other on the weekends?"

"I don't think it'll be easy. A lot of men feel more secure when their wife is there all of the time. She can go outside, work in the garden or whatever, but a lot of men interpret a woman's free will or independent needs as an affront."

"But my living alone would take the pressure off," she said. She looked like a little girl who had been caught in a sudden rainfall without an umbrella or even a jacket, and her expensive labels wouldn't do any good now.

"Yes, but he'd lose a lot of what he loves most: Control."

"I'm ready to explode!" she said. She looked at me as if I could solve her problems and help her make a painless transition from living in a relationship model most appropriate for nursing small children into a relationship model appropriate for letting two adults grow and thrive as individuals.

And that's what bothers me about The Reserve. The people here have so many unharvested resources for helping humans grow, and on the other hand so many resources used for keeping up appearances while drowning their dreams of a different life in a sea of pills, pelts, and alcoholic potions. The rich disappoint me. I always thought that people with so many resources could expand the parameters for deep love and finding a soul mate. But maybe that's just not possible. Maybe deep love is, contrary to what we believe, a flighty bedfellow who refuses to be entrapped. And anything that refuses to be controlled is treated with a firm hand at The Reserve.

At some point during the discussion, I realized that my currencies are worth very little at The Reserve.

My currencies are:
- Emotions
- Passionate about sex (has low value when you are a woman)
- Living in the moment
- Easy access to enthusiasm

The Reserve currencies are:
- Rationality
- Service-mindedness, satisfying others' needs (high value when you are a woman)
- Organize and plan for the future
- Moderate emotional responses

Fascinating that people have gone on believing that this world is the promised land. It's completely understandable that it is disintegrating these days. In my opinion, that' s only because we have yet to define a new model that it still appears that the old model works. As soon as the new model has been established, we'll all wonder why it took so long to change.

At the end of the evening, I felt a light depression setting in, but then Prince Arkan called and gave me a nice dose of sweet talk. I absolutely adore this phase of the courtship; the tension is rising and imagination takes off with the conversations, the flirting, the growing intimacy, the opening up. But is this real? Ohhh, it's tempting, maybe even inevitable to dream that he could be the one . . . I'm torn, my hormones are fired up with longing for him, to give myself to him completely. . . the Allinge Retreat starts tomorrow for me . . . and I'm so ready!

The Modern Breakthrough

IT'S ELIZABETH TIME NOW—my trip is really and truly about to begin. First stop: The Allinge Retreat Centre. I'm all packed and stopping for brunch at Rebecca's on the way. I have butterflies in my stomach, quivering with anticipation. The house is extra quiet without Mille; even the sound of her breathing would make a difference. Good thing I'm going away.

LATER

I ARRIVED ON THE island of Bornholm at 6 o'clock and as soon I got off the ferry, I drove full speed ahead to The Allinge Retreat Centre. A handsome, classic dark blue Jaguar Mark II wove in and out of lanes around my Peugeot, but as soon as we passed the town of Hasle, it started pouring and I lost sight of the Jaguar. While driving on, I remembered a piece of art by Sophie Calle, called *The Address Book*. She found some man's address book and contacted everyone in it, asking them to tell her about the man. The art is the documentation of everything they told her. I'd like to do the same thing with Arkan at The Allinge Retreat Centre. I bet somebody there knows him. I haven't even had time to google him yet.

I was already twenty minutes late for dinner when I pulled up in front of the retreat—and parked my car . . . next to the blue Jag! When I got inside I discovered that its owner was none other than the handsome Per M, who became dean of the university since we last met some years ago where we did some intense flirting—before he got married.

At dinner, Per was delighted to see me and vice versa. He's tall, dark and divine. After dinner he invited me to go for a walk—we ended up going straight to the pub. On the way, he told me that things had gone badly with him and his wife. Really badly.

"Ah, that's a shame," I said, and changed the subject. I'd rather talk about the Modern Breakthrough in 1871, which was the topic of his doctoral dissertation, than his modern break-up in the present time. I do enough talking about couple trouble already, thank you! A round of applause for me for refusing to lend my ears to the tale of his dysfunctional marriage.

I asked Per if the Brandes brothers were anything more than a trivial Danish historical interlude or if they had had an international impact, and he talked about them for twenty minutes while we emptied a bottle of California pinot noir. I absolutely adored listening to him; he's enthusiastic and scholarly and he's got the nicest voice.

According to Per, the Brandes brothers who played a key role in the Modern Breakthrough were pioneers of Danish modern times, with all of its options and the new moral choices it offered. Some people claim that the tolerant, liberal development of Danish society started with the thinkers, writers and artists who were involved in the movement. The Brandes brothers and those around them had a definitive impact on the future—they made Scandinavia a preeminent modern society before other regions of Europe. The Modern Breakthrough was a breakaway trend from traditional cultural themes, especially the literary period of romanticism and towards a more realistic bent. The period was marked by more liberal views on sexuality and religion initiated by research on new topics in social sciences, creative novels about more liberal subjects and art that showed more. At that time, female writers also gained unprecedented influence and a number of them chose to challenge the existing moral values. For centuries people had been living in large families, but the notion of the nuclear family was 'launched' in the 1830's and really took hold from the 1850's and onward, with the growing industrialization of work and people moving from the country to cities.

In the late 19th century, the increasing number of people living in the cities enabled access to more opportunities for interaction. Affluence increased, new novels and poetry appeared vividly describing the exciting night life in the cities—aided by absinth, opium and other substances—and homosexuality was starting to be addressed more openly. In derogatory terms yes, but addressed. The male dominance in the family and society at large was also starting to be challenged. Up until then, women were seen as baby factories, and women's lives were conducted according to the man's will. Newspapers, books, and other things gave people insight into how other people lived their intimate lives and that inspired some people to become more daring.

I always thought it is fascinating how ideas can come together and create a force that changes society. Sometimes I wish that I were living in that period of time among the people who refused to accept the given restrictions, as by refusing it they created better lifestyles for the generations to come. To me, this proves that there is nothing inherently fixed or absolute about the current couple model. In the past thirty years, for instance, both men and women have had many new opportunities to live out their talents, desires and emotions in different ways.

And for years, I've taken these opportunities for granted. But now I've become aware that I cannot take them for granted. There's more and more negative talk in the public discourse about sex that I can't accept; almost as if it were somehow filthy or wrong . . . something to be avoided. I want to do my part to promote sex as a precious encounter between two individuals who desire one another. What they choose to do together and how long they desire each other—well, that's something entirely of their own choice.

These and other thoughts ran through my head as I listened to Per. It must have stimulated my sexual indulgence, too. I noticed that he stole a glance at my cleavage now and then, and at a certain point I leaned over to give him a better view. He smiled intensely. I smiled back.

We had a magical evening, and when we had emptied the second bottle, we went on to another room in the pub that had an old-fashioned jukebox with oldies like the Tom Jones classic, 'Isn't She Lovely,' and hits from the Supremes and even Louis Armstrong tunes. The place was sleepy when we came in, but we started dancing and three songs later, the dance floor and the bar were full. Purely magical. Per's hands rested firmly on my body, and he gently pulled me closer during the slow songs. I knew that the old 'playing with fire' game was on.

His arms around me, his desire—it was too much to resist, and I let myself go a little. I wrapped him around me like a cloak, in case Arkan was a disappointment. A married man in reserve is fine, and he is leaving in two days, so he'll be gone when Arkan gets here. We went home together wordlessly, the Nordic night sky stretching endlessly above us . . . sentimental, but overwhelming just the same.

In front of the door to his room, however, I changed my mind and parted ways from Per with a gentle kiss. I realized a married man is not high on my wish list, regardless of how high I am on his! A recent feature by Alexandra Bagger in the Danish newspaper Politiken popped into my head, where she writes that a woman's desire is logocentric: it revolves around poetic words and intelligent conversation, while a man's desire is iconcentric: it depends on visual stimuli. Per can weaken my knees with his knowledge and talent for analyzing in convincing ways, and his eyes exploring my body for visual inspiration.

Back in my room alone now, I've read two text messages from Arkan: *Hello beautiful, sitting with a bottle of rum after a day of writing about Cuba. Miss you ardently. Can't wait to explore us again soon! Kiss, Arkan*

And the second: *Going to bed now to dream about us. Kiss A.*

~~~~~~

All of my body longs for him, misses him . . . and I hardly even know him! To be close to him, touch and feel him. He and I. The two of us against the world. My skin is tingling with desire, pining for him to come and take me! Ugh, how irritating it is that my fantasy is exactly that; why can't I fantasize about coming to take *him*? Taking liberties with every cell in his body to satisfy my desire? Theoretically, I *could* fantasize about that. But my mind, oh, my mind doesn't really work with it. Am I afraid of rejection? Would it really be that much of a disgrace if he refused me? Men are rejected all the time and yet they get up and try again and again.

I keep giving in. I've checked men out and shown them what I knew they wanted to see. I have years of experience allowing men access to me upon presentation of the key: a lustful gaze. I bow down to a man's desire, rush to get something out of it, without any requirements as to how. And then, when's he's had enough, I accept it. The hardy, indulgent and meek female. Another characteristic of the heterosexual middle-class bliss that makes so many people unhappy.

But now I'm changing that: It's time for me to try out new avenues. I'll be the proud, indulgent, demanding woman with high expectations just as I was with my former millionaire and to some extent with David on the house boat. Arkan needs to be able to handle my intensity, my fragility and my curiosity. Hope he knows how to do that! I need to hold my space without suffocating him. And maybe that means holding back a little . . .

There I go again, looking out for him and his needs. And preventing myself from giving myself fully to him on my own terms . . . I don't dare . . . but I have to dare. That's the next step: to dare sexual and emotional equality in a long-term relationship.

I truly hope that Arkan can take care of me. But I don't quite believe it. Maybe we should just be friends . . . I better put his name on the list of potential 2's and hope that it can stop my mind from constructing romantic castles. And I'll treat him lovingly with that in mind.

I crawl under the luscious comforter and my fantasies start rolling . . .

PHILOSOPHER	LOVER	HANDYMAN
	• Arkan • David from Belgium • Per, the married dean	• Lasse

Waiting for Arkan

HAVE HAD A GOOD first day at the retreat—lots of stimulating topics being discussed that I am fascinated by. Wish I could spend a month here.

But this place seems full of people who are battling with love! There's Ditte, the 35-year-old super artist who's in love with Professor Berg who's 50. She does everything in her power to grab his interest and around Christmas she succeeded but only for a short period of time, so now she misses him so much that it's practically an obsession. He doesn't notice, or doesn't want to notice, because he's now smitten with the mysterious 30-year-old Iben, who herself longs for a violinist whom she only met briefly and with whom she has had a tantalizing telephone relationship. Ah, what a great entanglement love can be . . .

Helene and Magnus are here, too—two kind and well-educated people who struggle with each other's shortcomings and their ideals of perfection. In a way I can identify with them. Are our exceedingly high expectations what stands between us and true love? I'm lousy at accommodating other people's shortcomings, ugly shirts, wrong words and misery—especially if the misery is existential. Concrete misery is a different story, it deserves compassion.

But I'm through trying to save everyone from themselves, and in reality it's rather arrogant of me to believe that I know better what's good for them than they do. The existential misery that a cowardly man who lacks self-insight carries around is difficult for me to respect. I think he is wimpy and unable to take responsibility for his own actions. I wonder what kind of man Arkan is? Hopefully he's too much of a street kid to nurture existential misery and play the victim card on me.

It's stunning here at the Centre; the aesthetics alone are alluring. I have mixed feelings about visual aesthetics when I'm the object of desire; feel like I'm practically enslaved to it. I love sparking a man's lust by leaning forward and letting things swell and surge, sending signals with the swing of my hip. It's a kind of body-flirting. And I cannot resist doing it. The feeling of enslavement comes later, when I realize that I have to keep attracting his attention, flirting and insinuating, luring and disappearing. It's fantastic, right up until you've gone to bed with each other. Then it might be fantastic for a while longer, but it becomes more and more demanding, and I have to keep at it if I want that 'look that can't let go.' Then it feels like a matter of life and death, even if I know that disaster is about to strike as soon as that look lands on another woman for too long. It's supposed to visit other women briefly, then return to me and my body again and again and again.

Some feminists refuse to accept male and female sexuality as building on this seduction game because they don't want it to be like that in the future. But for generations the seduction game has been a model for sexual exchanges between men and women.

I'm a feminist who believes that sex and gender are cultural construc-tions and not pure biology. That means that we can change the way men and women interact with each other if we want to. When I look at young people who are 10 to 15 years younger than me, I see some major changes happen-ing. A number of them have a more fluid definition of their gender and their sexuality. One day a woman may feel like being dressed in man's clothes and have sex with a woman. The next day she may dress like a woman and have sex with a man or any other combination you can imagine.

But for my generation and the ones older than me, sexuality and gender are not like that. We've grown up with specific roles and characteristics for women that are different from those of men. In my model I try to loosen the roles women and men play, both in terms of the expectations we have of each other and our actual actions in the bedroom. I do that because I want to push feminism away from being an intellectual construction that is serious and sexually impassive, into something more playful where curiosity and courage can be assets. Women need more instruments to play in the sexual field, not fewer. For me, feminism is the freedom for women and men to play with sexuality and gender to find a definition that fits each person as an individual.

With my three-men model, for instance, I find that I have more room to be myself. I can free myself from one man's look by being the object of three men's gazes. From being one man's wife, to being the partner of several. My three-men model challenges the patriarchal definition of a woman's role as Florence Nightingale, Lady Macbeth or the trophy wife. I think women should train their capacity for defining what they want out of love, spend time practicing how to get it and not limit the fulfillment of their desire for one man or any other cultural restriction society has created to restrain women and men from living their full potential. If we can agree that it is okay to try out new models, we can liberate our forces of love.

I know that changing the old dynamic isn't easy, since the opinion of others means a lot to most women and since we still tend to follow the same success parameter—the monogamous relationship from high school sweetheart till death-do-us-part. But I also know that all it takes is for each of us to be a little more daring. We need to challenge the areas we are not satisfied with. I've gotten a new sense of freedom by trying out this three-men model and I feel that I am really enjoying that now. I also have a new understanding of myself and my own challenges (e.g., how my old-fashioned dreams keep complicating my experiment).

When Per M and I are together, for instance, we talk about him as a construction and me as a construction—not *us* as a construction. His wife is always present, even if we don't mention her. It's different with Arkan because we have us-construction potential, and this is both attractive and dangerous, as the love symbiosis tends to erase the individual personality and create 'twosomeness.' This coupling is wonderful but it can also become a burden since it can be difficult to even briefly step out of it once you have lived in it for a while. But if you don't try, you risk stagnating in your personal development. And that will influence your contribution to the twosomeness, so a change to it is bound to happen anyway, no matter what you do. Therefore, to master love, we also need to master change.

What I am saying is that I want and need more tools and words to help me make the transition from the traditional symbiotic love twosome to having an equal love relationship between two (or more) individuals.

If Arkan and I form a relationship, I hope we can continue being 'us,' consisting of him as an individual and me as an individual, without getting everything all mixed up. Maybe we can take our personal relationships a little less . . . personally? And not bog each other down with expectations, no matter how hard that may be. I admit, this is quite a challenge, because frankly, I fall face down in the 'you-and-me-model' every time I think about him!

I wonder why my need for love is so urgent. It hasn't always been like this. Was it repressed? Or just subconscious? Nowadays I feel insatiable. Is it because I'm allowing myself to feel and recognize my need for emotions? I've mostly just accepted whatever kind of love I got on my partner's terms until it disappeared completely. Now I've changed my focus and I believe—naïvely or not—that I can succeed at finding love on my own terms. So even if my heart has put my three-men plan on standby for Arkan's arrival, my mind hasn't.

I shall not fall in love with him. I'll practice holding firmly onto myself. And that's why it's so important to figure out which role Arkan should fill. I'll ask him, see how he responds and then say yes or no, depending on how I feel. That's easy—as long as he is far away!

TUESDAY, MAY 12TH

Somebody Knows Something!

I'VE ALWAYS FOUND THE Mercedes Benz to be an attractive car. Rolls Royce is higher on the list, of course, as is a Bentley—but the best of them all is the old Mark II Jaguar from the 1960's that Per has. I asked him to drive me out to Østerlars to see one of the famous round churches—and to decide if I might still want him, despite his bad marriage, without alcohol in my blood.

Churches and castles turn my fantasy switch on. An organist started to play 'I saw a rose shooting from the frozen earth,' which is one of my favorite psalms, so I sang along. I love the poetry of psalms and the song's intensity—the physical experience of taking a tone to its absolute limit, feel it filling my breast and rounding my abdomen; the sensation of my vocal chords resisting and succumbing in full intonation, rising with the organ to the top of the church and releasing.

While standing there singing solo, I realized how similar singing good psalms are to good orgasms. The entanglement of sex and psalms is maybe something only a limited number of people recognize. I sometimes wonder about forbidden things—I mean, unless they're obviously dangerous, like putting your hand on a hot cooking plate, and I find it strange that they are forbidden. Forbidding people to experience their feelings is to restrict their free will, and when you add a dose of religious dogma, a potential hell on earth is created . . . personally I find the connection between psalms and orgasms quite obvious, but I'm not aware who shares my opinion.

As we drove back to the Centre, I made up my mind about Per; I was more enamored of his Jag than of him. Sorry, but it felt good to finally admit that materialistic emotion in myself. Should I tell him?

3.30 P.M.

WELL, WELL, QUITE A revelation! Or at least part of one! At lunch, a strikingly beautiful blond woman named Tine asked me if there are any men in my life, and I answered that I had just met a fabulous guy with boyfriend potential. She asked me to tell her more and so I told her that he's a journalist, he's just been to Cuba and his name is Arkan.

"What?!" she exclaimed, her eyes widening in amazement. And her friend, Sarah, who was sitting across from us, leaned toward me, her face turning beet red. I asked if they knew him. Tine looked at Sarah and Sarah looked back at her. Tine gesticulated vaguely and Sarah looked away for a moment, then leaned over to me and said she had been his girlfriend about three years ago! And that he is, or at least was, terrific in bed!!!

Then a tall, dark-haired woman, Suzanne, who used to be editor-in-chief at one of the big Danish newspapers advised me against getting involved with Arkan at all!!! She claimed he's pushy and always tries to negotiate for more money and benefits when he's out in war zones.

That's a weird reason not to get involved with him, I thought. It's fair enough to push for good compensation when you're putting your life in danger.

Must investigate further what all this is about. And try to get them to tell me about Arkan. That way I can know more of him before we meet.

8.30 P.M.

PER KNOCKED ON MY door. He wants to go for a stroll in the dunes to watch the sun go down. This is a most wonderful side of living in Denmark as we approach summer—very long days with more hours of sunlight than darkness.

On our walk, Per brought up the subject of 'us' again, telling me about all the benefits that come with him. He recounted a parable from the Bible, he said, about a man who had a hundred sheep. One of them ran away, and the man used all his energy to find that one sheep instead of being happy that he still had the other 99. Per then explained what he meant by the parable: with him, I'd have 99 sheep, so I shouldn't keep worrying about the one sheep that he heard is coming to join me on Friday—Arkan.

Of course, Per simply ignored in his little shepherd tale the fact that he has a wife waiting for him at home! And he didn't want to talk about it when I pointed it out to him. We walked back in silence, but it was a kind of awkward silence different than when we had gone out two hours earlier. Luckily he's working tomorrow and leaving the day after tomorrow.

Maybe Per could work as my talker, given how he loves spending time talking with me?

WEDNESDAY, MAY 13TH

Longing for His Embrace

AT LUNCH I MADE a point of sitting next to Sarah. I wanted to try to get something out of her about Arkan, but I was unsuccessful. I can't shake the feeling that it's important to get her to talk. She seemed edgy and talked without stopping with the woman sitting next to her on the other side, and only gave curt answers to my questions . . . and she left before the dessert and coffee were served. What's the story???

I spent the afternoon in my room, dozing off and dreaming about Arkan's embrace. To be embraced, accepted . . . it goes straight to my abdomen and to my heart. It's both disquieting and soothing, respectively. My breath becomes steady and deep, I've come home and feel the irresistible urge to give myself to him completely. As a woman, one is sometimes intimidated by a man's physical strength. But in his embrace, I imagine it's comforting. At that moment I am his; he can throw me on his back, carry me away and do whatever he pleases with me. It continues to peeve me that this image is part of my dreams—my longing is completely at odds with my feminism and my independence.

Must stop searching for black and white answers. The notion that there is one answer to everything is the cornerstone of fundamentalism. I must embrace the contradictions in my mind and body, and celebrate them—after all, those contradictions are what enable me to handle the diversity life has to offer also when it comes to love.

Maybe men are looking for an embrace, too? A harbor to dock in to take a break safely and be righted before he sets out in the world's adverse winds again to realize his ideas and have his way. In the harbor, his woman tends to him. She listens and takes care of him, spoils him—he gives himself to her, and he is hers for a moment. I wonder if that's the kind of short-term docking Arkan is looking for?

THURSDAY, MAY 14TH 5 P.M.

What a Tolerant Woman

TINE JUST LEFT. She showed up an hour ago at my door and something in her eyes made me offer her a gin and tonic.

"Make it a double," she said, and sat down in the room's only armchair. After a sizeable gulp she said, "I know Arkan, too. Actually, I have a relationship with him."

"A relationship?" I asked.

"We're not exclusive," she said. "You could say I'm his mistress!"

His mistress? I wanted to ask why she didn't tell me this at lunch and let only Sarah confess to being his ex from three years ago. Seemed odd, but I just stared at her for a moment, till she explained more. Turns out she was with him the day before he sent me the first email. She claims that it doesn't surprise her that he contacted me. Says she knows he has other women. "To fulfill different kinds of sexual relations," he claimed to her. I wondered aloud if that was alright with her? She told me she was in love with him this winter and they were together for three months before he broke up with her, and now she's not in love with him anymore. They just see each other from time to time and have sex, but she is about to end all that anyway.

I immediately offered to cancel his visit to The Allinge Retreat Centre, given how awkward it could get, but she wouldn't hear of it. Besides, she'll already be gone before he gets here, she said. And then she went on to tell me what a wonderful man he is, recommending me warmly to take the relationship further. I asked her how she could speak so highly of him when he no longer wanted her. But she was firm that he was caring, and for the right woman, he could be the perfect man. And she thinks that I could be the right woman and that he and I are in the same league! Oh my!

Now I'm disappointed that he may not be *the love of my life,* given how much he seems to hop around from woman to woman. Despite that, I can't seem to smother a foolish little hope that I am the right woman for him, like Tine said, and that he might therefore return to the position of being the 'love of my life.' Perhaps I can sweep him away from all of the other women and make him focus only on me, and violin music will be playing . . .

Hmmm . . . after she left I couldn't help but bitch to myself how I feel cheated by his messages. I ended up sending him a text:

Hi Arkan, I have spent the past few days almost in your company—with one of your ex-girlfriends, who speaks very highly of you, and an old colleague in the newspaper business who recommends avoiding you at all costs—plus I just had G&T's with your mistress! Love from someone who's no angel herself.

Then I turned off the ringer on my phone to go to Svaneke with four of the others from the retreat, including Tine and Arkan's other ex-girlfriend, Sarah. We were invited to dinner with General George, one of the heads of the Danish armed forces, who was attending the retreat today and lived nearby. Per has extended his stay, so he came along as well.

9.50 P.M.

NICE GUY, THAT GENERAL George who hosted the dinner. We hit it off and had some great ping-pong dialogue and plenty of laughs, but that marriage of his, what's he to do about that? They seemed like they despise each other.

At dinner, I read a text message from Arkan: *What you wrote is statistically impossible! Text 'Now' when you have time to talk to me and I'll call. We must clear this up!*

I put the phone back in my purse and sneaked down the stairs and onto the balcony of the General's exclusive house with its view over the Baltic Sea. It was a most romantic setting, and the moon reflected in the water, but there were no violins for me.

Suddenly someone grabbed me from behind around the waist. It was Per. He pulled me to him gently and kissed me on the nape of my neck. I let him, enjoying his arms around me and reveling in his embrace—ignoring the fact that I had made up my mind that I shouldn't be letting him kiss me at all. But it all seemed so complicated, with all of the women in Arkan's life, text messages and interpretations . . . and here was Per with a warm cuddle.

After a while, he held me at arm's length, looked me in the eyes and said, "Are you the kind of woman a man can share every day with?"

"Maybe," I said, "but *we* can't."

"What do you mean?"

"If you think your wife is bad, I'm much worse."

"Well, you're also better."

"Do you really believe that?"

"Yes, but I don't think you're the everyday type who keeps up a household and such."

"You're absolutely right."

"But maybe you could learn . . . ," he said, sizing me up with his eyes.

"I wouldn't count on it."

"No, I suspected as much."

He let go of me and left.

I think I'll take Per off my list as a potential number one; the fact that he won't stop wooing me is flattering, yet it adds to the complications.

11:30 P.M.

After Per left, I stood on the balcony for a while. At 10:30 p.m. I texted 'now' to Arkan. A minute later he called. He repeated that my claims were statistically impossible and asked who I was talking about. Right then Sarah came out on the balcony. How perfect! I handed her the phone. There was a glint of vindication in her eyes, but she held herself well and talked and laughed with him on the phone for a couple of minutes, then disappeared toward the beach.

"Oh, that was just Sarah," he laughed. "She doesn't mean anything to me anymore. She was three years ago!"

"Too bad you think like that of her," I said, "because she has quite a good opinion of you."

We laughed. Damn, humor is so disarming, though it made me wonder if he might say the same thing of me three years from now: *Oh, that was just Dixie; she doesn't mean anything anymore.*

Then he wanted to know which ex-colleague I was talking about, but I was not inclined to reveal who it was. I thought it would be good for him to steam in his own juices a while.

Then I told him that I had also met Tine.

"Tine? You met Tine? How?" he asked, clearly trying to find out how much I *really* knew.

"Well, it wasn't very hard, considering we're both at The Allinge Retreat Centre. She even said she told you she was coming here," I answered.

"Well, I thought it was a huge place, with 200 guests," he said surprised.

"15," I said, "We're just 15."

"Hmm," he replied, "she and I broke up a while ago, too."

He then proceeded to tell me how much he missed me and that he only wanted to be with me and how no one in his past mattered any more to him. I laughed. But was he being honest? Or just adept at seduction?

"Well then," he said, "I'd rather meet you back in Copenhagen, if you're uncomfortable about Sarah and Tine being there."

But when I told him that they were both going home tomorrow, he shifted again and said he'd still like to come, if I wanted him to. And I do.

Time for bed . . . but now with a somewhat smaller scoop of fantasies.

FRIDAY, MAY 15TH AROUND 6 P.M.

Marry Me

PER HAS JUST LEFT my room. He walked in 10 minutes ago and hugged me, but before I had time to set him straight, he let go and told me there was something on his mind. He looked straight at me and said:

"You must marry me before I turn 60, because otherwise you won't receive my full civil service retirement benefits."

"Okay," I answered, "but that's the strangest proposal I've ever heard, and I think your wife would disagree since you guys are already married."

"Yes, well, I was just thinking."

"You're really trying every trick to get me, aren't you, Per?"

"No, no, no. I'm serious about you. These things need to be planned."

To be planned . . . yes my friend, plan your divorce and avoid the loneliness that follows, I thought to myself. He just wants to sail from one relationship to the next—and even if his relationships last longer than Arkan's, he's apparently willing to let them overlap.

Ok, all this has actually helped me come to a conclusion. I've decided to send my romantic illusions on vacation and simply start a passionate affair with Arkan. If he's so good in bed, as those ladies say, he'll get a chance to show it! And it's probably the best thing for me to just have a fling. I had thought he and I were on our way to the romantic duet I've never succeeded in singing from start to finish with any man. But now I see that you always get what you wish for—and I've already sacked true romance, so it's no surprise that it's not coming around.

Maybe I'm just lucky. Arkan and I already managed to avoid the classic couple trap: romantic double accounting, where two people try to dominate each other's actions and each other's expectations. Arkan and I will be able to play instead. I'm no Miss Nice Girl myself—or I don't want to be. The romantic side of the spectrum has been eliminated, but the sexual side has been expanded—since he's apparently a master of sex. Maybe he'll even surprise me. Maybe I'll surprise myself. Such an open field to experiment is exactly what I've been wishing for.

LATER

Back and Forth, Again and Again

ARKAN FINALLY ARRIVED. I picked him up in Rønne and he grabbed my arms and swung me around like he had just come home from years and years at war. He kissed the hollow of my throat and I got chills everywhere. We got into the car and he leaned over, one hand running up between my thighs and whispered: "Take your underwear off."

Wow! That was sexy. I pulled over on the side of the road, and off they came.

We drove back to the Centre as quickly as I could—with him fondling me as much as he could the whole way. After that foreplay, I was in desperate need . . . but the retreat house was full of commotion. The Centre's manager, Marie, is not just a talented painter but a wonderful cook, and she sets the most fabulous baroque tables; this time overflowing with stones from the beach, seaweed and tea lights. She had made a warm borscht with pirogue and vodka, followed by delicious fish cakes and potatoes. The intellectual conversation flowed, and the paths that cross here certainly are exciting. Rune, a famous Danish writer of novels who just got here today, took part in the dinner, and I felt so lucky to talk with him. Per was also still there, and so was Iben, the woman who is pining for her violinist.

Arkan continuously touched me throughout the meal, and whispered to me, "Let's sneak up to the room and have sex." But I felt like postponing the moment and enjoying the buildup.

After dinner we went to sit by the fireplace that the professor had lit and where the vodka flowed freely. Arkan also pulled out a bottle of exquisite old rum and some cigars to share around. The smell of tropical tobacco made me think of Agatha Christie storylines. Outside the house, the wind began howling and Marie suddenly asked everyone: "What are your wildest dreams in life?"

We all looked at her and at each other, a little confused by the question and not knowing whom she was asking. She's played this game a few times before and I *love* it—it creates new connections between people and I feel like everyone comes closer when they speak from their hearts about their hopes and dreams.

"What about you, Arkan?" she asked. "What do you want to do with the rest of your life? What would make you happy?"

I found the question especially interesting. He shrank a bit and made a few glib remarks about his Cuban journalism experience.

"Not good enough, Arkan. Come on, dig deeper and reveal something really personal to everyone," Marie insisted.

"It's not a question you can answer just like that," he said, looking into his rum glass and taking a sip. She had really put him on the spot and she wasn't about to let him go . . . she sharpened her claws.

"Of course you can," she insisted.

I chimed in and said, "Yes, come on. Just tell us one thing, one dream you have for this year, Arkan?"

"Ok," he said taking a deep breath.

Maybe it was the alcohol talking, as his answer was astonishing.

"My dream this year is more sex; I want to have more sex this year than ever before. Like King Solomon, I want 900 beautiful women so I can choose exactly which woman I want and settle down."

"More sex, aha," answered Marie. "Well, how about that. That's really the least intriguing answer that I've ever had anyone give to that question. And believe me, I've asked quite a few."

Apparently, her sarcasm didn't hit him. His remark showed me that Arkan is not someone I want in my life. His dream was so simple-minded and crude, with no class, no courage, no ambition! My curiosity about him diminished rapidly as he talked about sex and women like that. As if the world were his toy shop and he could just grab women off the shelves. So four women aren't enough . . . 900, that's his model then. Good to know.

He smiled, and I saw hunger in the sideways glances he sent around to all the women sitting with us. Oh, I don't want to be one of those women who's always on guard because her man is always on the prowl.

"I want to make the world a better place by changing fundamental ways of thinking," Per said suddenly.

"That's exactly what the world needs!" I exclaimed, noticing that at that moment I wanted Per more than I wanted Arkan.

"It'll never happen," said Arkan, who clearly had a high blood alcohol level, and continued, "The UN's Universal Declaration of Human Rights says exactly the same thing, and there's a heap of other social change declarations too, yet nothing ever happens!"

"We need to find new solutions; the old ones are outdated; just look at the climate debate," Per said.

"More nonsense," said Arkan. "We need more nuclear power, that's a perfectly fine solution to climate change."

I was getting more and more surprised . . . how could I have wasted so much romantic longing on him? I walked over to the fireplace hearth as if I were cold, then I sat on the arm of Per's chair and kissed his bald head . . . I could see that Arkan noticed it . . . hehe.

"What about you, Elizabeth?" Marie finally got around to asking me.

"Speaking of changing the ways of thinking, here's my idea when it comes to relationships. I want three men: one for conversation—one for sex—and one for doing handy things around the house."

"Men don't want to share," Arkan said, emptying his glass.

Before I could ask him why he had responded to my ad if he didn't want to share, Marie asked me to explain how that would change our thinking. The conversation needed a little stoking, so I told everyone about an ethnic group in China where the people live according to a matriarchy. It's called Mosuo. Women are in charge and children grow up in large families that center on the mom and her parents and siblings. Relationships are much more loosely constructed than here. Both men and women can have more than one partner and you are free to start and break off a relationship when you want to. And interestingly enough, men seem to have a much better life there than here.

"How so?" Rune asked.

"Men have fewer responsibilities, they work less and spend more time with their friends. The men live with their moms and wear hats. At night, they go to where the women live and try to woo them. If the woman he chooses agrees, the man hangs his hat on a nail in front of her house so that others will know that she's taken for the night. And a woman need only open the door for a suitor if she is in the mood. In this manner, you can choose a partner purely for the sake of satisfaction," I said.

"Sounds perfect," said Arkan. "What did you say this place is called?"

"The interesting thing is that conflicts are resolved without resorting to violence there."

"How do you mean?" asked Rune.

"Because if one woman isn't in the mood, he can just continue to the next hut, huh?" Arkan exclaimed.

I looked at him, feeling relieved that I no longer wanted him.

"They call their relationships for 'walking marriages' since they can change at short notice. I think it is really interesting to see how it is possible to separate sexuality and romance from being a parent, financial matters and the whole set-up of a house hold. A woman's sex life can be purely voluntary, whereas her family life with parents, children and sibling is seen as a long term commitment."

"That is an interesting concept from a philosophical point of view," said Per and looked at me and I liked him even more for his analytical approach.

"Yes, how about if we decide to separate the bringing up of children from grown ups intimate relationships? Grown ups have romantic and sexual needs with passion and curiosity which don't really match the children's needs for stability and predictability which are similar to the needs of elderly people. Instead of following the Christian model of abstaining from fulfilling our grown up needs we just separate it so grown up needs are met between grown ups and the needs of children are taken care of by the larger family. In that way it is possible to have both," I said and felt that things can be as simple as that if we want to.

"The biggest challenge for implementing such a change is the way houses and apartments are being financed," Per said.

"Please elaborate," Marie said.

"Well, with 30-year mortgage plans it is not so easy to make a different model," Per explained.

"Well, children still need to live in the houses, it is just not a couple that takes on the mortgage, it is the parents of the pregnant daughter. That could also solve a number of challenges that families with small children have today. They need to earn money to offer the children a proper home, the children are small and wake the parents up at night so they find it hard to work a lot and they also want to spend time with the children. Such a simple change of things could fix all of this," I said.

"Fascinating," Marie said.

I smiled and then I turned to Marie and asked, "What about you Marie, what are your dreams?"

"When you've grown up the way I have, you want to do good things for other people," she said, and smiled.

"That sounds nice," said Per.

I was struck by Per's kindness to others, while Arkan, with all his battleships sinking, seemed to be plagued by existential self-hate. Suddenly I noticed the way his face just hung. He seemed old and miserable, sunk down in his armchair stuffed with self-pity.

I needed some peace and quiet, so I took the glasses into the kitchen, emptied and washed them. I was looking for a dish towel to dry them off and found a stack of small white aprons and suddenly had an idea. I folded one and put it into my bra. Just as I was closing the cupboard, Arkan came into the kitchen, put his arms around my waist and tried to kiss me. I didn't like it. It was a cold, demanding kiss. I remembered a line from the writer at dinner, Rune, in his book, *The Fight for Truths* where he writes: "Revolutionary art was supposed to liberate the people from the conservative art that presented women as a stimulant, like beer and cigarettes." The kiss made me feel like Arkan's stimulant. Now I've met Arkan's world. Certain things are expected of women who want to be a part of that world, where everything revolves around him, the sultan, who can command women as he pleases. I envy men for their ability to create a world around themselves. But I won't take on the role he's assigned me.

I gently pushed him towards the wall in the hallway where he slowly slid down to a squat. I sensed a rawness and disillusionment in Arkan. He's a victim of himself, and something finally snapped. But it won't do me any good to project solutions on him that he isn't finding himself so that it becomes *my role* to get him out of his shell. I've already been married to such a man!

When I got back into the parlor, everyone was splitting up and carrying things into the kitchen, passing by where Arkan had fallen on his side and was snoring. We left him there, and Per was happy about that. He grabbed the rest of the rum, took me by the hand and pulled me to his room. He put on a song and passed me the rum bottle—we had forgotten to take glasses. I took out the apron and put it on. I stood in the middle of the floor and rocked back and forth to the music, and started to strip; he drank, smiled and took off his clothes. His gorgeous body shone in the dark.

I lifted my jumper over my head and revealed my lack of panties from when I was in the car with Arkan. I stripped in tune with the music, taking a sip of the bottle now and then. He smiled and looked at me and took out a condom of his pocket and put it on with pride. When I was completely naked, I stepped closer to him and he buried his face in my breasts, licked and kissed every inch of my body until I exploded. Then he entered me and we gave ourselves to each other, and angels began to sing.

Afterwards he immediately fell asleep. I hopped out of bed, gathered my clothes and went back to my room, took a bath and now here I am, writing.

It's incredible. My first planned attempt at non-patriarchal sex doesn't happen with the man I planned but starts out with strip and a maid-fantasy with an unhappily married man whom I had sworn off. Pretty conformist, I must say, but I give myself a bit of self-praise for doing exactly what I wanted to, even I feel a bit sad that my tryst with Arkan had no future.

Looking for a Lost Reality Filter!

SOMEONE KNOCKED ON MY door at 10 a.m.—Marie with a breakfast tray. Curiosity about my new model? Nooo, she's not the type; but I think this is the beginning of a beautiful friendship. Told her about Per . . . haha, soon everyone around here will know, which is a good thing. Then I won't start getting weak in the knees—he's only an affair!

Ok, so what does this mean? Maybe it's just another example of our lack of language for many types of the interactions between genders. A lot of people just give up, saying: emotions are irrational, they're inexplicable! But I think giving up is too easy. In my experience, not only can emotions be described, they can also be explained. Certainly there are some emotions which we're not especially proud of, our Dark side, our Shadows, which might contribute to our disinclination to confess to them or go into detail about them in front of others. And sometimes we experience different emotions simultaneously, which can be very confusing. Maybe I should write a book about this? *Emotions Explained*: a reference work for when we confuse even ourselves and need straightforward answers and guidelines. I could start with my most recent experiences.

Emotions: Disappointment, insight, serenity, a bit of love: Traveling home from The Allinge Retreat Centre with a different man in my dreams than I came with. It was supposed to have been a worldly, well-known journalist, but he wasn't what I was looking for! His dream is of a woman whose most profound dream is to make his dreams come true. He'll have to look elsewhere.

Emotions: Hope, possibilities, romance, a bit of love, joy, vulnerability. I met Per, who says he can be the three things I'm looking for, but he's still married though claiming to be getting a divorce. Maybe there's a possibility there, if he can manage at his end, that is. And if I can put the brakes on my dreams for a while—which always have a tendency to get stuck in a romantic model I don't really believe in.

Hmm, maybe this is not the most enlightening strategy after all. But I just don't have the words for the type of love I'm looking for. For a while I believed that Arkan and I were looking for the same thing. From our conversations and texts and the first date we had, it seemed that we were communicating the same thing—that we wanted a wonderful relationship to grow between us. I think I was listening with a special filter in the beginning, the filter called 'I really, really want him to be the one to fulfill my dreams about love, so I'm paying attention to everything he says that supports the idea that he is the man of my dreams.' But only when I heard him through a reality filter ignited by Marie's question, only then could I hear who Arkan really is. I guess I forgot that he originally contacted me because of my three-men model. Maybe he thought that I was just like him, well you know, 900 women for him and 3 men for me!

I wish I had some sort of tool that would allow me to 'reality-hear' men from our very first conversation. Maybe I'll have to design such a reality filter hearing aid. I'm sure there is a worldwide market of women for it.

Next week I'm attending a course on social media at an old estate on another island called Samsø. It takes three and a half hours to get there from Copenhagen, half of it driving and half on a ferry. When I told Per about the course, he wanted to come along. A trip to a beautiful estate with my lover doesn't sound so shabby—except for the fact that it's much too conducive to romantic dreaming!

Well I'm still at the Retreat Centre, and tomorrow there's a choir concert outdoors on the grounds of the ruins of Hammershus Castle. The rain was falling all day but it has finally cleared up. I really need to get some fresh air, so I think I'll attend that concert.

SUNDAY, MAY 17TH

Au Revoir, The Allinge Retreat Centre

I SKIPPED THE CONCERT and instead I went to the butterfly park by Nexø, then to the beautiful Dueodde beach for a walk. I love walking barefoot on the sand and feeling the fine white grains surround my feet and slip between the toes. At this time of the year the sand is still cool, so you can really feel it against the skin of your soles that have been tucked into shoes and socks all winter and are now finally liberated. The landscape around the beach here is different than the rest of Denmark, since there are rocks and pine trees. The darkness of the trees against the light beaming off the ocean and the white sand make for beautiful contrasts. Today the dark shadows of the trees allured me as a symbol of the forces of my life that I cannot control while the light incites me to let go of control and enjoy the present.

I sat down in the sand enjoying the energies of the environment and being caressed by the cool, soft breeze coming from the Baltic Sea. Then I opened my eyes wide and saw a man walking towards me who bore a striking resemblance to Rebecca's brother Oscar. When he got near, I saw that it was him!

He stopped and we talked. He had been looking at houses on the sunshine island. An odd coincidence that we should meet here! I couldn't help but be moved by his warm sideways glances, his outdoorsy charm and smell. We turned around and we strolled back to the car park. Walking silently with him and enjoying the beautiful light was wonderful. Is this for real? Does he have a crush on me or am I imagining things? Do I have a crush on him?

We drove out to Siemsens Gaard in Svaneke, an old well-restored 17th century merchant store. Oscar told me that he is sure that if the walls here could speak, we would hear daunting tales about life in the time of the great sailing ships. Siemsens Gaard held a prominent position right on the harbor and was a vital trading post from 1650 through the next 250 years.

I'm glad he took me there since it was indeed an old house that has been restored gently with great attention to detail so it appears old and charming and at the same time functions as a renowned hotel and restaurant.

We decided to have lunch together, as I was ravenous and the restaurant's catch of the day—butter-grilled plaice, a delicious Baltic white fish—lured us inside. Just as we were going in, Mille called me. I told Oscar to go on in and I'd be right there. Back on the phone, Mille sounded ecstatic about everything, and she's completely hooked on swimming, and it sounds like she's getting a lot of encouragement—the future Olympic medalist, as Marianne calls her. Can't wait to see her again; I miss her so much, it almost hurts.

Walked into the restaurant and looked around for Oscar, and there was Arkan! He was sitting in profile, intertwining fingers with a young, apple-cheeked blonde whose ample breasts were about to swell out of her low cut blouse. The sheepish expression on his face when he caught sight of me was priceless. He quickly pulled his fingers back and the blonde looked at me with surprise, maybe thinking I was his wife or something. I led Oscar over to their table and made introductions, thanking Arkan for last night. The blonde's name, he said, is Aurora, which means goddess; and truth be told she did have a fantastic figure and milky-white skin.

"See you later," I said to Arkan, and pulled Oscar to the table furthest from theirs. It didn't take long before Arkan and the blonde got up to leave, sending me a stiff wave goodbye. Even if I found it incredibly comical, I was somehow... offended!? Me! Hmmm. I told Oscar that Arkan had paid court to me just yesterday. Oscar got up, went outside and came back with an axe, which he handed to me.

"Here, so you can sever the contact to pathetic men who neither understand nor appreciate you," he said.

It was moving, sweet and strange, and it made me laugh. Isn't there a law against walking around in public with an axe? Or does the law only cover knives? I left the axe on the table to see what the waitress would say, but she didn't bat an eye. Probably we didn't look like crazy axe-murderers.

Oscar told me he was thinking of buying a garden center here and using the smaller greenhouse for yoga lessons. He doesn't like living in the city, feels trapped. For me it's exactly the opposite. Small towns away from it all give me a trapped feeling. Copenhagen stimulates me; all of those impressions one gets in the city each day are fantastic. People, bodies, movement, colors, things to do, multiple flirtations everywhere you go. The countryside is lovely for a short time, but my imagination slows to a halt if all I have to look at are trees, sky and birds. But for Oscar, the city stresses him out. I had never talked with him in such personal detail like this before since we were kids. Rebecca wouldn't approve. She watches over the two of us like a hawk, but why? Does she think I'm not good enough for him?

It was surprisingly nice to be with him, and I felt completely at ease. He's down to earth and at peace with himself, not fickle and full of hot air like Arkan. Oscar believes in love, unity, commitment and the everyday in a relationship—but then why did his wife Bente leave him? Five years ago, after 16 years of marriage, she ran off with a man nine years her and Oscar's junior. Even if he was calm about it on the surface, I could see that it hurt him when he said that she had just gotten married and was already expecting a child.

It was 8 p.m. when I took a taxi home. When we said goodbye, he pulled me close to him and gave me a long, warm hug. I love it when a man embraces me like that, not *needing* but just warm and comforting. The strength of his body, his heavy arms, his chest. Maybe I should make a date with Oscar soon? Forgot to ask him which of the three he'd like to be, in the case of . . .

When I entered the retreat, I heard someone sobbing quietly in the parlor. I carefully opened the door and found Marie looking up at me. On the floor, his head in her lap, was Arkan. He stopped crying and sniffled when he saw me.

"Are you following me?" he asked, his voice stuffy. "Don't you understand I'm crazy about you?" he sniveled. "Without you, I'm nothing," he cried.

"Aha, and what about Aurora?"

"OHHH, she doesn't matter, I miss you."

Marie's eyes flickered with reserved amusement. To put it mildly, I was surprised and bewildered. Yet another woman whom Arkan talked about as if she meant nothing. I poured myself a Havana Club from what was left in the bottle and sat down. I looked Arkan straight in his pleading eyes and said quietly, "I'm sure you're quite a man. But we're just not going down the same lane in life. We wouldn't be good for each other. I need to feel special to a man, and with your goal of 900 women, I could never feel special."

I stroked his cheek. His eyes filled with tears. I had an almost uncontrollable urge to slap his face, but instead I just said, "You're still welcome to drive back to Copenhagen with me tomorrow as we agreed."

Thank God he didn't want to. Under the circumstances he decided to stay a few extra days . . . to meet with Aurora, I'm sure, hehehe. Such a cad.

Tonight, as I look at my list, it is not very long and there are too many question marks. I think I better tuck myself in under the luscious comforter at the Retreat Centre for this last night, enjoying the cold sea air, listening to the gentle crashing of the waves. I'm happy and ready to go home and check for new reactions to my profile. In reality, there are still so many options . . . I shouldn't give up; my model can still work.

PHILOSOPHER	LOVER	HANDYMAN
• Oscar?	• Per • David from Belgium • Oscar?	• Lasse • Oscar?

Life is Now

I TOOK IT EASY for the first few days when I got home from The Allinge Retreat Centre. One day I took Mille to a café after school, the next I did a little of this and that around the house. I organized a couple of closets and mainly enjoyed the evening sun and warming weather.

Tomorrow I'm going to a workshop at an estate on Samsø, a beautiful island right in the middle of Denmark. The estate is one of the biggest ones on the island. The island is a culture in and of itself, as are most islands of a certain size. Agriculture is the main activity, with more and more people growing fruits and vegetables sustainably. They have their own Energy Academy that over a 15-year period has made Samsø energy-independent from the rest of Denmark. The local government, local business and local committed people did this by implementing a broad variety of renewable energy projects, from wind turbines to CO_2 neutral district heating plants, to using tractors powered by rape seed oil and solar energy panels. Fascinating what people can do when they join forces to reach a shared vision.

Normally, they don't do workshops at this estate, but the owner's daughter, who knows social media inside out, was hosting a 48-hour one on the premises. It's only for executives; and I like being in that category. The estate owner and his wife will give us a grand tour, then they'll serve aperitifs in the wine cellar and dinner in the banquet hall.

And what could be more perfect than an estate to finalize having my three men without getting romantic about it? I've already got my handyman Lasse to help with handiwork, my first-lover Per is coming to the workshop with me, so I just need to find someone to talk with. It shouldn't be that hard. All I need to do is say 'Arkan' to myself and poof! The romance ghost vanishes. Every time that works, I feel a little giddy and enjoy that I'm not a part of his construct.

Not worrying about the future gives you the freedom to let go of the steering wheel and enjoy the moment. Life is now, as my uncle says.

Sincerely hope to meet an interesting man for stimulating conversation at that workshop! Maybe it was a bad idea to take Per along . . . but it's too late now, and he just texted to tell me he's looking forward to seeing me!

An Interesting Workshop on Social Media

I'VE JUST SETTLED IN the 'White Lady's Suite.' Apparently she was one of the former owners who always wore white linen dresses and is believed to haunt the place for wrongs that happened to her at the end of her life on the estate. There's a four-poster bed in the room and a bathtub with Jacuzzi jets—I like this modern estate living already.

3.15 P.M.

PER CANCELLED! TURNS OUT his boss, Ruben Pontoppidan, who is the headmaster of the university, will be here and Per didn't want the boss to know he was going to take the day off to be here. Truly hope the headmaster is not the most interesting person to talk to here; that could really get me into trouble!

6.30 P.M.

OMG, YES, HEADMASTER RUBEN Pontoppidan *is the most interesting person here,* given the fact that the estate owner is happily married! Ruben is curious by nature and wants to combine social media with the experiences he had as a young man in his father's photographer's studio. I don't quite see the connection, but it sounds interesting enough coming from such an attractive man's mouth. Damn!

This afternoon's workshop was great. Both the content and the other participants are all cool. There's Alf, who is self-employed and started his company selling nuts and bolts three years ago. In no time, he's gone from zero to ninety and now he wants to use social media to bring it all up to one hundred. Then there's a fireball woman from the municipal council who hasn't yet given up her goals due to endless battling with a bureaucratic organization. She's hoping to short-circuit some of the bureaucracy with the help of social media. There's also the woman from a theatre group in Jutland who heard that the messenger becomes the message with social media, which is highly appropriate for a world of big egos, so she is curious to learn more. And there's the official PR guy—the 'spin doctor'—from the Danish parliament who knows that you can never know too much about social media. At some point, the media is bound to strike at a politician and the PR fellow has to be prepared.

And then there are the organizers of the workshop. The estate owner's daughter Mathilde is running it. At first glance, that is. Upon closer investigation, it turns out that the estate owner is also chairman of and investor in her company. His training and education are more extensive than hers about business, and he intuitively understands new ways of doing things; a rare quality for his age group. His daughter is pleasant, but it almost seems as though she feels like they've already reached their company goals because they have clients and can arrange workshops like this one. The father knows they are not there yet, and so he is going all out to entertain us in the hopes that we will eventually hire their agency. He and his wife are serving a fancy Grand Cru champagne from Mesnil-sur-Oger as an aperitif in the wine cellar, and afterwards they have a three-course meal in the banquet hall. They'll be serving a rare 2005 Premier Cru Bordeaux with the main course, so the evening looks both tasty and promising!

LATER

A Stimulating Conversation

I SAT NEXT TO the estate owner father for dinner. I started the conversation by telling him about my three-men model as an example of innovation. He was sincerely interested in it and it was a pleasure to discuss my life with such a cultivated man.

"I like your constructive approach to what happens when love between two people doesn't work," he said.

"A lot of couples break apart and feel like failures after a divorce," I said, "when instead they could just admit that they love each other, but not for all things."

"Exactly, a number of our friends have gone through serious difficulties following their divorces, which could have been easier if they had been willing to face reality sooner and not tried to live up to all of each other's expectations."

"Imagine what it would be like if people could congratulate each other on having made a healthy decision to end something that wasn't working out. In a lot of other contexts, celebrating would be the appropriate reaction for coming to an amicable conclusion."

He smiled and said, "Yes, you may be right, though I think you're being a bit naïve. Relationships are the foundation of our society, and you can't change that with a snap of the fingers."

"Well, I think we could if we wanted to. We could just decide to stop insisting on seeing adults and children's needs as the same. Adults need passion, curiosity and courage; children need safety and predictability. How about if the two people creating the child don't have to take care of it full time, but leave that role more to the grandparents? In your case it would mean that your daughter could concentrate on her ad agency and an affair here and there, and you and your wife could look after the children."

He looked at me and seemed to contemplate my proposal.

"A change is already going on around us, and has been for a long time, with people saying one thing and doing something else. I think it is about time that we change the framework around love," I said.

"Haven't some people always challenged the way most people live?" he asked.

"Yes, for the noblemen and noblewomen who used to roam these halls maybe. But now it's happening on a larger scale in our society. And I think it's a healthy development. Imagine you had a factory or an organization with an operational model that just didn't work: you'd change that model. I would say that it is only in about 25% of all relationships, that the present monogamous relationship model works really well. The rest of the relationships accrue enormous debts, and society ends up spending billions picking up the pieces."

"Are you trying to start a revolution?" he asked, looking at me with a serious gaze.

"I'm merely describing what I see happening around me, and proposing a new model," I replied.

"90% of the resources in society are spent on maintaining what we already have," he countered.

"Precisely, and that's why so little energy is invested in finding other models. But you know that; you've worked with innovation for years."

"Innovation requires people to think and look across established boundaries. It frustrates me that the tools used in innovation aren't more widespread than they are; society needs innovation," he said.

"That's exactly what I'm saying, but about romance," I countered.

"And why do you think that we will be able to change our existing model?"

"Because most of us already have more than one sexual partner. People today often meet more people in a single day than people in the past encountered in their entire lifetime."

He raised his eyebrows.

"Having multiple sexual partners and many types of interactions teaches you that there are many different ways of doing things," I said and continued. "The same goes for living in another culture. All of your accepted standards about life are challenged: behavior, clothing, procedures, romantic sensibilities and for that matter different ways of courting and having sex. This gives people a chance to look at themselves and their world from the outside, to re-evaluate things and define how they want to live, completely independently of any traditions or fixed ideas they may have grown up with. You could call it the realization of personal freedom."

The butler came and demanded the estate owner's attention. Across from me sat Ruben Pontoppidan and apparently he had been following our conversation. His gaze got me. Clear blue eyes in a beautiful square face. He smiled at me and said, "You are a very special woman, do you know that?" From his gaze and flirtatious voice, I can tell he is interested . . . and my body is beginning to tremble.

I looked him directly in the eyes and smiled.

The dance begins again.

FRIDAY, MAY 22ND AFTERNOON

The Key to Life

I'M STILL SO STUNNED by my meeting with Ruben that I couldn't concentrate on today's workshop. But it's over now, and people are leaving the estate with more knowledge about social media and a better personal network.

Last night after everyone had gone upstairs, I sat in the banquet hall and was answering emails on my phone. Ruben approached and knelt down right in front of me. I was a flustered; after all, I barely knew him and wasn't prepared for his approach. A solemn ambiance that hadn't been there before set in.

He looked me in the eyes and said, "I would hereby like to invite you to Severin's World."

I looked at him and he laid a small box in my hand. The way he looked at me made me open it right away. Resting inside on a pillow of pink velour was a silver cross on a chain laid out in a heart shape. My heart leapt into my throat.

"What is Severin's World?"

"It's a world for people who are attracted to the extraordinary things in life," he said, and he draped the necklace around my neck.

"This is an ankh, or an Egyptian cross. In Latin, it's called a *crux ansata*. The ankh was made by combining the male and female symbols of Osiris and Isis, who in turn are symbols of heaven and earth. The ankh symbolizes 'The Key to Life'."

I was moved and stood up to thank him.

"No need," he said. "You and your model are extraordinary, so I'd like to introduce you to some people whom you will find interesting...and who will find *you* interesting."

"Thank you," I repeated, and I sensed that a door to a new life had opened right here, in the middle of the banquet hall of a 200-year-old estate. In my mind were images of Pandora and the white *pure spirits* in James Cameron's film *Avatar,* and they intermingled with people who smiled and greeted me in a hall that was a hundred times bigger than this banquet hall.

Ruben grasped my hand and kissed it. Both my consciousness and my heart swelled when I took his face in my hands and kissed him. Impassioned, he kissed me. We caressed one another's bodies and our breath became short. I slipped my fingers between the buttons of his shirt but he grabbed my hand and said, "Come with me."

We went outside, me in a cocktail dress and bare feet, him in his suit and jacket. He walked quickly and I almost had to run to keep up with his determined stride through the park and up to the garden pavilion. On top of the pavilion was a beautiful stone sculpture of a reclining woman looking over the park. Inside was a full circle of candles; the garden furniture that had been there earlier was gone and in the middle was a futon covered with gorgeous, peach-colored Indian silk.

Ruben bowed slightly and invited me inside. What happened next was so special, I can't even write about it now. Need to process it.

My Night with Ruben

I SPENT THE PENTECOSTAL weekend, the religious holiday that occurs exactly 50 days after Easter, being a full-time mother to my part-time daughter. We went to the zoo, puttered around the house together and she told me all about her swimming lessons. Marianne wants her to start competing this autumn. Then we played badminton and cards and went to a flea market.

On Sunday we were invited to lunch at Aunt Kate and Uncle Theo's, but he had to go back into the hospital so lunch was cancelled. A day at home suits me just fine: maybe I can finally begin to fathom what happened that night with Ruben. I haven't heard a peep from him since, and I haven't texted him either. Which seems alright. I've also procrastinated mentally dealing with what went on between Per and myself. Just a week ago I was almost ready to overhaul my life for a married man, and now it feels like what happened with Per was just an interlude of sorts. He has texted me nine times since Thursday—luckily a bit less during the holiday weekend where his calendar obviously says family time.

Ruben is something else. When I stepped into the pavilion, he invited me to lay down on the futon and make myself comfortable on the four huge pillows. When I had arranged myself I could feel that my body was already preparing to converge with his. But he sat at the foot of the futon and said, "In Severin's World, we worship women."

"Sounds good," I said with a smile.

"When a woman is provided with the right environment, she can work miracles. For centuries, eons even, society hasn't grasped the divine power that women possess. When a woman thrives, so does everything around her. Severin's World is a congregation of men and women who see these potentials and want to develop them."

"Why are men interested in taking part in it?" I asked.

"When a man has made love to and been with a woman who is thriving, he'll never again settle for anything less."

I smiled and was glad that we were soon to merge, or so I thought.

"How long have you been looking for like-minded people with your three-men model?" he asked.

"Just a short time, since after Easter," I said, and told him a brief version of what had happened with Thomas and his affair in Barcelona. Telling him reawakened my hurt feelings—but at the same time it felt like those feelings had belonged to me in another lifetime. So much has happened since then.

"At first, my model was somewhat of a panic reaction. But I've since grown quite fond of it," I explained.

"Why?"

"Having three men gives me the freedom to be myself. No man can demand from me that I adhere to his guidelines. From the beginning, I make it clear that the men in my life can't necessarily count on me. And that I have concrete expectations of them—which has two positive effects. First of all, it disqualifies a lot of men who are just looking for a safe, full-service base to come home to. Secondly, it opens up for new ways to talk about love with the men who want to try out the model with me. They are curious by nature, and those are the guys with whom I want to associate."

"Curiosity is precisely the quality that can lead to finding new ways of living together," said Ruben.

"But what surprised me is how hard it is for me to let go of the twosome model with all of its romantic ideals. And I need to get away from it, since it doesn't bring out the best in me. Or in men, for that matter."

"What alternatives can you offer?"

"Now I'm trying with three men. What alternatives does Severin's World offer?"

"The only way to find out is by firsthand experience with others from Severin's World."

"With you, for example?"

He smiled and didn't answer. Hmm, it seemed he wanted to test me a little. I was slightly provoked, but just as men get hooked on my model because it gives them new ways to get to know themselves, I was curious to find out what had to be done to gain access to Severin himself.

"I can't promise you eternal fidelity," he finally said.

"I wouldn't believe you if you did," I said, and I meant it because there was something ephemeral about him.

"Promising each other eternal desire is absurd. It simply can't be done," Ruben replied. "We never know what life will bring, how our partner will develop and change, what will happen to our own bodies. There will always be temptations and as long as our relationship is strong enough, we'll be able to deal with them. But as we change, so will our relationship. Holding onto a principle for the sake of principle seems foolish. We know that curiosity about others will always exist, and our ability to resist temptation may weaken, so there is a risk that one or the other of us will be hurt at some point. But that risk is there regardless of whether we've sworn our eternal fidelity or not. As it is, we haven't made any promises—that means that we both need to make an effort to keep our relationship alive and make sure we continue to respect each other's curiosity."

I enjoyed his calling our meeting a relationship. It made it grow larger and more important in a way that pleased my longing for him which was already soaring around in my body.

"You are a very special woman," he said and kissed me.

I kissed him back feeling very special to him. He let go of me and turned his back on me.

To attract his attention again, I asked, "Where does the name Severin's World come from?"

"My name is Ruben Severin Pontoppidan," he said. "Severin was my great-grandfather's name. The Danish priest and philosopher Grundtvig's middle name was Severin, too—and I've always felt a closeness to him and his psalms, his battle with demons and his greatness. The name comes from Latin *severus,* which means serious. In Severin's World, we take individuals seriously. When you meet someone deeply where he or she is and provide them with the feedback they need, they are capable of taking a quantum leap. I find that fascinating."

"How long has Severin's World existed?"

He stood up and took off his shirt. Yet again he surprised me since I thought that we might make love after all. But he opened his bag and pulled out two bottles of oil and a towel.

"What kind of massage would you like?" he asked.

"Pardon?"

"Craniosacral, shiatsu, Ayurveda or deep tissue?"

"Uh," I said, feeling stupid for not really knowing the difference and not being able to just casually say 'shiatsu with vanilla oil' or something intelligent like that.

"In Severin's World, we cherish our bodies because they are the source of pleasure and the best indicator if something is or is not as it should be."

"Which massage do you think I need the most?" I asked him.

"Shiatsu with vanilla oil."

"Yes, of course," I said, thinking: what a strange coincidence he said exactly what I had thought.

"Take off your dress and lay down, please."

He then gave me a sensational massage and served me a glass of Dom Perignon and some delicious Kalamata olives. We were enjoying the champagne when he asked:

"How did you get to be like you are?"

"Do you want the short or the long version?" I asked.

"The long one. We're in no hurry."

I looked him deep in the eyes and began to tell him about how, when I was young, I used to spend my time studying the periods before and after the turn of the 20th century—the years when we went through the modern breakthrough in the western world, with artists like Gustav Klimt and *l'apocalypse joyeuse—the joyful apocalypse*, the American photographer Alfred Stieglitz and his wife Georgia O'Keeffe who was a painter, the people around the Bauhaus school of architecture and design, Picasso and Gertrude Stein in Paris and all of the bohemians and offbeat characters who served as the advance guard of the upheaval of society that started then and lasted for several decades.

"Ansel Adams is one of my favorite photographers," Ruben said.

"The man who invented landscape photography. Did you see the exhibition at Gammel Holtegaard Exhibition Centre?"

"Yes, twice."

"I spent hours immersed in the way he captures nature's enormous power. Like a waterfall."

"Yes, but back to your life; go on."

"Well, like his images, I've always had my focus on the intensity of life.

When I was 21, I got up and moved to Paris one day. Free from restrictions and expectations of my parents and friends, I could experiment with becoming a version of myself I hadn't known before. For a couple of years, I lived life the sensual way. When I left France, I took sensuality with me."

"What kind of family are you from? How is or was your dad?"

"Ha! Now you get to the difficult part."

"Enlighten me."

"My dad lives in his own universe and always has. He gets frustrated when people don't see the world the same way he does. My mum never did."

"So your role was to mediate and mitigate?"

"Exactly!"

"Which meant there was never room for you to blossom and find yourself."

"Right again. That's why I had to move to Paris."

"And what about love?"

Again he surprised me. He treats each topic he touches with the same level of importance.

"Love has been interwoven throughout my travels and my work," I answered, fingering the new ankh cross around my neck. "Despite the fact that it's the most important thing of all and that it has, without a doubt, dictated everything else in my life, it's no longer on my CV. We divide and categorize everything, and along the way I've learned when it has been necessary and when it's not."

"You're avoiding my question. Where is love in your life?"

"Love is being seen for who I am—and loved for it. But I haven't met it yet. I start by not showing a man who I really am, due to some way back notion that it doesn't deserve attention, and then when I do take a stand and show the real me, the man doesn't seem to appreciate the change. I've found out that I do this because romantic love has played far too big a role in my mind. My three-men model will hopefully steer my attention away from losing myself to another man and the ideal of total bliss, and toward the joy of being myself with a man who is himself. That's the story I want to share with others."

"What is it with you and stories?" he asked.

"I love stories," I said. "I can't live without them."

"Which stories?"

"The grand stories from thousands of years ago. The trivial stories from an hour ago and how the two are connected when I draw a line between them."

"I write a journal," he said.

"Do you?"

"15 volumes to date. I write every day."

"What's in your journal?"

"Tonight I'll write that you and I have met."

"And what will you write about our meeting?"

"That it's special."

"Is it?"

"Yes, extremely. I don't really understand the meaning of it yet, but I can sense that it will be important for me. I've never met a woman like you before. But I still don't understand how you got to be like you are?"

"I've always followed my curiosity."

"But you know that people sometimes reach the end of the path when they follow their curiosity."

"Yes, and then it's time to move on."

"I'm there now, and it's overwhelmingly sad."

"Yes. Sometimes we have to say goodbye to some people in the process."

"Exactly!"

"Who do you have to say goodbye to?" I asked him, trying to fathom who he was referring to.

"I spent the evening before the workshop with a good friend of mine here on this island. We talked about it. He made me realize that I have to take action."

I could see he wasn't going to give me any details. I simply asked, "So where are you going next?"

"I don't know. What I do know is that you arouse my curiosity," he said, looking deeply at me. He was an exceptionally handsome man with that unruly blonde hair that's always been out of style and thus become its own hairstyle. His eyes are the clearest blue, and when they smiled at me, I soared.

"Time for you to go to sleep," he said, getting up.

Taken aback by the sudden shift and overwhelmed by the desire for him to stay, I stood up and embraced him. The sensation of holding him in my arms stayed with me for a long time.

I had come to the conference seeking to find a conversation man, and now I'm on my way into Severin's World! Whatever that really means, I am eager to find out.

My Father Found Me Frederic!

LASSE TEXTED TO SAY that he can't help me with handiwork anymore. He's moving back in with his ex, and she lives in the northern part of Jutland, about six hours by car from my house. Too bad for me—he and his son were nice, and he was efficient with all the tasks I asked him to do, including the one he took initiative to perform with me over my kitchen table. I'm fine with it and I'm also fine with not repeating it. Some things have a short life.

My father just called—he claims he's found a man for me! His name is Frederic. Guess my dad does it to keep me from my three-men model.

Frederic recently moved into a house on my father's street. He also has a summer house on Samsø, just like my Aunt Kate and Uncle Theo, and my father finds this very practical. "That way Frederic and you can spend your summer vacations on Samsø while I am at Kate and Theo's," my father said. The only glitch is: it solves a problem for my father, but not for me. And if summer vacations on Samsø are the most positive quality my father can think of, it isn't especially promising regarding the guy's character.

"Your uncle says he's not very good looking," my father continued.

"Aha," I replied.

"But looks aren't everything."

Considering that my father makes rude comments when people are just five kilos overweight, has told my girlfriends to their faces that he'd prefer it if they wore skirts when they came over, and likes women who wear makeup, I'd venture to say that he's misrepresenting his own standards in terms of the importance of looks.

"Frederic is coming over for a cup of coffee on Saturday; be here at 11 a.m.!" my father commanded. Then he hung up.

I felt a sudden stomach virus coming up on Saturday. At any rate, I'm going to Aarhus for a conference tomorrow—and Ruben will be there too!

I'm looking forward to getting to know him better and finding out what he and Severin's World are all about. Maybe I should invite him to Elizabeth's world instead . . . hehehe.

Oh, no. My father just texted that 'Katherine will be there' when I come to meet this guy Frederic. I texted back "Who" to find out who she is and received this reply: "My girlfriend!"

I called him back right away to find out where and when this Katherine had come from, but he didn't answer. Does this mean I'm having a double date with my father!?! Fortunately, it will only be a cup of coffee in the morning. Please don't let Katherine be Frederic's mother!!

PHILOSOPHER	LOVER	HANDYMAN
• Oscar • Frederic?	• David from Belgium • Ruben	

Ruben and His Friends

I GOT HOME LATE last night from a conference in Aarhus, on the main peninsula of Denmark.

I took the train to Aarhus from Copenhagen. It is about a 3-hour ride through the big island of Funen which is right in the middle of Denmark, and one of the biggest of our 1419 islands. Most of the islands are uninhabited, and some of the others have as few as 50 inhabitants. For all inhabited islands, the state has to ensure free elementary schools, kindergarten, daycare and quick access to a hospital in case of an emergency. The expense of all that is often debated in the media, as it costs an arm and a leg to give those Danish citizens the same privileges as the rest of us who live in the bigger cities. I'm fascinated by how it must be to live on an island with just 49 other people. How do you get along? And if you don't, what do you do, because there is nowhere to hide. Do people tend to accept most things and make compromises that would be unheard of anywhere else because they can't afford to become enemies? Or are the 50 people separated into two or more groups that fight each other because their great-grandfathers were enemies?

I was contemplating this as the train rode onto Jutland, the main peninsula of our country—it always struck me how it looks like a huge thumb sticking up from Germany. We arrived at Aarhus, the second largest city in Denmark. Aarhus has a big port that is very active and a charming 'old city' where you can get a real sense of what life in Denmark used to be like centuries ago. Entering the ancient houses, you have to bend over so as not to bump your head on the low door jambs, since people used to be much shorter then than they are today. Old kitchen utensils and recipes are on view along with clothes, furniture, and tools from the past so you almost feel like you can taste and smell how Danish life in the 1600s to the 1800s used to be around here.

Ruben and I both took part in the conference—or should have taken part in it to be precise; we ended up spending more time with each other than with the rest of the participants.

He showed up an hour late and I was so happy to see him. He lit up the room, and when he smiled at me it got even brighter. We were in the same breakout group and did our very best to contribute, but it was as if we were in a parallel dimension—even when we were addressing the group, it was as if we were talking to each other. At every break, we continued our conversation. We felt out each other's boundaries and challenged them, smiled and had our own thoughts.

The conference was taking place at the Aros Art Museum. Aros is famous for its daring architecture with an exhibit street separating the buildings where you can walk for free, and a spiral staircase that you follow to visit the artwork. Somehow the staircase transports your mood away from your daily activities into a more receptive state of mind. The top of the building is a circular skywalk called 'Your Panorama Rainbow,' designed by the famous Danish/Icelandic artist Olafur Eliasson. As you follow the skywalk, you see the views of Aarhus through different color tones. It is fascinating how it changes your view on things. The museum has a large collection of art from the Golden Age through today. You could say that Aarhus really entered the art scene when that museum was opened.

At lunchtime, Ruben and I took a walk around the place and looked at the exhibition. We soaked up the art like sponges, talking about them in a non-stop 'mind-meets-mind,' listening deeply to each other, and feeling each other's presence on an almost spiritual level. As we walked through the rooms of the museum, Ruben told me about his two best friends, whom he had known for 25 years.

One of them is an aesthetic and architect who finally found the woman of his dreams after battling life and love for years. "Anton just refused to give up until she said yes," Ruben said.

"Interesting," I replied, wondering if he was thinking about us like that.

"It took five years."

"Really! And is she everything he wished for?"

"Yes. I guess so, as they're expecting a baby."

"Aha," I answered. "And your other friend?"

"Frederic considers himself a pragmatic, but I think he's an idealist. He feels a deep solidarity with the weak at any rate. Liberty, responsibility and solidarity—that's his credo, and he's worked hard for it. He believes that you can measure the health of a society by how it treats its weakest citizens. But at the same time he's a pretty materialistic perfectionist."

"In what way?" I queried him.

"His standards are high. A perfectionist who can't come to grips with reality's grim imperfections. He's the toughest, but also the most difficult of us three."

"How so?" I asked. I could feel my curiosity being aroused.

"He lives life at 100%, all the time."

"It sounds like all three of you do that," I laughed.

"Well, he does it the most. He's a very special person. Often when he offers you advice, it may seem insignificant and understated—but each and every time it turns out to be excellent. We're all very close. I don't know why I'm telling you this," Ruben said. "I keep telling you things that I don't say to anyone else."

"I have that effect on people," I said with a smile. He smiled back.

"Would you tell me more about Severin's World?" I asked.

"It's a world which is patient with humans and impatient with systems. We belong to the first generation in which women and men both legally and practically have equal opportunities, but we've still not reached full equality—and it would probably be unrealistic to expect it soon. That's why patience is so essential: patience for the mistakes that we inevitably make while exploring our many options. Both women and men need to find new legs to stand on, alone and with one another," he said.

"What exactly do you mean by that?" I asked.

"Women need to apply for executive positions without asking for permission first. Men need to listen without being asked to first. Women need to perform their executive duties their way. Men need to listen in their way. When changes like these happen, the sexes will meet under new circumstances."

"So how do you see encounters between men and women now?" I asked. I sensed that my own options were being tested—because my conversational date was becoming more and more attractive as he was standing there in the museum surrounded by venerable pieces of art.

"Everything in Severin's World serves one purpose: to increase our self-insight so that we can use our talents as much as possible to benefit ourselves and others."

"That's what I use my model for, too. To increase self-insight," I said.

"You made that point the last time we talked. You said that your model helps you see reality and how you relate to it."

"How exactly do you go about seeing reality in Severin's World?"

"We meet and discuss things, we have parties, and we help each other with our daily life problems."

"Three different roles for the people in your world. That's a little bit like my three-men model, huh?"

"In a way. Severin's World is a meeting point for people on a quest, people who want to make a difference. People who are willing to make an extra effort; who aren't content with what they have."

"How often do you meet?"

"It depends."

"It's still a bit hard for me to understand what this world is all about."

"That's ok. It isn't static; it changes all the time. You can contribute and influence it with whatever you bring into it."

It was ironic that he was telling me this just as we were standing in front of one of Olafur Eliasson's mirror light sculptures. It was a box the size of a small elevator, covered in mirrors set up at different angles, so when you enter it, the artwork becomes you. Or him rather, since Ruben had just stepped into the mirror sculpture and all I was seeing and enjoying was Ruben, Ruben, Ruben in his infinite reflections.

I smiled at him. He smiled back.

When he stepped out of the sculpture I said, "I still don't really get what I can contribute to Severin's World."

He smiled and pulled me toward him.

"You're already part of it," he said assuredly.

I longed to kiss him, but I didn't dare take the initiative for fear of breaking the spell.

"Your first assignment is to tell me what you'd do for the rest of your life—if you could do anything you wanted?"

"I have a better idea: you take me out to dinner at one of Copenhagen's best restaurants and I'll tell you."

"What are you doing this Saturday?" he asked.

"Having dinner with you at . . . ?"

"Noma."

"The waiting list is half a year," I exclaimed, recognizing this was one of the most famous restaurants in Copenhagen.

He just smiled.

SATURDAY, MAY 30TH

Ask and You Shall Receive!

MY FATHER CALLED AND woke me at 8 a.m.

"I'll pick you up at 10!" he barked.

"Hello, who is it?" I stuttered.

I had been sound asleep. I took a late train back to Copenhagen and went straight to the Oak Room Bar where I stood around for a couple of hours talking to a good-looking guy until I left him in the middle of a sentence at half past nausea. And now I was a really nauseous and hung over.

"Frederic from Samsø is coming over, and I think you should wear a skirt," my dad exclaimed in my ear.

"Dad!"

"Were you sleeping? Aren't you going to get out of bed and make something of your day? You need a run in the park."

"I have to go . . . " I stammered and managed to get to the toilet in the nick of time.

I must have found my way back to bed and fallen asleep again because the next thing I knew my father was pounding on my head board and howling, "Get up! We're leaving in 12 minutes!"

Once again I regretted having given him an emergency key.

"Dad, I can't . . . I . . . "

"Nonsense. Go take a cold shower. Now!"

I dragged myself under the shower and it did make me feel better, even if I was loath to admit it. But when I looked in the mirror I thought: Horror!

Shortly thereafter my poor brain recalled that the man I was meeting was not known for his good looks—so my looks were almost a gesture of solidarity with him and his!

The only problem would be if he thought I always looked like this . . . oh well, I would most probably never see him again anyway. He didn't sound like anything I would be interested in, especially now that I had met Ruben. On the other hand, Ruben and I just keep on talking, and he hasn't even tried anything else with me. Is he expecting me to take the initiative? How does that work in Severin's World?

Then my father said that Frederic reminded him of Claus, which snapped me back a few decades. Claus and I had dated for a very short time when I was young. I had just finished school and I was still living at home—and when Claus and I met, he usually spent more time in the living room with my father than in my room with me. Claus dreamed of becoming a researcher. One day while they sat talking, I left my room and went outside. I took a long walk in the forest and when I came back they were still sitting in the living room, chatting away. I broke up with Claus, but my father didn't. He and Claus still meet regularly and my father never fails to mention when they've seen each other, complete with an outburst like, "What a shame it is that you didn't stay together—Claus is such a great guy!"

We arrived at my father's place at three minutes to eleven—his 'Estate,' as he calls it, since it has a large house, a shed and what others refer to as a garden but which is 'land' to my father.

When we arrived there was a man standing on my dad's land and the lights were on inside his house. I thought of my father's girlfriend and suddenly the heavy load of the entire arrangement came down on me like a hammer.

But it turned out I was completely wrong. Frederic was charming and handsome! And self-confident. He was a little taller than me and in good shape.

His dark hair was short and his hazel eyes were intense. I was attracted to his essence and his body, and when he smiled at me, my hangover evaporated like dew in the sunshine. I really regretted going out last night since I looked so worn out and tired, but was thankful that it could only improve from here.

My father and I almost raced out of the car to greet him. My father won, gave him his hand and welcomed Frederic to his estate. Why must my father always appear more important than he is? On the other hand, it was a good thing Frederic had already met my father—that way he wouldn't be the reason everything went downhill later, if it even turned into anything at all. After all, I had my conversational date, Ruben, and I wanted to have sex with him so maybe I didn't need another man other than a handyman.

Especially now that I'd dropped Per—I called him yesterday and told him that I've met someone else. He actually claimed that this was an excellent reason to continue our relationship: "After all, it puts us in the same situation, given the fact that I still have a wife at home," he insisted. But the problem is that he will always have a physical and emotional safety net in his wife, and he can't afford to provide me with that safety. And Ruben has definitely piqued my curiosity, so now is the right time to call it quits with Per. But back to Frederic, who was reaching out his hand and introducing himself.

We exchanged greetings and his smile struck my heart like an arrow. The smile formed by his lovely lips spread across his face and into his warm eyes, which looked directly into mine. Wow!

Then my father started getting impatient and interrupted, "Come inside and I'll show you around."

Show him around! . . . but Frederic got the complete tour, asked funny questions and challenged my father's dominant nature. It was far more entertaining than I had expected.

In between comments from my father, he asked about what I did and where I lived. I explained that I live in a rented terraced house and told him about my job. He was very well-informed on the topic and asked me some great in-depth questions about the success rate of startups in Copenhagen.

Then Katherine arrived. She was a sweet, round woman in the prime of her life, easygoing and full of smiles. On top of that, she seemed crazy about my father. She complimented and laughed and patted in all of the right places, and he shone like the sun. Once again I was struck by how talented some women are at getting others to thrive. She was very sociable and our pleasant morning coffee quickly developed into brunch—luckily for me it was scrambled eggs, bacon and beer—and while we ate I started thinking about bringing Frederic into the running for my three profiles. But as soon as Katherine and my father went into the kitchen to get the cheese, he was a step ahead of me and asked, "How's it going with your three men?"

"Um, alright. How do you know about that?"

"A friend of mine thought I should respond to your personal ad. So when your father got in touch with me I figured: well, now two people think we might have something in common."

"Interesting," I said.

"I much prefer meeting you like this. I find online dating a little weird. It's like a supermarket for romance, sex, and intimacy, and I keep finding myself in the wrong aisle. Maybe I'm just too much of a romantic."

We laughed and I decided to ask him, "So which of the three roles would you try out for?"

"I'm definitely all for good sex. And good food," he replied quite directly. He smiled and the rest of his face followed suit in that incredibly charming way.

Just then Katherine and my father came back, so I was spared a reply. If I hadn't met Ruben, I would have said yes to him without blinking an eye. But Ruben is technically still a conversational companion. On the other hand, he hasn't asked me to promise him anything, and he knows what I'm looking for.

At three in the afternoon, Frederic was getting ready to leave and I accepted his offer to drop me off on his way back. When we got to my house, he asked for my phone number, which I gave him.

Now it's time for a nap, then a bath so I can to get ready for dinner at Noma with Ruben!

SUNDAY, MAY 31ST EARLY

My Dinner with Ruben

THE RENOWN AND MICHELIN star-awarded Noma is a beautiful restaurant. It is located right on the waterfront in Copenhagen, and the restaurant is on the ground floor of a house where Visit Greenland and the Icelandic Embassy are. There is a certain roughness to it in the sense that the environment is creative in a messy way but that is perfect since it keeps the restaurant's ambiance at a level that doesn't get too shiny and smooth. Inside, the restaurant has a very simple Scandinavian look with tables, chairs, a bar and practically nothing else. You get a feeling of voluptuous austerity, if that is possible. Voluptuous for the feeling I had about the upcoming food, and austerity for the design.

Ruben and I certainly had our senses stimulated by the seven-course meal we ate last night. We started with dried scallops, watercress with organic grains and beech nuts and a 2007 Arbois 'Fleur de Savagnin,' Domaine de la Tournelle from Jura. The experience wasn't just beautiful; it fully lived up to the restaurant's reputation.

While we ate, Ruben told me the story behind Noma. The restaurant is based on a manifesto for new Nordic cuisine, created in 2004 by some people who felt that Nordic ingredients and gastronomic traditions deserved a renaissance so they decided to give the traditions a modern makeover. The chef at Noma was especially interested in using 'foraged' ingredients, so he'd go out to the forests and fields of Denmark for days looking for edible natural plants whose tastes and textures would delight and surprise. At one time, they even served live ants in honey for dessert!

Since Noma was founded, they've employed discipline, poetry and perfectionism in the quest for the ultimate gastronomic experience. Their recognition by Michelin is a clear indication that they succeeded. Even the names of the dishes are creative and multisensory—one dish is called 'Oysters and the sea.' Another is 'Ox cheek and endive pickled pear and verbena.' Or for dessert 'Gammel Dansk, powdered milk and wood sorrel.' Each course was accompanied by a wine that perfectly matched the taste or teased out the food's nuances so they seemed even brighter and more elegant.

While Ruben talked, I concentrated on watching him closely, soaking in every detail of his countenance. It made me think about what moves us emotionally as humans when we are with someone at close range. We get attracted to someone's slightest movement or expression. It could be a little twist of the hand, a turn of the mouth, a twitch of the nose, a certain pronunciation of a word, a smile, or a twinkle of the eye that promises a laugh about to happen. Ruben moved me with his gestures and little expressions, and somehow I felt that I wanted to open myself to him. I started to feel closely connected to him. I'm not often moved; usually I don't even want to be moved. I don't want to open that part of myself because it is vulnerable. Being moved isn't always fantastic—it can be excruciatingly painful. But with him it seemed as if I couldn't quite resist it.

He lifted his glass and we toasted cheers. Then he looked at me closely and said, "So, now is the time to tell me whether you think you might want to join me in Severin's World."

I smiled and said, "In Severin's World, you talk about mastering masculine power. That's a very important thing. In Elizabeth's world, you have to master the feminine manner."

"The feminine manner? Why not the feminine power?"

"Because masculine and feminine creation happen differently. 'Power' indicates determination and the release of energy. 'Manner' indicates that women form their surroundings and themselves in their surroundings to a greater extent. That's why you see so many women putting their energy into creating homes and making sure that everything works, keeping the fire burning."

"Position three in your three-men universe is the key to a good relationship, then?"

"You could put it that way."

"And position one, the conversation guy, what role does he play?"

"Let me explain the whole thing. First, the handyman contributes to creating a well-functioning context. The guy who can talk and listen fills the context with valuable content. A lot of women enjoy discussing things, being challenged and getting new information about a subject. The talker must also be able to take part in my social circles. To feel complete, most woman need an active social circle to which she can contribute in many ways. A lot of women, for instance, like to tend to children and their needs, see friends in town or invite them home for a meal, call a neighbor to wish him good luck on his upcoming driving test, and stroke her husband's cheek when he's having a dark day. The man who understands the importance of social functions for a woman's well-being can win her heart."

"And lastly, what role does the sexual companion guy play?"

"When a relatively attractive woman steps outside from her house in the morning, she goes out and encounters many men who are potential sex partners. She doesn't need to do anything to meet them except walk in the street, sit at the bus stop, or go to work somewhere. And when a man catches sight of a woman that attracts him, he instinctively begins to determine whether or not he has a chance at winning her, and his body will send out indirect signals. Not all women notice these signals, but when they learn to recognize and interpret them, they'll start noticing them everywhere—from the board room to the supermarket. If they begin to react to those signals, they will get more direct invitations from a man. It does not happen every time or with all men, but if a woman is receptive and open-minded there is no end to her being approached by men who want her. So when a woman during a day says no to many possibilities, of which some are quite blunt, and she decides to refuse them and go home to her husband in the evening, he should thank his lucky stars that she has once again chosen him over all the others to have sex with. But he can't assume that she'll continue to choose him, because people and relationships change."

"Quite a number of demands for men, isn't it?"

"Yes, but there are demands on women, too. A woman is responsible for keeping herself in good shape so she can meet some of a man's expectations. She does so by taking good care of her body and herself in general. Of course, men have to do the same; after all it's the first step to good sex. But back to women. When a young girl starts feeling the urge, she should start getting to know herself sexually by exploring her body and her desires. She can start by reading some books on different types of sex. It can be novels, practical instruction books, poems or whatever. While reading, her body will give her clear signs about what turns her on. She can also watch porn on the internet to find out what turns her on, but that is a much more direct medium, so I don't recommend to start with that. At some point she will feel ready to start experimenting with men and maybe with other women as well. After having experimented for a while, she's ready to choose a love partner and maybe one day she'll find a partner with whom she can spend her life and possibly have children if they want to."

"I thought it was supposed to be three men?" Ruben said and grinned.

"What I just described is the model for finding out what is important to a woman when she is young and ready to start a family. But after a while, a women's talent for making the foyer function well by catering to everybody and their needs has such a powerful negative side effect which is that she forgets to fill her own batteries. My three-men model is the antidote for that."

"Do you think that women have more complex emotions than men?"

I gaped at him, my stare providing the answer.

"Ok, I get it. It's true that most of the women I know operate on a more complex emotional spectrum. And it seems like they have more dreams and desires," he explained.

"They are also able to have more varieties of orgasms," I teased.

Ruben smiled oddly. He has a unique ability of making me unsure. Maybe because we've talked so much about sex without having had it. The closest we've come was that night on the estate, but nothing came of it. How would he react if I made a move? Am I reading too much into the situation? There's a definite physical attraction between us, but there's also more than that. When I'm with him, it's almost as if I'm a little better than the best I thought I could be.

"In Severin's World, we have a program for training young men," he said.

"Training them in what?"

"In harnessing their masculine energy and recognizing what satisfies a woman. Your model makes me think that it makes a lot of sense to define three different roles that men can have for women. We haven't done that up until now, so we may want to modify our program using your ideas."

"What has the focus been so far in your program?" I asked.

"Teaching men to say yes and no to women and feeling good about it so they can build respect and honor for each other. That's the greatest challenge for men to learn about women."

"And in concrete words?"

"Social tools aren't a priority in our educational system. That's up to families, but having a child doesn't automatically teach you to be a good parent. Many sons are let down by not receiving good feedback about their behaviors towards women. They need to have limitations set up in order to discipline them and give their rebellious energy a focus. Few young men are able to handle the total freedom of choice that modern society presents to them. By creating better training for boys, we help them establish a clearer identity. That is an important element for a young man in terms of establishing good habits and a good life for himself. And it's important in relation to women because at some point the young man may have to say no to a woman which will make her upset and frustrated. A man has to be able to handle feminine frustration in order for a healthy relationship to develop. When he is afraid of making her angry, he risks becoming unmanly, abusive, or cruel—signs of an emotional weakling. And you know, most women actually want to know where their man stands on important issues."

I was fascinated by Ruben's perception of how my model could be adapted for young men, and thought how amazing it would be if I could end up contributing to this program for young men in Severin's World.

As we sipped the last remnants of our wine, Ruben seemed to be deep in thought. He then turned to me and asked, "Elizabeth, what do you really want to do in your life?"

"I want to inspire people to look at things from different angles and see new possible models for relationships."

"And how do you think you can do that?"

"Emotions control 80% of what people do versus 20% of behavior that comes from the analytical part of the brain. But only 7% of society's resources are used on teaching people about emotions and how to use them well. 93% of society's resources are invested in picking up the pieces after people have lived according to their emotions without being able to handle the consequences. Just look at all of the criminals behind bars, the investors who are driven by the conviction of their own greatness, people who use food to comfort themselves and get obese, children who are neglected because their parents can only think about themselves . . . these are all examples of how urgently we need a compass to find out what is important to us in terms of other people."

"So you want to increase the 7%?"

"Just look at how far Noma has gotten redefining food by gathering elements in nature which suit each other sublimely. And all because they took the time to step back and look at things from the outside to redefine for us a vision of what eating can be."

"And what precisely do you want to accomplish?"

"You'll have to come further into 'Elizabeth's world' to find out."

"Touché," he grinned.

I smiled in return, but my smile immediately stiffened when he said, "This has been very interesting, Elizabeth. But for now I'm afraid I'll have to say no thanks and cut off contact with you."

"Now?" I asked and straightened in my chair.

"I need to take some time to reflect on whether I can choose you completely. If I can, the consequences will be substantial. And if I can't, you deserve somebody who can."

I looked at him and felt my eyes fill with tears. I tried to stop them, but that only made things worse. I let them fall. He looked back at me. Which somehow hurt even more. We had had such magical encounters so far and now this rejection. But wait, it's not a rejection—it's the postponement of a decision. How long will he need to decide? Can I do anything besides wait for him to figure out his emotions?

"I'd like for you to do the same," he said, "to decide if you can choose me completely."

He's a special man, unlike anyone I've ever met before. So he's probably right. But I was having a hard time with it, so I stood up and bowed slightly before leaving. It felt awful and fantastic at once, and I needed to get some fresh air.

I still do.

SUNDAY EVENING

A New Handyman in My Garden

ANTON CAME OVER AFTER lunch and he turned out to be even better that I had expected. He had just responded to my profile saying that he was an architect and loved to do practical tasks around a house and that he didn't have one yet, since he and his pregnant wife had decided to wait until after the birth, so he had some spare time for me. He's a funny, stocky man with dark hair and cool, green eyes. He's somewhat taller than I am and when he asked me about the details of my practical needs he looked me straight in the eyes, which made me weak in the knees. I was feeling so vulnerable after last night, so it's possible than any man who gave me any attention could have made me weak in the knees today.

I didn't have any plans for today, just enjoyed that he had come over to help me with the handiwork. And he was great at it; it took him just two hours to complete everything on my list! That included bringing some heavy stuff up to the attic, clearing out the shed, cleaning the garden furniture, repairing the stuck lid on the grill and fixing the loose plank by the door-jamb. I served coffee and cake and he told me that he had lived in a house for years but was now in an apartment with his wife. He had studied building and construction, which was why he knew so much about handiwork.

I got a text from my father that Uncle Theo is much more ill than the doctors had thought at first, so I should visit him in the hospital tomorrow. Apparently he's been asking for me.

PHILOSOPHER	LOVER	HANDYMAN
• Frederic? • Ruben?	• David from Belgium • Ruben	• Anton

MONDAY, JUNE 1ST

My Wonderful Uncle Theo

UNCLE THEO BEAMED WHEN he caught sight of me. And even that took an effort—he clearly doesn't have much time left. Aunt Kate went out and left us alone and it was lovely to spend some time with him. My uncle and I have always been close, and it hurts me to see him so weak. The doctors say that cancer has spread everywhere and there's nothing they can do to help him.

I sat down and took his hand. He dozed off but then suddenly awoke and asked:

"Are you still planning that thing with the numbers?"

"1789/1909/2029?"

"Yes."

"I thought you were going to do it with Thomas?"

"He's gone. It just wasn't meant to be with him."

"So what are you going to do?"

"I met another man. If all goes well, he and I will do it together."

"Is he a good man?"

"He's fantastic," I said with a smile.

"And will he understand why these years are important? I mean you've read so many books to prepare for this and we have had many conversations. It's a pity if it doesn't happen."

"I'm sure he knows why the French revolution in 1789 is important for our possibilities of personal freedom today. And in 1909 women got the right to vote. I'm not sure he knows about that, but we will talk about it."

"And 2029?"

"I haven't told him that I believe that by 2029, we will be living in a world completely different from today and that I want to influence in what direction we are moving."

"But will he agree with you on the important ideas you've had, Lizzy?" He loved calling me that nickname and it touched me to hear it.

"We agree that men and women should have equal opportunities. And that sex is a key parameter in the lives of both men and women. We haven't covered other topics yet, but his approach to life is as tolerant, curious and grand as mine."

"That's my girl," Uncle Theo said and grinned from ear to ear as he patted my hand. Then he drifted off again.

When I got home there was an email from Frederic, who wants to go out with me on Wednesday. I accepted right away—it helped me abate my disappointment that Ruben hasn't written.

TUESDAY, JUNE 2ND

An Email from Ruben

RUBEN WROTE THIS MORNING!

Dear E.
Respect yourself.
Love R

What in the world is that supposed to mean? I wanted an answer, an invitation, a clear signal about whether he wants me. And all I get is one-line schoolteacher rhetoric! What is he doing? Why can't we just meet and take it from there?

What an odd guy. More than anything else I'm baffled. I simply cannot understand why it should take him so long to find out that he cannot live without me. There are so many things that connect the two of us, and not just the usual stuff. When I think about him and our time together, I realize that I've been missing something for a long time without quite being aware of it. I feel a loneliness on many levels, a loneliness that's never really been abated. I like the way he resonates in my mind. Is that the respect for women he's talking about? Respect for what I feel deep inside is important? A sensation which I, in my haste, have drowned because I shy away from the conditions and efforts it requires to make it grow? What is it that he wants me to respect?

A Message from the Past

RECEIVED AN EMAIL FROM my former boyfriend Jens today:

Dear Elizabeth,

I often think of the good times we had together. Do you remember the night we made love in the forest at Charlottenlund after that party at Denmark's Aquarium? You leaned up against a tree with one leg on a fallen tree trunk and looked so beautiful and happy. The forest floor was fragrant and I felt like a teenager in love. I'd like to spend a night with you again. Get in touch if you're interested.

Love, Jens

Interested, oh yes. He's perfect for profile #2—we used to have great sex. The only problem was that I fell in love with him, and he didn't fall in love with me. Instead, he chose to be with one of my girlfriends for five years. Even when he was with her though, we always talked and flirted with each other, but quite innocently. I don't remember why, but I lost contact with my girlfriend—we weren't on bad terms or anything, we just stopped calling each other.

One evening I ran into Jens in a bar and he told me that things were going badly between him and her and that he had decided to move out. Something just clicked between us and we released five years of pent up mutual lust in one night. It started a sort of avalanche and soon we met at all possible and impossible times. We got very close. At first I didn't take it as more than an impassioned affair, but when he moved out of their flat two weeks later I thought we would become a couple. I visited him in his rented room and we had a great time when we met. We knew each other well, so we could let our lust take over in an easy manner.

He had a rich and fascinating inner life, and I loved him for it. He spun fascinating stories around himself, with ancestors and props from the past like a white straw hat to match his white linen suit, a Drachmann poem he just happened to know by heart, a way of speaking to me as a woman that made me feel womanly. It was as if he had stepped right out of the impressionist painter crowd that gathered in Skagen, the northernmost town in Denmark, around the year 1900. They were the Danish 'artistes'—free thinkers and creative souls who invented a lifestyle that few can live today. They came to Skagen to take advantage of the beautiful landscape and the famous northern light that allows one to experience colors without a filter.

I believe 'without a filter' also characterized their lifestyles. They created art, drank, partied, had arguments, kissed, made love, separated, got back together, were happy, got hurt, and so on, constantly living with all their senses alive. Life for them was about being challenged and provoked in your viewpoints, getting hurt, feeling overtaken by somebody more talented, falling in love, and taking your own talents to the max. Life in the ordinary lane is seldom like that.

Jens was one of these kinds. I longed to be with him and soak up a drop of his life without a filter. I wanted to shower him with love, to be there for him through thick and thin. And thick and thin there were.

But each time I left his place, it was almost as if I ceased to exist. He didn't ask when I'd come back, he didn't call me when I wasn't there. We carried on like that for some months. New Year's Eve rolled around and I assumed we'd spend the evening together, but at the same time I wasn't sure. And when I finally asked if he had plans for New Year's, he said that he'd be spending it with his brother, who lived next door and whom he saw all the time anyway! Then I realized that I had been just a kind of raft for him, something he used to get him out of his shipwrecked relationship. I sat down and cried.

And now he wanted a ride on the raft again . . . was it because he was ready for more with me? Am I ready for more with him? No, I'm not. Right now I'm trying to find out if I can handle Ruben. And respect myself . . . instead of respecting Jens. I wonder what Ruben will think of this resolution of mine? Can he really handle me when I respect myself?

Another Email from Ruben

Dear E.

*Tu peux avoir tout ce que tu veux, tant que tu ne veux pas tout. You can
have all that you want as long as you don't want it all.*

Love R

Are admonitions in French part of Severin's World?!

And what is this cryptic sentence supposed to mean, anyway?

Frederic has asked me to meet him at the organic restaurant Bio Mio
tonight, near the train station in an area that is being gentrified and turned
into a little Paris, cobblestone streets and all. The restaurant is situated in
the old slaughterhouse brick buildings of Copenhagen, which are now filled
with fancy art galleries, cafés and restaurants. Bio Mio has a relaxed section
of sofas and comfortable chairs and an eating section with long tables that
you share with anyone, like in a school or camp facility.

I can't get my mind off Ruben; on the other hand, I'm not getting very
clear signs from him. Is it cruel to meet Frederic when I'm this unsure of
what I want from Ruben? But I haven't promised Frederic anything. He
said he loves to talk and he is good at it. And if Ruben turns me down,
Frederic is next in line. Ok, it is a bit cruel to juggle two potential lovers.
But isn't that the way everyone does it?

Meanwhile, David has just invited me to Paris this coming weekend!
And I said yes! Friday is a national holiday because our constitution was
signed on June 5th, so I'm free to travel for some hot sex with David.

My Dinner with Frederic

WAS AT A BOOK release party in the beautiful and flowery King's Garden in
the center of Copenhagen this afternoon for a book about how to divorce

well. The garden started as the King's Garden for growing vegetables and fruit, and for riding and other forms of entertainment for the king and his friends. But in 1770, it was opened to the public.

I've attended many private picnics and public events here and today it was a book launch at the Orangeri restaurant in the eastern part of the garden. We can't have too many books on how to get back on the horse again after a divorce, so I wanted to support the launch. Drinking champagne on a warm afternoon, we talked about divorces and affairs and the juicy rumors circulating about a certain prominent politician's infidelity that recently got the famous Copenhagen journalist Baxter sacked for reporting on it. That'll show him.

Got an email from General George, the general in our Danish armed forces who hosted the dinner when I was at The Allinge Retreat Centre. He wanted to go on a date. He didn't mention if his wife would be coming along ;) and given the amount of quarrel there was between them at the dinner party, I won't miss her.

LATER

MY DATE WITH FREDERIC was pushed back to Thursday evening. When I got to BioMio, Frederic was already sitting at one of the long tables looking good. We ordered a couple of their delicious organic entrees and I enjoyed the crowd and the laid-back atmosphere. Frederic ordered us beer from their more than 20 home brews in huge silver fermentation tanks in the back of the restaurant.

As soon as we said cheers, he told me that he had thought out a new model which would make it possible for everyone in society to benefit from new inventions. It entails having 15% of all annual budgets in the public sector devoted to doing something radically different. In my mind, he's a bit vague about what 'different' means, since it's a subjective term. But he insisted that if all companies invested 15% of the revenues on a radical new ways of business, it would start a chain reaction. We spent two hours discussing his model, turning it upside down and trying to translate it to a doable paradigm.

He didn't flirt with me. Or maybe he did, but it wasn't easy to read. He was very focused, even when staring at my breasts. Maybe I was just reading too much into it.

At one point, he looked at his watch and said out of the blue, "We can still catch a late show. Want to?"

"Sure," I said enthusiastically. "What should we see?"

We found a newspaper and picked out a film. I suggested that we leave his bicycle there and drive to the cinema together in my car.

"Good idea," he said. "Maybe you'll get a roll in the hay later."

I looked at him with surprise. It came from seemingly nowhere, from a man who may or may not have been flirting with me. I decided to play hard to get and said that I wasn't sure if I was interested.

He looked at me sideways and said with a smile, "Of course you are."

I smiled back and couldn't help but laugh at his smugness.

"My boundaries are different than other people," he said.

"That suits me just fine," I said. I was beginning to like him more and more.

"I think you're a wonderful woman," he said.

"Thank you," I replied with a smile. Ruben had better get moving if he wants me, I thought.

We went to the cinema and saw *Good Night and Good Luck*. I had wanted to see it when it originally came out but missed it, so this plan worked for me.

The darkness of a cinema can be dangerous for a man and a woman. It creates an intimate environment which can be overwhelming to a new relationship. And that's what ours was, given that it wasn't even a relationship. On our way into the darkness, Frederic handed me my ticket and said, "I'll meet you inside in a minute."

I went in and found my seat.

Five minutes later, I felt a warm hand caressing my neck that startled me. Frederic sat down next to me and I could smell his cologne. I could barely concentrate on the film, the warmth between us rising. I wanted his hands on me and his hot words in my ear. I did manage to catch that the film was a drama set in the McCarthy era in the U.S. in the 1950s, and was about the two journalists who finally brought down McCarthy. George Clooney was sublime as one of the journalists, but his presence on screen made me yearn for Frederic. At one point, he held my hand for a while, then he laid it back on my leg, and his occasional whispering of comments about the movie in my ear were interspersed with other sentences, like, "There are so many things I want to do to you."

I suddenly felt Frederic gently pressing a morsel of chocolate between my lips and into my mouth. He let his fingers rest briefly on my lips and I could feel it in every molecule of my body. That sensual, masculine way of delivering a piece of chocolate increased the probability of intimacy dramatically.

When the film was over I was ready to go to my place or his right away... but we didn't—he said he had someplace else to be! I don't understand it. What does he want? First, he said I was wonderful and he wanted to do all sort of things to me. First Ruben, now Frederic. Tell me, are there no willing men in this city???!

PHILOSOPHER	LOVER	HANDYMAN
• Frederic	• David from Belgium	• Anton
• Ruben?	• Ruben	
	• Frederic?	
	• Jens	

FRIDAY, JUNE 5TH

Paris, Here I Come!

ON THE WAY TO Paris. I only had to buy the ticket, as David would take care of the rest, he told me.

Hotel du Roc is where we will meet. It's right by metro Dufrennes in the 6th arrondissement. I'm curious about what kind of place it is, and whether it will be easy to find.

On my way to the airport I got a text from Ruben.

Dear E.
Open your inner circle to others who respect themselves.
Love R

Yes, alright..., I will, thanks. Christ, Ruben's really a character. In reality I don't know much about him. He's the dean of the country's largest university, he lives downtown somewhere and his father was a photographer with his own studio. Is he married? I didn't ask and he hasn't mentioned any wife . . . so far. He behaves like a single man; independent you might say. And he created a world of his own, Severin's World—which I still don't really know a whole lot about. Some people would advise me to steer clear of a man like him. My intuition says I should sail a steady course toward him. I want to open my inner circle to him; I assume that he respects himself. But I'm no good at waiting, so I've decided that the best way forward is for me to figure out what initiative to take with him. Then it's all or nothing.

Right now it doesn't really matter since I'm on my way to a weekend with David in Paris. I have to return Sunday morning, so we don't have too much time. Which is probably for the best.

Must admit that David does things with a lot of confidence. He texted me again when I was on the metro on the way there, and by the time I came out from the station, he was already walking towards me grinning like a lion about to mate. It felt a little too forward though. I know he did it to be nice, but it seemed in some way, as if he thought we were a couple. A boyfriend picks you up at the station. A mistress can find her own way.

Fortunately, he had bought champagne, which he opened as soon as we had entered the suite he reserved. He dimmed the lights in a nice subdued manner, uncovered the bed in the proper way, and when we had drunk half a glass of champagne, he left me there alone so I could unpack while he went down and got a bottle of wine at a store nearby. When he came back, I had put on my transparent pink negligee and placed myself on top of the covers drinking my champagne.

"You're very sexy in that nightgown," he gleamed.

"Nightgown," I replied, "it's called a negligee!"

"Usually I don't really care about sexy underwear, but that one is very . . . uh, naughty."

I smiled, and he crawled into bed with me. He seemed so excited that he had difficulty getting rid of his clothes fast enough. I laughed at his efforts.

I kissed him, he kissed me back, but when he started to embrace me, I jumped up and poured him a glass of champagne.

He looked at me. "Aha, so you know that the best satisfaction is postponed satisfaction," he said and smiled at me as I handed him the glass.

I smiled and made sure my negligee moved a bit to show some bare skin on my breasts. It felt really good to be me and showing it.

He leaned back in the bed and took a sip from the glass.

This will be a good weekend, I thought. It was very different than such intimate encounters normally are for me, because I was not the least bit in love with him. There was nothing at stake, as there normally is when I'm naked with a man. It gave me a sense of freedom to enjoy. We were more like equals. I just had to disregard the fact that it seemed like he was about to fall in love with me. That was not my problem. I was just playing the same game that he plays with women all the time.

I asked him what he had been doing since we last saw each other, and within a short time, we were talking, caressing, drinking, and touching each other all over. My heart was beating rather normally as I sat there in my negligee, thinking we would soon make love. It was nice that we had no urgency to get to it. We had met in Paris to make love, so at some point it would happen. Since it was weeks and many text messages since we last saw each other in Copenhagen where we had great sex, I felt quite sure it was going to be good. I was enjoying my lazy lust.

My clarity about this tryst differed from my previous experiences. Whenever I've been with a guy I was in love with, I was never quite sure what would happen. I had not recognized until now that by listening to "us," I was failing to listen to "myself." That meant that I was never sure if we were going to make love or not. Of course I could have taken the initiative myself, and on occasion, I had done that, but with a guy I was in love with, I was afraid of doing something wrong so I often ended up doing nothing.

I guess it comes from a feeling that respectable women are not allowed to be horny, so when I'm horny I try to wrap my desire around the idea that it's something the man wants. It's his desire, not mine. Or maybe it's just me, having grown up in a chaste suburb where women who expressed desire were unwelcome.

Here in Paris, I felt that it was a lot easier to take initiatives with David, since it wasn't so important if I succeeded or not, or if what I did was exciting to him or not. In this meeting with David, there is much more space for me to be and act exactly as horny as I feel. I like that! In fact, I will try to bring it back with me when I go home.

As we talked lying together in bed, I could even feel that the boundaries for my initiatives were growing by the minute, as I sensed that David was falling in love with me. It was fun to think that he had met his equal, namely a woman who takes what she wants, which was normally his role.

"Do you make a lot of money in your job?" he asked suddenly.

"Enough," I replied.

"Enough for what?"

"For leading the kind of life I want to live."

"You are quite independent, huh?"

"Yes," I replied, and kissed him.

We emptied the champagne bottle and soon our bodies found each other as we embraced. It was hot and intense as we made love a first time and we released our sexual energy quickly. Then we fell asleep.

I woke up later and he was caressing my back, my legs and my inner thighs. His touch was soft and nice.

I could tell he was excited, but it had to wait a little more for a second round.

"Why did you want to know how much I earn?" I asked.

"You seem very independent. And wise. So I wanted to know if you are smarter than me," he said, and laughed.

I smiled at him and asked "How can you find that out?"

"I would judge it based on how much you earn."

"Tell me what you earn, and I will answer you."

"Approximately 65,000 Euros per year."

"Then I am smarter than you," I answered, smiling.

His smile froze.

"But I have my own company," he said teasingly.

"Oh yeah, great for you, Mr. CEO."

He grabbed me again. This time a little harder and kissed me. I could feel he had a real hard on again.

"Why are some men provoked by strong women?" I asked.

"I like independent women," he replied, and stopped caressing me.

"Do you?"

"Clearly. The victory of conquering a strong woman is more thrilling than conquering a weak one," he replied, grinning.

I looked down at his cock that suddenly was no longer hard.

I got up and made coffee for us.

He looked at me.

When I came over to the bed and sat down, he reached for me.

"Come on," he said. "Again?" He took my hand.

I put the coffee cups on the bedside table and he pulled me down on the bed and got on top of me while he grabbed my hands and lifted them so they were stretched out over my head on the pillow. He said, "I love strong women like you."

"Do you now?"

"Hell, yes!" he almost shouted and held me tight, but no signs of arousal in him materialized.

I looked up at him, realizing what he needed to hear from me. "I'm a manager with ten people under me. I have a difficult board of directors that I have to manage closely, and I have meetings with the Ministry of innovation and research, sometimes with the Minister herself."

"Okay," he said, but still no arousal. We rolled over so we were now lying next to each other.

"I manage my budget closely and have so far exceeded my sales projections each year while never exceeding my expense budget," I taunted him.

"Great," he said.

"And you find all that attractive?"

"Hell yeah!" he shouted again.

"It doesn't really look like it," I said, staring at his flaccid cock.

"But . . . " he said. "I just need more time . . . "

"Sssh," I told him. "Let's try something different. Close your eyes."

He did it.

"Now imagine that I'm a dumb blonde with low income who is five years younger than you."

"Yes . . . "

"Is that a little more exciting?"

"No," he said.

But his cock showed the opposite, as it began filling up and rising.

"This blond has perky tits, with nice nipples and she wears a lot of makeup and bright red lipstick."

"Ok, I see her," he said, his closed eyes fluttering.

His cock grew bigger. I grabbed it and yanked it to make him open his eyes.

"David, when we were talking about strong women, you lost your excitement. Now that we are role playing me as a young, dumb blonde, your cock gets excited."

"Well . . . "

He looked at me and realized that I was right. His body spoke its own language.

"Bloody hell," he said and looked at me.

"Yeah, right."

"Well you see, it's because . . . "

"You don't have to explain anything," I said and laughed at him.

"Shit!"

"Well, let's leave it for now. How about if we get up and see if we can find a restaurant?" I asked.

"Sure," he said and looked a little relieved.

LATER

As we sat at the restaurant, he brought up the subject again.

"You know, I really do have high respect for intelligent women," he said.

"Yeah, we are interesting to talk to, right?" I said, my sarcasm clear to him.

"You are also good in bed!" he said.

"Sure."

"It's true. You and I made great love in Copenhagen on that house boat. It was super."

"Yes, because I let you control the process."

"What do you mean? Why?"

"When two people don't know each other well, I find that it works best if the man is in control."

"I don't think it has to be like that all the time."

I thought a little and looked at him. He looked back at me like a willing dog, and then I got an idea. "Okay, let's swap roles then."

"What do you mean?"

"Between now and the next six hours, it is I who decide."

"Decides what?"

"*When* we have sex and *how* we do it. You just do as I say."

The idea turned me on; it was unpredictable and rather exciting. I also felt the power in it. Now I could get things to work out just like I wanted it.

He sat for a minute, looking at me and smiled a little. He seemed hesitant as to whether he thought it was a good idea to accept my offer.

I wasn't sure that he would, or how I would really feel if he did as then I would really have to take control. I wasn't used to being so unchallenged in the driver's seat. Usually it was a man taking the first step with me following, and then we would adjust to each other's behavior. But if David said yes, everything would suddenly be up to me. Intriguing thought!

I looked at him and asked, "So are you up for it?"

He was still considering, but there was no real alternative for him actually. If he said no, he might as well go back home, because we both knew that my respect for him would be quite diminished.

"Alright, let's do it," he replied.

"Ok, then finish your meal and let's head back to the hotel," I said and smiled at him.

I could see he felt provoked by me commanding him, so I softened my tone of voice and smiled at him. I had to be careful not to push him so much that his desire for me completely disappeared. It had to be something of a balancing act, I thought and smiled to myself.

On the way back to the hotel, he tried again to take my hand, but I didn't want him to, and pulled my hand away. When he later tried to kiss me, I looked directly at him and said, a bit coldly, "Not now."

"Oh, you are tough!" he lamented.

"Yes," I said, thinking that now I understand people who get high on power. "That is why it requires a responsible mind to manage power."

Back in the hotel room, I went to the bathroom and changed into my negligee.

When I came into the bedroom, I sat on the bed and asked him to get me a drink.

"Okay, what do you want?" he asked.

"Whiskey on the rocks."

I needed something to strengthen me if I was going to implement this. It was exciting and scary—and therefore even more exciting. But I wasn't sure I could carry it out so I chose to let the alcohol relax my inhibitions.

He prepared the drink and brought it over to me on the bed. I took the glass, as he sat down beside me and started to caress my body.

"Not now," I said again.

"When, then?"

"You will find out."

"Hm."

It was a new situation for him and I could see he had no idea how to react. He got up and prepared a drink for himself.

"What now?" he asked.

"I don't know."

"But couldn't we do something?" he said reaching out to slip his hand onto my breasts.

"Nope. You just have to wait until I find out what I want," I said and looked at him, cherishing my power.

"Oh, you are one tough cookie."

"It can get a lot worse," I said and smiled.

He looked at me, and I could see his imagination starting up, except he was not sure what to expect. I wasn't either. But that was the fun.

I took a big gulp of the drink. Finally, he came over to me, leaned over me and kissed me.

"Sit," I said.

"Sit??"

"As a dog."

He looked at me to see if I meant it. I did. I had to go all-in with this experience. Could I get him to sit like a dog who obediently waited for orders from his master?

He sat on the floor.

"It does not look like a dog," I said.

He squatted.

"Still doesn't."

He raised his arms in front of his body, straightened and bent his two hands in front of his chest, so it looked like two front paws.

I kissed him and said, "Good dog."

"Ahhh!!!" he cried, and I could see it both provoked and excited him.

"Okay," I said. "Now I want you to find some music and then start stripping for me."

"Stripping!?!"

"Yes."

"What do you mean?"

"You strip by taking your clothes off one piece at a time . . . "

"Yes, yes, but are you serious?"

"Yes. And I want you to touch yourself while you do it."

He emptied his drink and poured another for himself.

Then he started. Hesitantly at first, but when I smiled at him and the rhythms of the music picked up, he got more into it and started dancing with more emotion. I sipped my drink and watched him. He was muscular, attractive and well proportioned, but he was also beginning to develop an obvious stomach. His cock was of the big, long type, and it was getting erect and tall, so by the time he was down to his underwear, he had difficulty keeping it inside. We looked at each other and smiled. The cock grew longer. My excitement grew. And at the same time, I knew that I could prolong the process as long as I wanted to. It was fun!

He had some difficulty in stripping off his boxer shorts, stumbling over them as he took them off one leg. I smiled. He got up, just as the music ended, and removed his shorts completely. I saw that he was about to jump up in bed ready to get his reward.

"Not so fast," I said.

"Ouch, you are worse than a she-devil!"

"So is that what you think of strong women?"

"No, I mean, you know . . . "

"No, I don't actually."

He stood looking at me. He was clearly baffled.

"What now?" he pleaded.

"I want to look at you and your cock. Stand at the end of the bed and play with yourself."

"Seriously?"

"Yep. Cheers!"

"Cheers."

He grabbed his cock and began to move his hand rhythmically back and forth and up and down, masturbating himself.

It was exciting to watch, because this is such a very private thing for a man.

He began to groan.

"You must not come," I yelled.

"Then we have to quit this soon."

"Ok, stop."

He stopped and got into the bed and grabbed my body.

"Take it easy, I'm not ready yet," I said.

"Shit, this is hard—and I'm hard, too."

"Yep, I can see that."

"What now? C'mon, let's make love."

"First lavish me with compliments and caress my body with your hands."

"What compliments?"

"That's up to you. They must be personal, and I need to really feel appreciated."

"You are so beautiful," he said in a meaningful tone.

"Thank you. I know you mean it."

"Your breasts and vagina are perfect."

"Keep going."

"I desire you."

"Yeah . . . "

"Your smile is enchanting, and you are very wise."

I looked at him and smiled, giving him approval. He beamed back at me, and pulled me in closer.

He began reciting all kinds of compliments to me, and with each one, I slowly guided his capable hands all over my body, so he got me to burn with passion. But every time his cock approached my thighs, I pulled away and said, "Not yet."

He squirmed and panted from the desire building up in his body.

"Stop," I said suddenly, as I was tired of a movement he kept repeating.

He looked at me, his frustration mounting, so I was almost afraid to go on.

"I want you to move to the other side of the bed and touch yourself again, but you cannot come," I said.

"Ai, that will be almost impossible."

"Do it. If you come, you will miss what I have for you."

It was incredible to see that he continued to do everything I said. So this is all that it takes to have your desires met, hmmm? You just need somebody to accept the role of fulfilling your fantasies.

It was a wonderful new experience to watch him dancing and stroking himself at the side of the bed. There was something completely uninhibited about us now. As stimulating as a porn movie when it is a good one, which is rare. This was like my personal porn movie, but the roles were reversed.

"Don't you think this is a valuable lesson for you?" I asked.

"What do you mean?"

"Now you can actually explore how far your desire for strong women goes."

"For one strong woman, you mean."

"Oh yeah."

"And yes . . . I desire you very much," he said, and grabbed his big cock. I smiled at him and said, "Okay then, come on."

~~~~~~~~~~~~~~~~~~~~~~~~~~~~

David had a relaxed relationship with his own body, which makes sex more enjoyable. He was completely and totally present. It was also great that he could control his dick and what he did with it. It was as if it were an instrument he played like a maestro. And he knew just what notes he had to play on my body. As he arched over me, swaying his hips back and forth, penetrating me deeply, his face lit up like a man who had come out after a long period of captivity. He was rocking and rolling all over me, kissing me everywhere. We caressed each other till total satisfaction, and as he came, he roared like an animal.

SUNDAY, JUNE 7TH

Ruben is a Mystery to Me

I'M NOW ON MY way home after an incredibly sensual, erotic and satisfying weekend. I wonder why I haven't tried the type of role reversal that I did with David long ago with my prior lovers? It was fantastic! And without problems. He didn't care for more of it, though. He said that he had proven to me that he found me very attractive as an independent woman. And I must say that he continued to prove it, even when the roles reversed back.

I now understand why men like the patriarchal model. It's fulfilling to have your needs met by somebody who aims to please you.

But as interesting as the weekend proved to be, I'm not so keen on meeting David again, as I think there are other men who will be better suited for my position #2. He likes me too much to fill just one role.

I WENT TO UNCLE Theo and Aunt Kate's for dinner today. I drove straight there from the airport. But only Kate was there in their beautiful country house just 10 miles from Copenhagen's City Hall Square. On the way, I picked up Mille from Sebastian and Marianne's, then the two of us picked up my latest efficient and kind handyman Anton at the train station and drove up to the country house. Kate had said that she needed to clean the attic, and I can understand why: there was so much furniture, so many boxes and books and bits and pieces in every color, shape and size—things they had saved for a rainy day during most of a lifetime.

Kate had made coffee and her specialty—a delicious, buttery cake with meringue on top called 'the emperor's beard.' Anton and Mille competed to see who could eat more, but when they each had gobbled up four pieces I put a stop to it.

Kate explained that she wanted everything taken out of the attic. She wanted to get rid of as much as possible, and we were welcome to take anything that she didn't want to keep. Anton was efficient and Mille just had a good time carrying as much as she possibly could at once. I, on the other hand, was melancholic. I recognized Theo's favorite armchair, and when Anton brought out the worn-down footrest that belonged to it, tears started streaming down my cheeks. Kate noticed and asked if I could come and give her a hand in the kitchen.

She poured each of us a shot of Gammel Dansk, a bitter alcohol that you drink in small glasses mostly in the morning or when you are feeling cold. We emptied the glasses and she poured us a second that we drank more slowly. She also put on a pot of coffee. I dried my eyes.

"You know that Theo is very ill, don't you," Kate finally told me.

"Yes," I nodded. I felt the tears welling up in my eyes again.

"I won't be able to stay here alone," she said.

"But what will you do? I thought this place is your life and you'd never want to leave it."

"*Our* life, yes. But not mine. I've never really liked living here."

"What?"

"I don't need a big place and I'm not a handy person. If I touch something in the garden, it withers. I'm much more suited to an apartment."

"What are you going to do with the house?"

"Your Uncle Theo has plans."

"He always does," I said with a smile.

"Yes, he's been a marvelous husband. And because this is his place, I want to respect his wishes."

"I've always loved being here," I said. "You're so good at making people feel welcome."

"As Theo says: 'Old bricks like these are not for keeps.'"

"He's always treated them so well."

"Exactly, you've always been able to understand that sort of thing. But you're not much of a handywoman yourself."

"That is why I've got Anton," I boasted with a smile.

"That three-men model of yours is certainly something. Do you think of him as your boyfriend?"

"No, I think more of my lover as a boyfriend, and right now there's no one in that position. But I have my eye on one or two men for a lover, and I have my conversational man Frederic and my right-hand man Anton."

"And the three men are alright with it?"

"They appreciate the clarity of my expectations. And also, I always have a minimum of two potential candidates for the position of lover, which is great. I'm never overly dependent on one guy, since I have an understudy ready to take over."

"It all sounds quite intellectual."

"I have to admit, I think I've gotten in over my head with the first lover I've got my eyes on now, a guy named Ruben."

"How so?"

"He's of a different, higher caliber than the others. He relates strongly to me, and he has a whole world, a sort of network of people, of his own—you have to qualify to be admitted."

"And haven't you passed the admission test yet?"

"No, and it really irks me."

Kate smiled and looked at her watch. I could see she didn't want to hear more about this strange paradigm of mine. TMI for my aunt.

"I brought a picnic basket," I said.

"You didn't have to do that."

"You have three guests, so of course I did."

We set the table and Mille and Anton came inside. Anton had completely thrown himself into the task of emptying the attic, so after a quick lunch and two beers, he went back to work.

By three o'clock we were finished and headed back to the city. I thanked Anton profusely for his enormous help.

"When Ruben says our help is needed, we're always there," Anton said. My ears suddenly perked up. What?

"Ruben? You know Ruben?!"

"Sure."

Suddenly a light went on. And I asked—"Are you Ruben's friend, the architect? The one with the pregnant wife?"

He nodded.

"Why didn't you say anything before about that?"

"Ruben asks for help with a lot of things. There is no need to be curious."

"I hadn't seen this coming," I said, feeling a little overwhelmed at the coincidence. "But then you need to tell me a little more about Ruben."

"What do you want to know?"

"Is he married?"

"He was."

"To whom?"

"The astrophysicist Maria Martinsen. And before that to the French phi-lologist and marathon runner Daphne Dufour."

"Has he got any children?"

"Yes, three. The youngest is 18. You can drop me off here, right around the corner."

After I dropped him off, Mille asked, "Who's Ruben?"

"A man I met who's a little bit strange sometimes."

"Is he your boyfriend?"

"No, he's not."

We were quiet for a while. Then, breathlessly, Mille blurted out, "Dad says you have three boyfriends. Is that true?"

I looked at her and smiled, trying to hold off on answering her a bit. She didn't smile back.

"I'm *looking* for three men," I finally said. "I was so sad when Thomas left us. And my relationships with other men have not really lasted, so I thought it was time for a new model. With three boyfriends, I have more options."

"I don't understand."

"Anton is super at practical things, so he comes and helps with handi-work. I also spend time with Frederic, who's smart and interested in every-thing. We can sit and talk until three in the morning, drinking red wine and discussing life. I like that."

"So who's Ruben?"

"Well, that's a good question."

"Can't you just ask him if he wants to be your boyfriend?"

"It's not that easy."

"Ahhh, you grown-ups!" Mille said and laughed, just as we pulled up in front of Sebastian and Marianne's. She was about to get out of the car, but I paused her and said, "Some people may find this model of mine with three men a strange thing to do, so if anybody asks you, feel free to plead ignorance, honey. If they insist, just say that your mom has always been a bit odd."

Mille stared at me with a "duh-yeah" look, hugged me and said, "Of course, Mom."

Driving home, I was happy about our lovely afternoon at Kate's, finding out that Anton is a friend of Ruben's and talking to Mille about my relation-ship model and giving her a back door out so she didn't have to be involved. Also, Anton and I had a good time and spent just the right amount of time together. If Anton had been my boyfriend, we would have had to spend the rest of the day together, figure out what we wanted to have for dinner, go shopping and cook together, probably getting on each other's nerves since what I needed was to be alone for a while. We would have eaten while watching the evening news and fallen asleep in front of the TV. No romance there.

Instead I went home and made myself a simple bowl of penne arrabbiata and a green salad and now I'm sitting on the sofa. I put on my classical music playlist on my iPod and I'm going to listen for a bit, thinking about my day.

A light bulb suddenly lit up in my head. Ruben must have summoned Anton to become my handyman. And they are old and close friends, so close that Anton doesn't ask any questions, he just does what he is asked to do. Why is this? I wonder what else Ruben has lined up for me. He truly is a mystery that I have to figure out.

Changing Tracks

I WOKE UP EARLY this morning with a new conviction that I must seduce Ruben like he's never been seduced before. That's what I'm wishing for, so I have to do it in a way that makes room for me in his life instead of just waiting and hoping that he can figure out what should happen between the two of us. I'll take the initiative and start creating the life I want to have with him.

In order to do this, I'll need to find out everything I can about him. I left Anton a message this morning to give me a ring. I found a phone number for the astrophysicist and two for the French philologist Ruben used to be with. I hope they will talk to me and share who Ruben really is. And finally, I wrote and sent an invitation to him.

Dear Ruben,

Put on a dinner jacket and meet me at Nordre Toldbod at the end of Esplanaden on the 23rd of June, at 4 p.m. Bring me a gift, which you haven't yet bought.

Love, Elizabeth

That's just two weeks from now, so I have to hurry up and figure out what exactly we'll be doing. If he doesn't want to come, that will probably be the end of our . . . acquaintance . . . relationship . . . encounter . . . future?

Anton just called and it turns out that Ruben isn't the dean of a university at all, but the director of a large IT company! The dean's name is R. Pontoppidan so people often mix them up, but the dean's first name is Rune, not Ruben! Things are becoming more and more strange. Why hadn't I figured this out before?

LATER

I JUST TALKED TO Frederic and he could hear that something was bugging me. I told him a bit about Ruben and now it turns out that he also knows him! Actually Frederic is the Frederic friend that Ruben told me about. And Ruben visited Frederic the evening before the workshop on Samsø Island!

After the workshop, Ruben called Frederic and asked him to get in contact with me. The same day my Uncle Theo had asked if Frederic wanted to meet my dad. Frederic took having several people tell him about me as a sign that he should meet me. That's what he told me, but I hadn't realized how small the world is.

So what I have now is three men, or rather I have what I wanted: Frederic for conversation, Anton for handiwork and Ruben for sex. Except for the fact that so far there is no sex with Ruben . . . and quite some heavy sexual flirting with Frederic!?

Ruben is more like my invisible third man. And now Frederic says that Ruben's last name isn't Pontoppidan! Or that this is only his middle name, to be precise. His real name is Ruben Pontoppidan la Cour! And he's not the director of an IT company. Tell me, does this man have multiple identities? And if so, why? Maybe the world he created doesn't even exist? And now I've invited him out on June 23rd! The biggest problem is that this all makes him even more mysterious and attractive to me.

This is exactly some of the mystery that I was longing for when I created this model. I wanted my three men to be different, so I am always pleasantly surprised when I am with each of them. But I cannot figure Ruben out, he surprises me too much . . . by not behaving like most men do—i.e. wanting to get me in the sack as quickly as possible. And how odd that he takes it upon himself to mobilize his friends to fill my two other positions. I cannot figure out if he is wonderful, caring and in complete control of things or if he is scary, egotistical and a control freak.

My mind is working overtime now, as I can imagine all sorts of things happening. I might be the queen of his universe—or the opposite, with me being the one in control of him and his actions. It is all really exciting! And a bit scary . . .

TUESDAY, JUNE 9TH

Uncle Theo Finds Peace

MY BELOVED UNCLE THEO passed away early this morning. I'm so glad I got to see him the other day. And that he didn't have to suffer long. I feel like calling him and having another of our wonderful conversations about the big things in life.

When I spent time with Theo, he was always present and could remember everything we had talked about last time we met. We often picked up right where we had left off when we saw each other, as if only a few moments had passed. With Theo, you lived in the now moment, with direct access to what was going on around you.

I often tried to talk to Theo about his energy because I wanted more of it in my life. He explained it as a kind of adjustable energetic flow that you could tap into any time, because it is always around us. Call it a carousel of action, people, emotions and interests that whirl around like a rocket in orbit. Every activity has its own orbit which is forever crossing other orbits and creating energy. Sometimes it's harmonious, but with everything traveling at its own speed, the harmony is sometimes compromised. It's like when two lights are blinking at different intervals. They blink at different speeds, become synchronized, blink in unison for a while and fall out of sync again.

Now Theo's light has been turned off, and I feel a strong responsibility to manage his estate. This was not something we discussed. We actually never really talked about him when we met. We discussed the French Revolution and how very revolutionary it was that liberty, equality and fraternity became fundamental values in that period of time. In Theo's opinion, we're still struggling to give everyone in the world liberty, equality and fraternity. I pointed out to him that fraternity might have been taken a little too literally, as it was only in 1909 that women were allowed to vote in local elections in Denmark, and it took many years after that for women to earn the right to vote in other countries, even in the US. Interestingly enough, it was also in the beginning of the 20th century that Freud found out women had a sexual desire of their own.

Theo and I could spend hours talking about what society might be like in 2029. This was the conversation Theo and I were always having, in fact, so we were always ready to continue where we had left off no matter how much time had passed.

Equality is a key word for the world of the future we were hoping for. And now it's up to me to carry out our plans. I believe that Ruben has what it takes to be a part of them. Maybe that's why I met him right before Uncle Theo's death. What is it Ruben says? Oh yes, he wrote me these things:

Respect yourself.

You can have everything you want, as long as you don't want everything. Open your inner circle for others who respect themselves.

Could these points, coupled with equality, be the keys to a better future for everyone?

Theo's funeral is on Friday. I find it so strange that we still don't know enough about cancer to prevent it or stop it from spreading. We can send a man to the moon and clone fruits, animals and vegetables, but cancer remains a mystery. I'm looking forward to the day when it gets solved!

LATER

FREDERIC JUST CALLED, AND this time he really wanted to talk. Turns out he's worried about his mother. She's lonely, but she's chosen to live outside of her little town so she can be closer to a married man with whom she's been having an affair for the past ten years. Frederic finds it hard to help her.

"My mother hasn't got time to find friends because she's always waiting for this married man to find time for her. And he rarely has time for her, because his wife is ill. It's such a pity for her. She really should get out more."

"My mother went through a similar phase after she and my father divorced. But last summer, she spent two weeks in Skagen and by the time she got home, she started painting again. On June 20th, she's having an opening at Gallery MJ."

"Wow, I wish my mother could take charge like that."

I've also taken charge today and scheduled two appointments in the coming days: one with the astrophysicist and another with the philologist.

WEDNESDAY, JUNE 10TH

The Wedding is Cancelled!

KAREN HAS CALLED OFF her wedding with Mr. Perfect! Four days before they were going to tie the knot she broke it off. What's going on? Rebecca called and told me the news. And Rebecca just split up with her boyfriend of three months. I called Karen, and she and Rebecca are coming over for coffee in an hour.

LATER

Rebecca and Karen showed up at the same time and before they had even sat down, Karen blurted out at me, "I don't think I could live like you do! I like knowing that he'll be there when I come home, cooking together, eating together, cleaning up while he washes the car, sitting in front of the TV and watching a good movie together."

"Great for you if that's what your life is like," I said. "But if you're completely honest with yourself, how often has it really been like that?" I looked her straight in the eye.

"Sometimes it is," she said, but it was clearly dawning on her that it was maybe more her dream than reality.

"Karen, I want to know why you're not getting married now," Rebecca interrupted.

The question alone made Karen start to cry. Rebecca and I got up and held her and each other while she sobbed. I brought her a box of tissues and made her a cosmopolitan, but as she sipped it, she started to cry again. Rebecca and I toasted anyway and then all three of us took a swig of that wonderful symbol of celebration and single life. How odd that all three of us are single again, even at our age.

It turns out that Mr. Perfect had cheated on Karen not once, but several times! We all thought everything was going so well between them. Karen kept telling herself that he'd straighten up. And he kept insisting that he'd straighten up. But the last time was with a good-looking single mom whose child attended the same day-care as theirs and Karen wouldn't stand for it anymore. It was one too many times, too close to their wedding day, so she called it off.

I didn't say this to Karen because I didn't think she was especially open to a new viewpoint right then, but if she could see him for who he is and just say to him and herself: 'Alright, you do your thing, I'd like to see you sometimes anyway.' Then she could look forward to seeing him regardless of what he does when she's not there. Twosomes are so proprietary: you're mine because you promised. As if life just stops when two people meet each other.

"I don't blame you for throwing him out," Rebecca comforted Karen. "I broke up with Carl last week, but that was just because I was bored."

"You get bored quickly, don't you?" I asked, taking another sip.

"Yes. Men don't seem to hold up for me in the long run," Rebecca said.

"Of course not," I said. "Look at how men learned to act. While modern women have gone through four levels of liberation, men are still following the footsteps of their father, grandfather and beyond. They learn to be men using the same old rules of ancient men."

"What four levels of liberation did women have?" Rebecca asked.

"The first level was bra-burning and women's lib. The second level was the yuppie era, when women started having careers. The third level was Sex and the City, with women earning money, being single and when having hot sex was ok. The fourth level is now, when women start living the lives we want to. Men have had to make adjustments to find their place in the different levels of women's freedom but many men haven't really seen it as the new reality or understood that they need to take a stand."

"And what about security?" Karen asked rhetorically. "That's what I've been missing since I discovered his first affair."

"Security is possible if both parties in a couple agree that they're creating a secure relationship and they're ready and willing to make compromises to protect that security. If those are the premises, the relationship can be fine. But often it is the women making men promise something that men apparently find it hard to keep. Maybe a lot of people aren't prepared to make the necessary compromises."

"You and your compromises!" said Rebecca. "Can't anyone ever get their way?"

"Sure, when you're single you can. But relationships always entail compromises."

"I don't believe that," said Rebecca.

"Listen closely the next time someone you know has a conflict in their relationship," I said. "A lot of the conflict is about unmet expectations . . . For instance, his ability to listen is unsatisfactory to her, or her interest in sex is absent. Something is always missing. How about if they look at the things that are there, the points they have in common and celebrate what they like about their relationship and each other, and let the rest go. Then I'm sure the world would be a much more peaceful and joyous place."

We all took a sip of our drinks. "How's your work going?" I asked Karen. She has an internet company selling children's clothes online.

"Business is fine," she said.

"Maybe it's time for you to find security in your success," I said.

She shrugged, as if she didn't get what I was implying—that her career was never really very important to her and how she needed to find her security in a man. Not so with Rebecca; she's a sales executive of an engineering firm and is quite competitive. When things are going well at work, she is ready to conquer the world, which to her also means men. And that's what she does, she devours them.

"What about you and men?" Rebecca asked almost as if she knew what I was thinking. She looked me up and down and emptied her glass.

"The one I want as my lover says that I must respect myself. We all must respect ourselves, of course."

"So why isn't he your lover now?" she challenged me to answer.

"Good question. Maybe he doesn't want me as much as I want him. Maybe he already has someone else. Maybe he doesn't like the idea that with my model, I'll always have two other men close to me."

"Which goes to show that your model doesn't work; it scares away men," Karen jumped back in.

"It does work at least most of the time. I'm forever getting offers of sex, and if that was the most important thing, I could just say yes, thank you and get a lot of sex. Meanwhile, I can call this guy Frederic any time of day and he and I can meet and talk about everything life has to offer. That's fantastic. And then there's Anton, who is also just a phone call away, and he will come and help me with handiwork."

"Well, what about the potential man to be your lover? What's his name?"

"Ruben and he seems to really want me. He even invited me to a special world he calls Severin's World. But he doesn't really do anything with me. Yet."

"That does sound a bit weird," said Rebecca.

"On top of that, he asked his two friends, Anton and Frederic, to sign up for my other positions and that's how I found them."

"Haha! He has got an ironic sense of humor!" exclaimed Rebecca.

"What do you mean?" I asked.

"In that way, he makes sure that you only sleep with him."

"Then why isn't he sleeping with me?" I asked.

"He may not be quite sure about you, so he is waiting to see if you pass the test," Karen said.

"It certainly feels like that," I said.

"And if he doesn't want you?"

"Then I'll have to find out why, cry and move on."

"If it's love you feel, though, you can't just move on," Karen said.

"Cowardice isn't love."

"What do you mean?"

"A lot of people don't dare leave their partner because they'd be faced with uncertainty. So they claim that 'love' keeps them in the relationship. I think they should be more honest and admit that cowardice or the need for security keeps them in their relationship. Maybe they're more afraid of losing the summer house than losing their partner."

"I would be more active towards that Ruben guy to figure out what he wants," said Rebecca.

"I'm doing exactly that," I answered and felt a sudden alertness arise in me, since I had no idea what I was going to meet.

Before going to bed I updated my board. It looks much simpler than it feels!

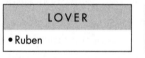

PHILOSOPHER	LOVER	HANDYMAN
• Frederic	• Ruben	• Anton

FRIDAY, JUNE 12TH

What a Surprise!

I WAS AT UNCLE Theo's funeral today, competition crying with Aunt Kate. The church was filled, there were flowers in all colors of the rainbow spread around the coffin and on the stone floor of the church. The priest, who had known Theo, delivered a stunning eulogy that made me cry even harder.

Afterwards we had a wake at the country house and it was wonderful to see that so many people wanted to pay their respects to Uncle Theo. When everyone had had coffee and cake, Aunt Kate tapped her cup to make a speech.

She thanked everyone for coming and said that Theo had asked her to make this speech, so she was respecting his wishes in doing so. She told us how important it was for Theo that the country house stayed in the family and he knew that Kate herself was not much of a handywoman, so he had left the place to me!!!

I was shocked and happy. Not because I can even begin to fathom how Mille and I will be capable of taking care of such a large place, but the fact that Theo wanted me to have it warmed my heart. And it was generous of Kate to allow him to give it to me. I suddenly understood the importance of our last conversation. And why Theo had asked about my plans to gather some people to make the world a better place. It was from my conversations with him that I ended up defining the years 1789, 1909 and 2029 as key years.

My father called me later and I could tell he was miffed that his brother had left me his home. He said that Theo's sons probably weren't very happy about it. I didn't have the energy to get into it, so I said goodbye quickly.

And now I must prepare for a lunch date tomorrow with General George.

SATURDAY, JUNE 13TH

Dating the General

SPENT FOUR HOURS AT the swimming pool with Mille today! Feels like I've still got chlorine in my whole system. She was brimming with pride because she improved her racing time by 17 seconds. Marianne was even prouder than she was. And neither of them let me feel left out—on the contrary, their enthusiasm helped me understand how fantastic it is that Mille is a natural. I was moved.

Then Sebastian showed up, just as positive and energetic as he had sounded on the telephone. We had a beer in the swim center cafeteria and he told anecdotes about his band that were truly funny and we had some good laughs. He asked about my work and listened when I told him about the exciting projects the entrepreneurs have been working on. At one point Mille looked at Sebastian and at me and back at Sebastian again and said, "Wow, what a flow between the two of you!" Given that we were sitting by an indoor swimming pool and water was flowing everywhere, we all exploded with laughter at Mille's unintended pun. Mille beamed and we warmly hugged goodbye. They went home to prepare for the next day of swimming while I went home, an overjoyed mother!

The general had invited me for lunch at Peter Liep's in Dyrehaven Park, about 15 minutes outside of Copenhagen. The restaurant has been there for centuries, originally to ensure that the coachmen driving the royal stage coaches could get something to eat and the horses could be fed before going back to the center of Copenhagen. The restaurant is located at a beautiful spot where two roads cross and is bathed in sunlight beaming through rows of trees.

We got a table outside and had a big lunch with the works, complete with beer and schnapps.

"So, your model is interesting," he said, looking at me as he pierced his grilled filet of fish with his fork.

"What is the most appealing part of it to you?" I asked. I was curious to hear his answer.

"My wife has more of me than she can handle. If we could modify the model, turn it around, she could maybe share me with other women."

"In what way are you too much for her?"

"From the outside, it might seem strange. It hasn't always been like this, but the older I get the more present it is," he said. He took a last big bite of the fish filet and I raised my beer glass to say cheers, but he insisted that we start with the small glasses of schnapps. So we emptied those and he waved to the waiter to come and refill them. We toasted again, and I could feel the aquavit alcohol flavored by dill and coriander warming my whole body as it went down.

I noticed the general was having a hard time sitting still. He twisted and turned in his chair. What's with him? Is he a drinker? Does he cheat on his wife? What is bothering him? I guess it's either something very normal that seems unusual because he's an army general, or it's something very unusual that seems especially unusual because he's an army general.

"What were you like when you were little?" I asked to open him up a bit.

"My father was very strict. Everything was subject to rules and regulations and the only place I could relax was in a little house I built on the island of Bornholm. When I was 16, I went there whenever I could."

"But what were you like?"

"I read a lot and wondered constantly about the direction of my life. I didn't understand why there were so many rigid rules. But my father insisted. So I studied politics and got a gold medal for my dissertation on the rights of nations in relation to the creation of the European Community in 1958. I met my wife Else at a party while I was studying. She was a law student and she came from a good family. We got married, and as you know she's a partner at the Junior Counsel to the Treasury today. We had a great marriage for years. We had our children, Carl Christian and Marie Louise. And with the exception of the fact that Else has always hated my sister Nina, who changed her named to Andrea and is a bohemian with chaos in everything from her love life to her finances, everything has been fine."

"Well, then everything is alright."

"No," he said. He lowered his head and a sudden sadness crossed his smile.

"No?" I asked "How so?"

He hesitated a second, then looked right at me. "Three months ago, my wife came home from work two hours early. I had worked at home all day because we had some workmen coming in the morning to fix our bathroom. They spent an hour there, fixed it and left again. So I was alone in the house after that. I didn't hear her come in. But suddenly, there she was."

"Aha, and so?" I said, unsure where he was going with his story. He had indisputably piqued my interest. He lifted his schnapps glass and gulped down its contents without toasting, so it was clear he really needed it.

"It didn't go well," he said softly.

"Why not?"

"I don't even know why I'm telling you this . . . "

"Because you trust me. Go ahead."

"You seem like someone who can handle things that are, shall we say, a little out of the ordinary."

"The sooner one accepts his or her emotions, the more natural a role they can play in one's life. And sooner or later they're bound to come to the surface anyway."

"Well, my wife glared at me because I think she got a bit of a shock at what she saw."

"And what did she see?"

"I had put on a pink cocktail dress and draped a feather boa around my neck, a shiny brunette wig with curls on my head, and I was about to step into stilettos."

"Wow," I said, "that sounds beautiful."

"I thought it was."

"But she didn't think so."

"And I understand her. She had no idea I'm into that kind of thing."

"Because you didn't tell her."

"I kept thinking my desire for it would go away. But the more I thought about it and the more beautiful dresses I bought, the more alive it became. And I never really felt like it was the right time to tell her."

"That's a shame for her, isn't it?"

"It's been really hard on her. Couldn't you tell when you came over for dinner?"

"I don't know you, so I figured she was always that cold and harsh towards you."

"My yearning for this alternate life goes against all that she believes in."

"Isn't it the same for you? An army general wearing women's clothes isn't something you hear about every day."

"I don't think it's such a big deal. I mean, it's only clothing that I want to wear sometimes."

"But clearly it's important to you."

"She doesn't understand that. She's begged me to forget it."

"But you can't?"

"Quite the contrary. It makes me feel free."

"I know what you mean. I was surprised at the feeling of freedom my model gave me. One man is a limitation, like the strict role of being an army general is for you. The three-men model expands my options as an individual. My encounters, challenges and the attention I receive are all different. Women's clothing gives you a strong counterbalance to all the discipline in the army and from when you were a boy. You might say that because your position as an army general is so sharply defined and you always need to stay within the lines, you feel the need to compensate somehow. And a silk hanky in your suit pocket doesn't do the trick; you need the whole feminine ensemble."

"I knew you'd understand! Have you ever been with a man in women's clothing?"

"No, but I have a feeling that can soon change," I said with a smile.

"Not a lot of people understand this kind of thing."

"How do you know? Have you talked to others?"

"Not many. It's still pretty taboo. But you understand it. Just imagine how fun it could be to play around with the roles, I mean sexually?"

"I'll consider it," I answered, smiled and emptied my glass.

SUNDAY, JUNE 14TH

Should I Choose Oscar?

GOT AN EMAIL FROM Ruben today. He thanked me for the invitation and he accepted from 4 to 6 p.m. because from 6 p.m. and onwards that day he said he already had his own plans for us. I guess that is okay, as it leaves me enough time to do my surprise thing with him.

Then Oscar, Rebecca's brother suddenly showed up. He was supposed to go to Karen's wedding at the manor house, but since it was cancelled, he had some spare time. I took him and Mille out to my new country estate. He's an attractive, dark-haired man with a muscular build and a calm presence. Right now, Oscar is trying to start up a yoga center here in Copenhagen after living in Jutland for a number of years. He had considered opening one on the island of Bornholm where I bumped into him on the beach but reconsidered when he discovered that there were already two centers there and no need for more.

After he left I started thinking. Should I invite him to open a yoga center at my new country estate? I'll have so much space there. He's handy and attractive—another man who can do two things. But things would become a little too close for comfort with Rebecca. And then there's the risk of him attaching more to the invitation than I do. I should probably just let it be.

LATER

Coffee with the Philologist

DAPHNE DUFOUR JUST left. A French philologist and marathon runner, an attractive woman. We talked a lot about France, which we both love, but after about 20 minutes I steered the conversation to Ruben. She softened up and said that he's fantastic in bed! And that she's never experienced anything quite like it—he knows the female anatomy like his own, and the effect that words and compliments can have on women. She added that he never made any special demands and was always willing to try the things she wanted to do. Once in a while, he left for three or four days and he never said where he was going, but since he always came back full of energy and eager to seduce her, she accepted it.

MUCH LATER

Coffee with the Astrophysicist

I MUST SAY THAT Ruben has made quite an impression on the women he has met. The astrophysicist was also full of positive words and almost bragged about their wonderful sex life.

But neither of the two women could really tell me much about him as a person. He appears to me mostly like a chameleon that changes color based on the people around him.

David keeps contacting me by email and texting me, so I've now informed him that I no longer want to remain in touch. I wished him good luck in finding a proper girlfriend. He wrote that he preferred to continue having me as a mistress. I responded that I didn't.

MONDAY, JUNE 15TH

My Mother

MY MOTHER CAME OVER to my place last night. She's ecstatic about her opening at the gallery on Saturday. I had promised to help her with the preparations. I adore my mother today. She's sensitive and aware of colors and forms and light no matter where she is.

It hasn't always been like that—when I was a child and we were out driving, she always commented on the view; sometimes she would frantically grab my father's arm while he was driving to get him to stop the car if the sun was shining in a certain way through the clouds or through the leaves of the trees in a particular pattern. He would get furious because she startled him with her 'Stop, stop, stop the car' calls as if she were having a heart attack. It made no difference, the next time it happened she did the same thing.

And she could lose herself completely in a color on the canvas on her easel. When I was a child, I didn't like this. If I wanted to get her attention, I had to call her name several times, and even when I had succeeded it was almost as if I wasn't there. Later I understood that she was struggling with life and sometimes life was too overwhelming, so she had to look deep into a bottle. She also spent a lot of time in bed on her own, which wasn't good for her.

I think she's a fantastic painter. But while she was married to my father, she refused to show her work in public. As she always said, "I'm my own worst critic, I don't need anyone else."

My mother, that fragile creature with no earthly contact, is full of excuses. If she ever believed in herself, it cannot have lasted long. At irregular intervals she turned into a kamikaze pilot who didn't know up from down in her own chaotic universe. I never quite felt at ease with my mother as a child. Many years later, I realized that she probably would have been diagnosed as bipolar since she alternated between being creative and painting in an exalted way, to sinking into apathy and whiskey. For many years I tried unsuccessfully to help her battle out of apathy and back into her creativity, but the whiskey won the war. I tried to cover up the emotional fluctuations that she couldn't control and which made my father furious. I shed many tears before giving up on saving either of them.

When I got older, I started being able to see her wounds, and that made it easier for me to forgive her for those she unwittingly had inflicted on me by making the wrong choices, being too egocentric or just not having the resources . . .

But I love my mother, who should have been a fortress for me, a place where the chaos of the world is blocked out—even if she was everything but. I feel like I've learned to steer clear of the pitfalls her life laid out for me and create my own life instead. In school, mathematics and many other 'difficult' subjects were easy for me, and it was a breeze to get my masters in Economics in four years and get a job right away and then be promoted over and over again. And Mille is happy, even if it's hard to be her age, with all of the raging hormones and increasing demands. So most things in my life are going well. I just hope this new model will help my love life run more smoothly.

Before leaving, my mother said I was welcome to invite everyone to her show at the gallery. So I called Frederic and asked for his mother's address. There's no reason for her to sit alone in Vordingborg when she can come to an art opening.

Frederic was thrilled and just called back to say that his mother would love to come. He also asked when the two of us could meet again; I said soon. I just don't have time and I don't really know how close a relationship I want with him before I'm clearer about Ruben. I also don't really have the time to see him, since I have so much to do at work and with Mille when she's with me. And now I've got to help my mother, and plan a surprise picnic I want to do with the General tomorrow, and I need to make preparations for my afternoon with Ruben coming up. I've gotten a really good idea of what to do, I think.

TUESDAY, JUNE 16ᵀᴴ

A Picnic with the Army General

THE ARMY GENERAL IS a distinguished, well-read, experienced, good-looking man with dark hair and a body that just belongs in a uniform. I had told him we were going on a picnic and to meet me at the big parking space by the sea at Tisvildeleje. The spot we are going is near the sea, about an hour from Copenhagen. The village is swarmed with Copenhagen jet-setters in July, but if you walk ahead for just 15 minutes, you can have the entire beach to yourself.

"Where are we going?" he asked when I started walking. "You seem to have a destination in mind."

I smiled at him, a picnic basket and a blanket under my arm. On our left side was the ocean, the waves rolling violently, and on our right side were high dunes and beach grass. Fortunately, the air was mild and there was just a light breeze. He didn't know where we were going. When we had made our date I had mentioned that we'd be visiting one of the 'darker' areas of life, the Shadow world as experienced reality. I told him about some of my darker sides; it was a long conversation. In the end, he recited Goethe's *Ginko Biloba* for me:

> *This leaf from a tree in the East,*
> *Has been given to my garden.*
> *It reveals a certain secret,*
> *Which pleases me and thoughtful people.*
> *Does it represent One living creature*
> *Which has divided itself?*
> *Or are these Two, which have decided,*
> *That they should be as One?*
> *To reply to such a question,*
> *I found the right answer:*
> *Do you notice in my songs and verses*
> *That I am One and Two?*

With that poem, he offered me some pieces to his puzzle, which I used to fill a picnic basket with decadent and challenging remedies for him. Time will tell if they're the right ones, I thought.

"I don't have much of a choice, do I?" he asked, looking at me sideways while we walked.

"Nope," I said and smiled.

He squeezed my arm. He seemed slightly nervous and looked at me expectantly. I squeezed back. We left the frothing waves behind and proceeded into the dunes.

I asked him to find a quiet place where we'd be protected from the wind, and we spread out the blanket and sat down. He took my hand and pressed his lightly in mine as I took out a bottle of wine, which I asked him to open. He poured the Chablis Premier Cru in our glasses. We raised them and toasted. I looked at him and said, "I could use a really good girlfriend."

"I'm the one!" he blurted out ecstatically.

"I was hoping you'd say that," I said with a smile.

"What is my name?"

"How about Christina?"

"Christina . . . "

"Or would you rather have a different name?"

"Christina is good."

"Fine, Christina. Listen, I brought some clothes for you."

"Truly?" His eyes lit up.

"Yes. You said you really liked my black silk skirt, so I brought it along. Do you want to try it on?"

"Yes!"

"I brought you a top, too. It's low-cut and it clips up in the back like a corset."

"Oh, I love that model," he said, grabbing for it.

In no time he had torn off his shirt, thrown the low cut top around his body and begun doing up the hooks. He joined the hooks with an experienced hand, breathing in a shallow and concentrated way. He veritably glowed with excitement, and his excitement was contagious. We were in deep water, he and I. Or Christina and I.

When he was finished dressing, we stood up and he spun around to show me how good he looked. He begged my pardon for not having high heels. I told him that it was no problem given the sand and all. We packed up and started back toward the town where we had started our journey. I was curious to see how long he would continue walking in the clothes. We met other people and he just continued. When we arrived at our cars, he asked if he could borrow everything. I agreed and we embraced one another warmly. He held me at arm's length—or rather, she held me at arm's length and said, "Thank you. Thank you with all of my heart."

"You're welcome," I replied, and loosened myself from his arms.

On the way home I realized that his joyful reaction to the women's clothing I brought had relaxed me and made me feel uninhibited, too. We have so many possibilities if we just follow our natural curiosity and respect that of others.

In some ways, the General is a highly cultivated man whom I can talk to. And his thing for women's clothing adds an extra dimension. Imagine a shopping trip to New York with your girlfriend/boyfriend. I wonder what he's like in bed? And how would it actually feel to have sex with a man dressed up as a woman?

Learning More about Ruben

I INVITED FREDERIC FOR lunch today to try to get more info about Ruben. But I didn't get much out of him. He wasn't interested in talking about Ruben; he wanted to talk about himself. But he did say that Ruben tends to wear women out with all his energy and that he's impatient with people who have less energy than he does. He also said that Ruben is curious by nature and that he bores of women quickly. When that happens, it's just a matter of time until he leaves them.

I'm sure that will not happen with me, since I'm normally the first bird to fly off.

THURSDAY, JUNE 18TH

An Invitation to Go to NYC

THIS EVENING I TRIED on dresses for my date with Ruben in five days. I'm sure he will be really surprised when he sees me. And he should be. Will I scare him off? If I do that's fine and then I'll know we have no future. It will be interesting to see how the afternoon and evening goes. And has he planned a midsummer's night party with a lot of people for the rest of the evening? Or will it just be him and me watching the traditional bonfires that we Danes light on June 23rd to celebrate the longest day of the year?

The General called earlier and invited me to NYC in August. I told him that it sounds like a great trip for us, but I can't decide yet. I need to do some soul-searching to figure out if that cross-dressing male thing really turns me on, or if I just think it's fun because it's new and different. At any rate, if he wants me to go with him to NYC he'll have to book the ticket when I'm ready to make a decision.

There is also Frederic, but I feel like there's so much open to question with Ruben right now and I want to clear things up before I start getting close to another man. But it feels great to be me setting my own pace with men!

Gone with the Thorn

I WENT TO THE 10-year celebration party for one of our entrepreneur partners tonight. It took place at the concert hall Vega in Copenhagen. The 1950s architecture of the hall is a fascinating combination of the simplicity of art deco and the serenity of the workers' movement that struggled hard to ensure proper working conditions back then.

The workers' union hired the famous architect Vilhelm Lauritzen to design the place and he did so meticulously. It has an astutely simple exterior design and a unique interior design filled with special details such as beautiful wooden panels on the walls, fine door handles and an impressive system of staircases that fits the design of the floors. The architecture itself offers a most rewarding experience to see before you even hear the music you came for. The workers' movement called it the People's House, and for two decades, people could rent it for parties, conferences, and concerts. Then many people got their own homes to host their parties, and so Vega was transformed into a concert hall for all sorts of bands and events. I enjoy going there since the building itself adds an extra condiment to the experience. The house is listed as a national monument, so no one can touch it, which I think is great.

I was in a really good mood, too, because I had just found out that Horn the thorn, that annoying bugger colleague of mine, is stepping down from the Board of Directors after two years of making my life miserable! I hummed to myself and celebrated with such amusement that my colleagues and partners asked if I was in love or had gotten promoted or something. I just smiled.

I talked to my mother a few times and made plans for her opening. It turns out her gallery is taking care of almost everything, so I'll mostly be there for moral support.

The Art Opening

WHAT A PLEASURE MY mother's art opening was today! She looked spectacular in her grey silk outfit, her hair coiffed elegantly and with beautiful make up. MJ, who owns the gallery, fussed over her before, during and after the doors opened. He's at least twenty years younger than her and straight, so my mother basked in his attention.

There were more than 150 guests, so her excitement was boundless. Mille arrived with Sebastian and Marianne. And my father and his new girlfriend Katherine joined, which didn't seem to bother my mother at all. Frederic's mom noticed that my mother needed a hand in dealing with all of the flowers and wine people brought, so she helped out. She had come by car, and when it was over, she offered to take my mother and all of her gifts home. I think they could become good friends, being both 'women of a certain age.' And best of all, mom's paintings are first-class and she had already sold five by the end of the opening.

TUESDAY, JUNE 23ʳᵈ

My Big Night is Approaching

I SLEPT LATE, ATE a leisurely breakfast and did a bit of this and that. While I was in the bath it was clear to me that I'm looking forward to tonight. Midsummer's Eve is one of my favorite evenings, full of bonfires and celebrations. This is a major holiday in Denmark and throughout Scandinavia. We celebrate it as the longest day of the year, when the sun has reached its furthest climb into the Northern hemisphere. In Denmark, we have nearly 20 hours of full sunlight a day this time of the year, and even the darkness is only twilight dark. In northern Sweden and Norway, daylight can last the full 24 hours as the sun never appears to set.

This day used to be the time when pagan traditions ruled. Nature was believed to be full of mystical forces, both good and bad. Herbs and natural water sources were thought to be holy, and it was a tradition to seek them on this evening.

Some of these pagan ideas are kept alive today through many joyous activities. Most of Scandinavia celebrates it with large picnics outside, enormous bonfires on the beaches on top of which puppet-like witches are burned in effigy to shoo off bad energies, bad luck and any sort of negative presence. People host big dinner parties and sing ballads to the sun gods, their voices assisted with lots of beer and aquavit. It is a bit unclear where these traditions come from, but we repeat them every year with delight.

At 11 a.m. someone rang the doorbell—a courier with a huge bouquet of red roses! And a card that read:

Dear Elizabeth,

I'm looking forward to sharing this evening with you.

At 3:30 p.m. a limousine will come to pick you up to take you to our meeting place.

Love, Ruben

Wow. That was unexpected. I knew he had style, but the gesture surprised me anyway. I need to get changed and be ready when the limo arrives. We were going to meet at Nordre Toldbod. I picked that place because it is beautiful, airy, and there is an ornate building of rococo architecture with a green copper roof by the seafront. The structure is from around 1860 and sits there overlooking the harbor. It used to be the customs clearance house. In front of the building is also two romantic pavilions in white painted wood and copper roofs. They used to be the place for receiving prominent guests who arrived by boat to Copenhagen. Today the Queen sails out from between the two white pavilions in a small boat that transports her to her yacht called 'Dannebrog,' which is the name of our Danish flag. When the dingy leaves Nordre Toldbod, the flag is raised on the ship to signal the Queen is now leaving shore. Dannebrog then sails the Queen around Denmark, or to our province Greenland or to the Faroe Islands that used to be Danish. They both still have two seats in our national assembly.

I chose that place to meet Ruben because I want to feel like a queen today!

WEDNESDAY, JUNE 24TH

An Exceptional Midsummer's Eve!

IT IS NOW THE day after and I am still reeling. My evening started in the limousine that arrived at my door at 3.30 as promised. In addition to the driver, another man was already inside when I got in. He introduced himself as 'This evening's butler, Madame,' and immediately offered me a glass of chilled champagne. He put on some classical music and invited me to sit back and relax. I thoroughly enjoyed driving through Copenhagen, on my way to a fairy tale to which I hoped I knew the ending, but whose beginning was already surprising me.

A half hour's drive and a couple of glasses of champagne later, the car pulled up to Esplanaden, one of the most expensive addresses in Copenhagen and the street that leads to Nordre Toldbod. The entrance is flanked by arches in light limestone on both sides and a wall painted a deep Nordic yellow. The car rode between the columns, stopping in front of the old building at Nordre Toldbod. The sun shone from a clear blue sky and a gentle breeze blew in from the sea and twirled around the two white pavilions.

I got out and placed myself between the pavilions with my back facing the water. Yes, I was wearing a white wedding dress with its little train, a veil covering my bare shoulders, and with a small red suitcase standing next to me. I looked up and saw Ruben walking towards me. He looked like a man of the world, wearing a sharp black tuxedo and I held my breath, waiting for him to catch sight of me.

He must not have recognized me at first, as his eyes searched the area along the Toldkammer building and down to the harbor. Then he spotted me, though at first he seemed merely to be enjoying the sight of an unknown bride-to-be. As he came closer, I smiled.

"Elizabeth? Is that you?"

"Welcome," I said, extending my hand. He took it and kissed it without skipping a beat.

"Come on, we're going sailing," I said, holding his hand in mine.

In front of Nordre Toldbod, I had arranged for us to meet a handsome mahogany sloop with wooden sideboards and a gorgeous deck made of ash wood. The captain stood at attention at the stern, and after we got on, a sailor began to set off at the prow. Inside, the salon was furnished with silk-cushioned rosewood benches. On a matching rosewood table were canapés and a bottle of champagne. I asked Ruben to open the bottle and by the look in his eyes, I could tell that my boat ride had pleasantly surprised him. He poured champagne in our glasses and we toasted.

I kicked off one of my shoes and pulled my foot up under my dress which I spread across the rosewood bench. With a smile I pulled the dress up so that I could gently stroke my bare foot. He looked at me. And at my hand on my foot. Then at my face again. He lifted his glass. I lifted mine. I put my glass down and let the veil and my hair fall delicately over my bare shoulders. He stood up, but I gestured to him with my hand to stay seated. I could see it frustrated him. I smiled.

"To what do we owe the honor of your fine attire?" he asked and remained standing.

I had a feeling that he had intentionally avoided the words 'wedding dress.' Was he worried?

"Welcome to our symbolic wedding," I replied.

"When did I say that I would marry you?"

"Don't you know?" I teased, fingering the ankh around my neck.

"Well, everyone wears an ankh in Severin's World. We put them on when we're searching and take them off when we've found what we're looking for, and then put them back on again when we're searching again."

"And where is your ankh?"

"Right there," he said, pointing to the ankh around my neck.

"Exactly. You took it off that night at the estate and gave it to me. You found what you were looking for," I laughed.

He looked at me, perhaps not quite understanding my implication. Clearly, we had just broached a deeper dimension of our potential relationship. He filled our glasses again and leaned over me to stroke my cheek as he handed me my champagne.

I looked up at the captain, who noticed nothing and continued to steer a steady course toward the Middelgrund fort on the island in the middle of the sea between Denmark and Sweden. The fort is more than a hundred years old and was built on nearly 25 feet of water, right where Kongedybet meets Hollænderdybet. Nowadays it's a big tourist attraction with its own restaurant.

"And why should we get married now?" he asked.

"It's important that the clothes, the traditions and everything else is right."

"Okay and why is that?"

"To exorcise the romantic dream from our relationship."

"Why is that so important?"

"The dress and the ceremony are both symbols of two souls joining. And the dream is strong in me. Every time you say or do something, I can't help but trying to interpret it in terms of that dream—and then the dream grows stronger until it overshadows reality. By doing this symbolic wedding, I'm hoping that we can fool my dream. Because then we will be free to focus on our reality."

"So the present I brought is my wedding gift to you?"

"Exactly."

The sloop slid gracefully across the waves and I was enjoying just sitting and talking to Ruben. The two of us seem to be able to talk about many of the topics I've read, learned and experienced in my life, and he easily sees, understands and expands on them. One of the things we both love talking about is photography. For years, I've been fascinated by the technical and artistic aspects of photography, so I've read quite a few books on the subject. Among others, I read a great book about how photography came to be. It all started in the 1830's with the invention of daguerreotypes, images produced by a process in which silvered plates were used as film. The plates were sensitized and then exposed to light in a camera, creating a latent image in the silver-halide coating. The images were developed using mercury vapor, creating a fine-grained layer of silver amalgam. The process actually resulted in a negative, but from a certain angle it looks like the mirror-image of a positive. Ruben knew all about this process and how the development of this technology had affected art, slowly making photography a feasible alternative to portrait painting.

In particular, I told Ruben about the American photographer Alfred Stieglitz, who spent hours outside in the bitter cold NYC winter to get a picture of the famous triangle-cornered Flatiron Building in the snow. This was made possible by a new type of film invented by Kodak, with which light could be captured even in difficult conditions. Another Stieglitz masterpiece was his 1907 image *The Steerage,* showing a crowd of people departing NYC on a steamer boat. The scene shows an upper deck and a lower deck, both crowded with people, and a gangway leading from upwards. A highlight of the photograph was a sailor's suspenders crisscrossing on his back used to hold up his pants. They were white, even though he was standing under the upper deck of the ship. Up till that point, it would have been impossible to see these on a photo given the inability of film to capture details like that. I could tell that Ruben loved talking about photography as much as I did, and he knew Stieglitz's work like the back of his hand, so he had a lot to contribute to our talk.

Our boat soon docked at the fort, and we disembarked into underground stone tunnels that were part of the fort, now the restaurant. Along the tunnels were a series of side caverns, like the little chapels along the nave of a cathedral. I had reserved one of them; inside it was a table covered with a white tablecloth and two large silver candelabras, each with seven candles. These were the only source of light in the pitch dark cavern, but they provided us with the ideal ambience. We sat down in our private 'chapel' and more champagne was served. Ruben raised his glass and toasted me. When I put my glass down, he handed me an envelope, his gift. Inside was a thick, crème-colored card with a message written in calligraphy:

Gift Certificate

One entrepreneurial project

By Ruben Pontoppidan

*This gift certificate is good for the realization of
a large project in your home or garden.*

The project may be completed with the assistance of man no. 3.

I read it twice and blinked away the tears in my eyes.

"How did you know that it is exactly what I need?" I asked him.

"Didn't you just inherit a place in the countryside?"

I smiled and thanked him and raised my glass.

Although our conversation flowed freely, and despite our laughter, I could tell that Ruben was a little tense. When we poured a second glass of champagne, he admitted that he was expecting an actual priest or a mayor to show up so that we could get married! I assured him that there was no need to take my dream that far. After that he was more relaxed.

We talked more about this island that had just been sold to the international scouts' movement. Then the crisp ring of a bell told us that the boat was ready to set sail again back to the mainland.

We entered and sailed back to Nordre Toldbod where the limousine was waiting. Ruben and I got in, and I appreciated that the butler now served cold sparkling water with lemon.

After about a half hour we arrived at a large estate at the end of a long stone driveway. Before I knew it, the butler had opened my car door and was helping me out. Ruben escorted me to the front door of the estate.

On each side of the large, green-painted wooden door was a tall white column. The green door opened and a servant stepped aside and bowed to Ruben. He went in first and I followed.

The estate was as grand on the inside as on the outside. We entered a beautiful, long hallway with Bordeaux-red walls with gilded crown molding, a black-and-white checkered floor and a wide, winding, white stone staircase in the distance. The place had such a grandness to it that my stomach jumped. The servant took our coats and it made me regret that I wasn't wearing the fur coat I don't even own!

He led us to the stairs and just then the doorbell rang again. We turned back towards the door, and in came Frederic and Anton! Ruben looked at them, then back at me with a smile. I grinned from ear to ear, amazed at his cleverness to have arranged a dinner party for all four of us.

"Welcome to our evening," I said to the two men.

"Thank you," they answered in unison and laughed.

"I apologize for not bringing a gift but I didn't realize it was your wedding," Frederic said looking a bit upset with Ruben.

"Neither did I," Ruben said and smiled at me.

Frederic looked slightly surprised at Ruben.

"This place is beautiful. Whose is it?" I asked.

"Frederic inherited in from his grandfather. They are noble. But tonight it's ours. Come on, drinks await us," Ruben said.

He extended his elbow toward me and together we entered the banquet hall with Frederic and Anton in tow.

In the banquet hall were four large pillars ornamented with gold. The walls were painted a luscious green and adorned with gilded edges at the ceiling. In the middle of the room was a carved cherry table, maybe 15 feet long, elegantly set for just four despite its grandeur. At the far end of the hall, a string quintet was playing Mozart's Divertimentos, which is one of my favorites!

Frederic and Anton came over to greet me properly.

"Bonsoir ma chérie," said Frederic, kissing me on both cheeks in true French style.

"Buona sera, signorina," said Anton, giving me an Italian-style hand kiss. The butler appeared with a tray with white wine and canapés.

"So please tell me exactly how you all know each other, since I now have all three of you together," I prompted them.

"We've known each other for 25 years," said Ruben and lifted his glass. We all toasted to their friendship.

I looked at the three men and felt powerful. I had arranged a symbolic wedding with Ruben and having the other two men there made Ruben seem slightly less important to me. I still found him very attractive, but now it seemed less important if he wanted me or not. There was no sign that he had lost interest, but it made me feel great to be less dependent on him and his decisions.

"I would like to show you the estate's paintings before we sit down," Frederic said.

We followed him into another wing of the estate. It looked almost like a museum, with the walls covered with dozens of famous Danish paintings. Apparently Frederic knew all about them, as he started to give us an informed talk about some of the masterpieces of the Danish Golden Age: Hammershøj's *Sunlight*; a charming self-portrait of Wilhelm Marstand at five years of age; two Christian Købke tableaus from Frederikstaden and one Eckersberg tableau called *Møns Klint ¾ of a Mile from the Coast and a Sailing Corvette*. Frederic pointed out unique details in each of the paintings—in Hammerhøj's painting it was the sunlight that fell through the windows, bright yet so delicate that you could almost feel the dust tickling your eyes. Or the skin of the five year-old Marstrand that made you feel he was there in the room with us. I was struck by the poetic nature of one of Eckersberg's landscapes and the precision in Købke's representation of Frederikstaden and its residents.

Waltzing through the museum room, I felt inspired and it lifted my spirits even higher. In a magical way, it felt like I was being courted and attended to by three 'knights' of the Arthurian Round Table. The men made certain I was well positioned to see the paintings when we moved around. Ruben was especially attentive to me and held me lightly around the waist, guiding me across the parquet floor. He gave me all the attention any woman could wish for.

After half an hour of art gazing, Frederic announced, "Shall we sit down?"

We returned to the dining room and stood at our chairs. There were place cards on the table. I was seated next to Ruben on the side of the table closest to the fireplace, in which a warm and crackling fire burned. Frederic sat across from me and Anton sat across from Ruben.

The butler appeared and, reading from a parchment sheet, announced the evening's menu: creamed potato-leek soup, smoked wild salmon, turbot carpaccio with red onions and Russian beluga caviar, braised venison with morel compote and new baby potatoes with a balsamic stock, followed by a cheese plate, and a dessert of beetroot ice cream with slices of Tahitian mango, plus white and dark chocolate mousse with a passion fruit coulis.

Riesling was to be served with the soup, followed by a Piesporter Michelsberg to accompany the salmon. Then Chateau Batailley, a divine Pauillac Grand Cru would accompany the main course and the cheese, and a Muscat de Beaumes-de-Venise with dessert.

As the string quintet played at the far end of the hall, we ate and started talking and debating what was happening in Denmark. The conversation felt like a tennis match at Wimbledon with our back and forth, or a ballet at the Bolshoi Theatre with the dance of ideas punctuated by leaps of brilliance.

Frederic commented, "Let me make an analogy about Denmark today. Venice was at its pinnacle for centuries, but then they stopped taking care of the weaker members of society, and it all went downhill from there." He raised the first mouthful of potato-leek soup to his lips.

"Why was that?" Anton queried him, and suddenly I felt Frederic's foot caressing mine under the table. I peeked discretely under the tablecloth to make certain that it was his foot reaching across the floor, and not some stray dog. It seemed like anything was possible here so I could take nothing for granted. It was indeed his foot, running up and down my leg. I had a few mouthfuls of soup and took a sip of wine. What a dinner!

Frederic responded, "Because when society doesn't take care of its weaker members, things become unsettled, which in turn scares off businesses. Money is conservative—that's why it's invested where profit is most probable and loss is less risky."

"I think as a society, we owe it to people to take care of people, when they fall ill or are very unfortunate," I said.

"If you help people in the beginning and give them the right tools, they can get back in gear. If you don't offer them help, many people risk staying behind," Anton agreed.

"I'm all for helping people as long as they don't feel they have the right to stop trying to help themselves," Ruben said.

After a few more volleys between political views, Ruben interjected. "I'd like to ask the bigger question," he said, looking at Frederic. "Should society allow the existence of an elite?"

"Can the masses be the elite?" Frederic replied in question.

"The elite is made up of a small fraction of the population who are endowed with a greater intellect, if you need a definition," Ruben reminded him. "They govern and make policy for the rest of the population."

"I don't think your definition is valid anymore. The internet is giving voice to the crowd and democratizing democracy. Soon we will all be expressing our opinions online about every issue and everyone will be able to vote on every decision, allowing a true majority opinion to decide how society functions."

"Isn't the crowdsourcing movement the antithesis of elite? It enables many ordinary people to join forces and produce more efficiently. But doesn't that make education so much more important?" I asked.

"The ideal society operates on the precondition that each and every one of us can make a contribution to create results. That's why we should all have a share in the values that we create," Frederic agreed, while Ruben stroked my thigh. An electric shock ran through my body and at the same time I held my inner peace.

Just then, the waiters cleared away the soup bowls and began serving the salmon.

"Can we ever reach this ideal society, though?" I asked.

"For me, an 'elite' has a strong disinterest in creating value for society as a whole. That kind of elite demands scorn. I think what you're talking about is more an intelligentsia than an elite: people with means at their disposal who choose to do things beyond their own interests," Frederic said.

"How about creating a kind of co-operative movement for societal innovation? People interested in stimulating change in a certain area can team up and make it happen," I suggested.

Ruben took my hand and caressed my fingers and said, "Interesting thought." And it looked like he meant it.

"I think defining how to live a non-materialistic life of happiness for oneself is the first step," Anton said. "It starts with yourself."

I felt Frederic's foot rubbing against mine. I had taken off my shoes and felt that I was relaxing more and just enjoying being a cherished guest.

"What is a life of happiness?" Frederic asked.

"For me, it's sitting with my best friends and a beautiful woman, eating and drinking and talking about the good life," Ruben answered and smiled. "Can we all accept that definition?" he asked.

We all nodded.

"Good, then we don't need to talk about it anymore," said Ruben and smiled. He raised his glass and clinked it against Anton's.

Anton drank a toast with him, but it was obvious that the conversation wasn't exhausted for him yet. As soon as he had set down his glass he said, "Well, there are other aspects of the good life, too."

"Aha, which would those be?" Ruben inquired.

"A good job, for example."

"Are you sure? Would you work if you didn't have to? If your grandfather had left you 100 million euro when he died, would you still go to work?"

"Yes, but I would work differently than I do now."

"Please elaborate."

"I would use the money to make a difference," Anton replied.

"Or buy a castle and a yacht and enjoy your life by eating and drinking with your best friends and a beautiful woman on an estate somewhere," said Frederic, pointing to the banquet hall surrounding us.

"That too, but it's not enough. I want to make my mark on the world."

I slowly noticed that it was as if Ruben were invisibly conducting the evening. He imperceptibly nodded assent to each topic before we began discussing it. He kept the conversation moving, and he did so elegantly. There was no doubt that he was in his element. We talked freely and easily for hours, interrupted only by the arrival of each course or a new wine to sample and appreciate through a series of toasts and deep, lingering gazes between me and the three men.

At the same time, I got a bit provoked by Ruben's role. What Rebecca had said about him taking charge of me and my life by attributing the two other roles to two of his friends circled around inside my mind. It came up when I felt how his friends followed his smallest wink. Then I forgot it when he caressed me or paid compliments to me. But then again it came up, when I realized how the whole evening was happening according to his wishes.

After the courses, we were satiated, both physically and spiritually. I was giddy from the wine and the excellent company. We rose from our chairs and Ruben clapped his hands once. Immediately there was a waiter at each chair.

~~~~~~~~~~~~~~~~~~~~~~~~~~~~~~~~~~~~~~~

We left the banquet hall and retired to the library, which was slightly smaller than the banquet hall but no less grand. Bookshelves lined the walls from floor to ceiling and an elegant wooden sliding ladder allowed access to the highest shelves. Vivacious classical music played but from what source remained invisible to us.

In the middle of the room was a beautiful Chesterfield sofa with matching chairs arranged around a low mahogany table which was set with coffee and chocolates. To the right of the sofa was a globe in a polished mahogany stand. The globe was half open and inside were several bottles of Cognac, Armagnac, Calvados and other liqueurs.

"Have a seat," Frederic said, pointing to the sofa. Ruben and I sat on the sofa and the butler served coffee and *petits fours*. Frederic and Ruben studied the bottles, trying to decide what to taste first. They recommended the Cognac XO, but the Calvados was also unrivalled, they said. I asked for a Calva and they began discussing whether or not Cognac XO was truly superior to the Cognac VSOP that was also there.

"If you sip the two side by side, you can instantly tell the difference," said Ruben indignantly.

"But is it worth the difference in price when they are really so close in taste to each other? The next day, do you really remember the taste?" Frederic asked with a wry smile.

Anton was busy with the books, and after a short time he brought three to the coffee table.

"Anton, what can I offer you?" Ruben asked.

"For me, I prefer the Armagnac. Cognac drinkers are such snobs."

The friends smiled at each other.

"Here you are. What have you brought us, Anton?"

"Well, it's difficult to choose in a library filled with masterpieces, but *The Importance of Being Earnest* is a must."

The men laughed and I smiled politely influenced by their feeling so close.

"And then I came across this. It's been a long time since I've had it in my hands, but it's perfect for our lovely guest," he said, looking over the top of his glasses and then he continued, *"A Room of One's Own,* by Virginia Woolf. And it's a first edition from 1929, signed by Ms. Woolf herself." He leaned over to the sofa and showed me the signed book.

I smiled and was impressed. Not only by the signed first edition, but by how well he had understood what I like.

"And we'll wrap it up with a little pearl: Chapter 9 of *Madame Bovary,* where Rodolphe Boulanger has been gone for six weeks without giving a sign of life. He comes to visit Madame and convinces Monsieur le Docteur that his wife needs a ride in the forest, and that he would be willing to assist . . . a stunning piece of literature, and you are fortunate enough to hear a translation of the rare original edition of Revue de Paris in which it was published before the book came out," he said, pointing to the magazine beside him. "The first chapter came out on October 1st, 1856, and it was published in increments until the last chapter was published on December 15th. The book was published in April of 1857 and quickly became a bestseller, doubtlessly due in part to the lawsuit against Gustave Flaubert for distributing indecent documents.

"Sounds promising. Cheers," said Frederic.

We toasted, and Anton took off his dark blue suit jacket, perched himself on the arm of a Chesterfield chair and began reading animatedly from *The Importance of Being Earnest.*

His reading provoked great amusement among his two friends who knew the book by heart and chimed in enthusiastically from time to time, especially Ruben. My affection for him began glowing strongly again. On the other side of me, Frederic drew patterns with his finger on my stocking in plain sight of the others. I looked at him and he flashed me a smile. I smiled back, feeling that his attention intensified my feelings for Ruben and for the entire evening. Ruben looked at Frederic's hand on my thigh and smiled.

When Anton had finished reading he put down the book, picked up another and moved next to the globe where he began reading from *A Room of One's Own.* He proceeded to read the book's pivotal passage—where the heroine gets a room of her own and can refuse to participate in the goings-on of the house. It was great listening to a man reading that passage.

Afterwards Ruben pointed out how essential it is for people to have a room of their own, a place where they can be alone with themselves and their soul.

Anton sat down next to me and put his arm around me. So there I was sitting between two men who were both caressing me while I was looking at Ruben who got up and stood in front of the fireplace reading *Madame Bovary* to us.

By the time Ruben had finished the excerpt, I wanted Frederic and Anton to leave so that Ruben and I could be alone and explore our desire. But before I had a chance to finish my thought, Ruben stood up and clapped his hands. The doors opened. Frederic and Anton got up and left the room bowing to me and Ruben.

Ruben extended his hand to me. I stood up, a bit shaky on my feet from the wine and the Calvados, the words of literature ringing in my ears and the sensual companionship. We left the room and ascended the wide white stone staircase in the foyer, passing by doors on the first floor and proceeding up the next flight of stairs. He held my hand in his and I stroked his arm.

At the top of the second floor, we arrived at a room that seemed to be used for storage. I didn't understand why he stopped there with a perplexed look on his face, and I was about to pull on his arm to get him out. But then Ruben succeeded in opening a door in a huge armoire in the room. It just stood there, seemingly innocuous. "Come," Ruben said, opening one of its doors. Then I understood that it was a secret passageway. The armoire wasn't an armoire at all: inside was a graceful wooden staircase leading up one more flight.

He went up first. At the top of the stairs was a large room, and in the middle was a raised round platform on which was a four-poster mahogany bed with a velour roof hanging above it in various shades of ruby red. On one side of the room was a large, white porcelain fireplace, over which hung a gold-framed mirror. A fire was burning in the hearth, which meant that someone had prepared the room for us. I had to pinch my arm to be sure that this wasn't my wedding night—all the ingredients were there!

The bed was covered with a thick white silk bedspread and a lot of cushions in beautiful red, orange and golden shades. Ruben stopped at the entrance to the room, pulled me toward him and kissed me deeply.

"You are such a beautiful and smart woman," he said to me. "I am drawn completely to you."

"Thank you for a lovely evening!" I said. "My plans had been somewhat different than yours, but this is surprising and wonderful. You fooled me. I don't know how I underestimated you."

"It's not over yet," he replied, leading me deeper into the room.

We glided through the room, kissing and caressing each other. He loosened his tie and tossed it aside. Slowly and without touching his skin, I undid the first button of his shirt, then the second and third. At the fourth I let my fingers skim across his chest and kept unbuttoning him. When the shirt was completely open I grabbed it by the collar and pulled it over his shoulders and down his arms, letting it fall to the floor. I looked at him standing there and a warm feeling spread throughout my body. The sight of his naked torso over the waistband of his dark trousers turned me on and I began running my fingers along the inside of his waistline.

Our breaths became heavy and uneven as our arousal grew. We approached the bed. When we reached the platform he stopped. He grabbed my shoulders and led me onto the platform where he began to undress me. My clothing fell to the floor piece by piece. When I was nude, he took a step back and looked at me, his eyes glowing with desire. I sizzled under his gaze. I wanted him; I wanted him now. I stretched my arms toward him but he was faster. He wrapped his arms around me and swung me in the air. I grabbed his head with both hands, but he whispered, "Let go."

So I let go. And the next thing I knew I was flying through the air and landed on the pillows. He smiled and stood on the platform at the end of the bed, slowly unbuttoning his trousers.

He took them off slowly and sensually. Watching him from my reclining position opened my floodgates.

Ruben stood nude at the far end of the bed, his lance proud and straight and so full of lust that it was almost trembling. He looked at me and smiled, reveling in his own nudity and me lying there watching him. He stood for a few seconds, then bent and kissed my feet. He kissed me up and down my entire body, sending waves of pleasure throughout.

I became aware of a movement next to me and turned my head to look. It was Frederic without clothes on! And with a cock that was as large and throbbing as Rubens. And on the other side of the bed stood Anton naked and erect as nature on one of its best days.

Wow!

I looked at Ruben.

He smiled at me.

I looked at Frederic.

He smiled at me.

I looked at Anton.

He smiled at me.

A cautious smile spread on my lips.

"Lay back and relax," said Ruben, "we will give you the royal treatment like you may never have been treated before."

Tentatively I lay back on the pillows and wondered how and when Frederic and Anton had come into the room. Had they been there all along? Had they seen Ruben and me undressing each other? It was a bit too much if they had, but at the same time, I noticed that it excited me. I looked at the three men. I thought that I could just get up and leave, or I could lay back and receive. Now that I had finally gotten three men, maybe it was something I should try. It also seemed at bit cowardly of me to just get up and leave. I might as well enjoy the ride, so to speak.

Ruben continued to kiss my feet and my legs and stroke my skin with a light touch that made me quiver. Frederic and Anton took each of my hands and caressed and kissed them tenderly and intently, and continued up the arms, while they whispered to me that I was beautiful and lovely and very appealing, as I lay there all naked.

With his other hand Frederic took hold of his lance. It was sexy to watch him caress himself. On the other side of my body, I felt Anton. He had crawled into bed with me and his hands caressed my breasts, which swelled avidly. He began kissing my nipples and I felt his hard member, which was thick and throbbing against my body every time he moved. I grabbed his cock and he moaned when I got hold of it. Frederic whispered to me that I was clever and lovely and that it was wonderful to be next to me. Then I registered that Ruben had stopped his kisses and now just stood at the end of the bed with his cock raised, watching his friends and me. I moaned and felt that I would burst.

Frederic then got up and I followed him moving to the head of the bed, where he approached me offering his cock to my mouth.

"Not yet," Ruben said to Frederic. "Lick her."

"And you do this," Ruben said to Anton, and showed him two fingers. "I'm sure she'll love it," Ruben said looking at me.

I continued to try to understand and rationalize what was happening, before I just gave myself up to the total enjoyment.

Frederic licked me as I have never been licked before. He was soft and caressing with his tongue and then more insistent. I had one orgasm, and one more and all of a sudden I started squirting while another orgasm filled my body. It was awesome.

"Yeah," said Frederic and stopped licking.

Anton then inserted two fingers in my vulva, and moved them back and forth so I dissolved into ecstasy. Three orgasms he gave me. Ruben watched us every now and then commented on how wonderful I looked when I stretched my body in yet another orgasm.

Without my noticing it, Ruben had now squeezed himself behind me so my head was resting in his lap. He stroked my hair and kissed me and said, "You are such a hot, sexy and wise woman."

I smiled at him.

"Is it too much, or you can take a little more?" he asked.

I got nervous but the next second I was longing for more. I felt so satisfied but still my curiosity soared. Could I take whatever came? What were they planning to do? I knew instinctively that I had to have confidence if I wanted more. I looked at him and felt a deep desire. I smiled gently and said to him "More!"

He smiled and said to the boys, "Alright, we change tracks."

The other two looked at us, as Ruben nodded and directed them.

Then he got up, and went down to the foot of the bed and ordered me to get down on all fours. I obeyed and went down on all fours right at the edge of the bed.

Frederic stood at the left side, and Anton lay at my right side.

I looked at Frederic and saw that his cock was right at my face. I looked at Ruben who nodded and said, "Yes, suck it."

I took him in my mouth and licked him. At the same time Anton caressed my breasts, as Ruben slowly kissed my pussy and began to stroke it gently with the tip of his cock. I licked Frederic and he groaned. Anton caressed me and I groaned. Ruben went in a little bit and then out again and back in, and then out. It felt so nice. And suddenly it happened. He penetrated me and filled me so fully that I squealed. He drove back and forth and held me tight on the hips and yelled "let go" to me.

At that moment it was as if there was an explosion in my head. It catapulted me into my subconscious, to a place where I had never been. My pleasure was so different than any other I had experienced. I was disarmed; all rules were broken. I wasn't in charge of what was happening in the room, but there was no doubt that I was at the center of it.

Colors, forms and figures flew and merged with one another. Suddenly a dream from my childhood came back to me. In the dream I am standing amidst a flock of imaginary animals, all of them with round bodies. They moved around me, all of them constantly changing size, going from tiny to gigantic. Sometimes there was only one animal and sometimes there were many that were swelling and almost squeezing me to death. I reached out for Ruben. I needed him to hold on to me so I wouldn't get smashed, but I couldn't explain it to him.

I saw that he nodded to the other two, and while Ruben took me so firmly yet tenderly, Anton and Frederic were stroking themselves. My body was sputtering with desire and Ruben was pushing his hard member further into me. He came just as I hollered with the intensity of my orgasm and his two friends likewise climaxed, shooting their semen over my body.

Ruben took me in his arms and the imaginary animals disappeared as I slowly came back.

A while later, or maybe it was much later, only Ruben and I remained in the room. We opened our eyes at the same moment from a warm, cozy, wet, after-sex sleep. Great waves of happiness rose in me and I remembered how different the evening was than I had imagined.

~~~~~~~~~~~~~~~~~~~~~~~~~~~~~~~~~~~~

This morning, I woke up in the bed next to Ruben. He was awake and he took me in his arms and kissed me passionately. Then he held me at arm's length and took in my naked body and I became aware of my love handles and my round belly and my thighs, but I don't think that was what he saw.

He burst out, "Your body is even more splendid than I could have imagined. You are so sensual, so womanly. I've dreamt of making love to you since I met you at the estate."

"Why did it take you such a long time?"

"I just came out of a relationship and I had been looking forward to being alone for a while, but you changed my plan."

I smiled at him.

Gently but firmly, he began caressing my breasts, whispering "I think you're a gorgeous and intelligent and I wanted to make you squeal with delight."

He began caressing my throat and without being asked, he complimented my body. The curve of my breasts, he said, was like the roundness of the softest silk pillow. He longed to rest his head on it; my skin was aglow with life and energy, and the elevation of my vulva was so inviting.

Every time he mentioned a part of my body I moved my hands there. Slowly and without ceasing his adorations, he drew nearer to me. I trembled with longing. When he finally slinked towards me like a panther, and we exploded rainbows together. It was as if we were flying through infinity, unified with each other and everything around us.

THURSDAY, JUNE 25TH

A Friend's Pact?!

TODAY RUBEN AND I had breakfast after spending all day yesterday in bed together. Then he gave me a lift home early so I could change before going to work.

The last thing Ruben said when he dropped me off was that it wouldn't happen again.

"What do you mean?" I asked.

"When Frederic, Anton or I meet a woman with whom we want a relationship, a welcome dinner is made."

"So last night was the fulfilment of a friends' pact?!?"

"You might call it that."

"Have you always done that?"

"We also did it for Anton's wife."

"But why?"

"The three of us had our sexual debut with the same woman. We were 17 years old and spent our summer holidays on Møn, as we always had.

That's where we all met. That year there was a woman there—Marlene. She lived alone in an old, run-down estate and loved having some visitors."

"How old was she?"

"Five years older than us. She was spending the summer there, and in the fall she was going to the US to study at a graduate school at Harvard."

"And what happened?"

"I got lost in her park one day and suddenly, there she was on the path in front of me. She invited me home for coffee and two hours later I was no longer a virgin. When she heard that two of my friends were there too she instructed me to send them up, one at a time; one the next day and the other the day after that. She gave them the same treatment. And then she started from the top with me again. Once in a while she took a break and we didn't hear from her for days at a time. Can you imagine how close we three young men were to exploding when she turned up again?"

"I sure can," I answered, smiling to myself.

"She was gorgeous. She taught each of us how to satisfy a woman—it was sublime. And of course we talked about it afterward—every time! That kind of thing bonds men. But then when the two months were almost over, she invited us all over for dinner, and the evening ended with a *ménage à quatre*. We were all so intimidated at first, but we got used to being naked in front of each other, with her at the center or our desire."

"What happened to her?"

"We haven't seen her since."

I suddenly felt that this was all becoming a little too much. It seemed like I had just been a prop in a private ritual Ruben and his friends were having.

"I'm not sure I really like this," I said.

"What part don't you like?"

"It seems like you want to control me, by arranging your two friends to fill two of the roles in my model. And then making me another conquest for the three of you to have together."

"And you performed very well."

"And what is my next part?" I asked.

"It's up to you. You know in Severin's World, it's all up to you."

"I'm not really sure it is a world for me," I said before thinking it through.

"Okay, suit yourself. You don't have to."

"Well you know, I'm really looking for deep relationships with each of my three men. I'm not looking to be somebody's tool."

"No problem, bye-bye," he said. Then he turned around, got in his car and drove away!

I was really shocked and just stood there looking at his disappearing car. What had just happened? Where had I missed out?

~~~~~~~~~~~~~~~~~~~~~~~~~~~~~~~~~~~~~

I've been thinking about it for a while now. And I'm not really sure what happened. Or how I feel about it. Last night I decided I should update my board to this:

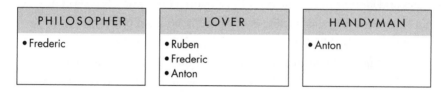

PHILOSOPHER	LOVER	HANDYMAN
• Frederic	• Ruben • Frederic • Anton	• Anton

But tonight it seems more like I should update it to this, given that I am back to Square One with all my three men:

PHILOSOPHER	LOVER	HANDYMAN
• ?	• ?	• ?

I felt so many frustrations soaring around in my body that I knew I needed to move around. But I didn't feel like going out. I put on 'I Want to Break Free' by Queen and danced and danced around the house. Then I put it on again and danced some more. And again. That song makes me feel like I'm on top of the world breaking free from all restraints—including the ones my own dreams put on me! Then I danced to Aretha Franklin's "Respect." I had fun with Ruben, but it was his fun, so it lacked the respect I was seeking.

I put on 'One More' by Elliphant and Mø. I love listening to and watching those two young women behaving like men, behaving like women, being uninhibited, doing what they feel like, kissing, fighting, laughing while looking cool—thank you!

The two final songs for my resurrection were 'Run the world (girls)' by Beyoncé and 'Bo$$' by Fifth Harmony, since I really need to be the boss in my own love life again!

Back on My Two Feet with Three Men Again

I'M NOW BACK WHERE I started before meeting Ruben, looking for all three men. I've just looked at the latest responses to my profile about possible dates and cleared out in the ones I'm no longer interested in. I will now set up dates with the new entries, as there are once again quite a few.

Rebecca just called. She wanted to hear how far Ruben and I are in our future plans. I told her that the future had turned into past tense and why.

"Well, well," she said, "I wondered how long it would take for you to meet a polyamorous man."

"Poly-what?" I asked.

"Polyamorous people have more than one partner for sex. There are also polyamorous couples where both of them agree that they can each have more than one sex partner."

"Do they continue to have sex with each other?"

"Yeah, just like married people who have a lover or a mistress, except that they are honest about it," Rebecca said and laughed.

"What about jealousy?" I asked.

"Big issue also for polyamorous people. It's interesting how easily people feel left out, even when they agree that it's ok to have sex with other people. I mean, it's only because they know that their partner is with someone else that they have a problem. If they thought their partner was attending a meeting in the bank, there would be no issues. And maybe a bank is a good allegory because in some ways, that is what they are doing: filling up their personal accounts with pleasure while continuing their involvement in a relationship."

"Maybe they are just separating their needs as grownups into intimate sexual needs they can fulfill with other grownups, and their needs for having a family which they share with one person," I said.

"Maybe, but jealousy seems to be the most difficult part to get rid of."

"You sound like you aren't jealous?" I asked.

"Not really. I think the people I'm with want to be with me, and if they don't, then they will go somewhere else."

"And what about it if one of your affairs does that, I mean just gets up and leaves you?"

"Then I hope we had fun while he was still around," Rebecca said and laughed. "I'm aware that few people feel like me."

"Maybe you haven't really fallen in love?" I said.

"Maybe. But I want to congratulate you on sticking to your own values and not living up to that guy Ruben's wishes since that is the only way forward for anybody exploring new relationship models."

"Thank you," I said.

"So was he good in bed?"

"Oh yes," I said, "I never had such intense orgasms before."

"But you still dumped him?"

"I don't think I could ever quite relax around him with all his agendas, his secret world and more than one partner and all."

"Can I have his number?" asked Rebecca.

I thought a bit. Then I smiled because I could feel that she and Ruben might be just right for each other and said, "Of course, then we can always compare notes if you get the foursome approval, like I did."

Rebecca laughed and said, "Yeah right, thanks! So what now for you?"

"Back on the dating horse!" I said.

"Okay, anything lined up?"

"Yes actually, men keep contacting me."

"Great, looking forward to hearing all about it. Do fill me in!"

"Will do."

LATER

A Date with a Talker

I'M GOING ON A date with William. He is a candidate for my talker position. I wonder what he is like. His response was quite straightforward. He wrote: "Funny model you have, I would like to talk and listen, so let's meet for coffee."

Since I am back to square one, I don't have any expectations to this date. Which might be a good sign as my expectations so far have taken up most of the space. I had my romantic mold that one man needed to fit into, but I sense that that it has diminished to next to nothing after the symbolic wedding. Which is great! I also longed to surrender myself to a strong man. That urge is much less since I was part of Ruben's circus. Now I know that a strong man can also have a strong will that leaves me the role of passive submission. That may be fine in the bedroom, but it does not appeal to me outside that space.

LATER

IT WAS A NICE date with a nice guy. William was seriously interested in hearing about me and my model and my job. He talked in an engaging manner about his life as a successful salesman. The most interesting part of our talk was hearing how he feels stuck in his present position where he has been for eight years. Things are going fine and the sales are increasing but he feels restless. He had googled me before our meeting and found out about my CEO position so he wanted to hear my advice on his own next career move.

He didn't mention sex or a relationship. I asked him about it since his passive approach to that part of his life intrigued me. It was rather different from most of my other dates who all, more sooner than later, brought up sex themselves.

It turned out that William divorced two years ago and since then he has had an occasional affair but isn't really interested in any closer ties. He hasn't had sex for a couple of months and frankly speaking, he would prefer to have dinner with friends than prioritize another affair. His emotional needs are met by his having his two kids every other week, he told me.

I enjoyed meeting him and didn't really feel the need to go any further than the career counseling, so that was all fine. Now I'm off to meeting Rebecca and Karen, since apparently Karen has met a man!

SATURDAY, JUNE 28TH

My BFF's

IT WAS GREAT SEEING my friends. They have known me for so long, which means that they are not afraid to say exactly what they think.

First we talked about Karen and her new boyfriend. He sounds great and just right for her. I look forward to meeting him.

Then I told them that Thomas had contacted me again and wanted to have a cup of coffee with me. I was really keen on it. Rebecca was quite frank about her views of Thomas and me. She said that she never grasped what I saw in Thomas. He was not a particularly accomplished painter and he was not very loving to me.

"Well, I knew he loved me," I said.

"Yes, he just had difficulty expressing it, right?" Rebecca said.

I got tears in my eyes.

"You've always been a sucker for romance," said Rebecca.

"I think you have been addicted to romance," Karen said.

"You may be right, but things have changed after my three-men model," I claimed.

"In what way?"

"When Thomas told me about the affair, he also said that he couldn't feel me. I didn't understand it at first, but since then I've understood that I was too preoccupied with him and what others were thinking of him and me. I was also too focused on his life and him becoming a successful painter. In this way, I expected a lot in return without actually saying it. My three-men model has changed that. When I meet a man, I look at him realistically now. I force myself to be frank about what I want and don't want in relation to him. And if a romantic mold starts to form itself in my head and I try to squeeze him into it, I immediately stop myself."

"Good for you!" said Karen

"And I only kiss if I can't help it!" I laughed.

"Well, of course," Karen said.

"That was not so obvious for me earlier."

They stared at me.

"Why not?" asked Rebecca.

"Well, it was part of this romantic storytelling that I started in my head as soon as I saw a man who was in any small way acceptable to me. I can't tell you how good my mind was at convincing myself he could change any quality I didn't like and become the man I was longing to meet. I kept at it again and again, and with Thomas it was even so much that I refused to see the signals that he had met someone else."

"And how is it different after the three men?" asked Karen.

"First of all, I have to face reality now in order to find out which of the three roles a man wants to fill or that I think he is best at fulfilling."

"Go on."

"Second, I can no longer follow a clear path in dealing with the men, since I'm not used to dealing with three men. That means I have to focus on what I want and not what they want. Once I know what I want, I'm much better able to say yes or no to suggestions. And I don't have too many expectations towards the men. They like getting a clear answer and it is much easier to do since I no longer have so many expectations going on in my own head."

"Sounds good," said Karen.

"The third reason is that my sex life has seriously improved," I said and grinned.

"How so?" Rebecca asked.

"I had absolutely unrivaled orgasms with Ruben and his friends even though I'm not in love with the guy or with his friends and am probably never going to see them again. I've also had other interesting sexual experiences, for instance with a handyman on my kitchen table, with a Belgian guy with whom I did some role switching, and I had the best sex with my former boyfriend Peter after I started using my model. And I could have had sex with a lot more men, if I wanted. Sex just like I want it, that is a big change for me and much more fun," I said.

"So do you want to continue having three men?" asked Karen.

"Oh yeah, it is the perfect model for me," I insisted.

My BFF's didn't contradict me.

LATER SATURDAY

A Surprising Party

ONE OF MY EMPLOYEES, Rita, turned 40 today and she threw quite a big party. There was a delicious buffet, great drinks and a fun DJ who played music that got a lot of people dancing. At the party, I had been talking to a number of my colleagues from work when a man suddenly walked up to me. I noticed him out of one eye—and when I faced him, I saw that it was Oscar, Rebecca's brother.

We hugged and I asked what he was doing here. He told me that he had started his own company and he was now looking for an office and was considering using my agency. He had been here to see the premises earlier today, and apparently Rita had shown him around. They hit it off nicely, so she had invited him to the party and there he was.

His company will be selling 'Stress prevention programs' to managers. This gives Oscar the chance to combine his knowledge of management with yoga and help business people who have too much on their plate. I welcomed him to our offices and wished him luck. He asked how I was and I told him that I was still practicing my three-men model.

"What do you want to achieve with that model?" he asked.

"Clear expectations," I answered.

"I've always had clear expectations of you."

"And they are?"

"That you be yourself."

"Yes, but . . . "

"But what?" he asked.

"I'm not so good at being myself with a man."

"Why not?"

"I was raised in a culture where you have to take care of the man, first."

"That sounds good."

"Yes, but I'm also brought up in a culture where women and men are equal."

"That sounds good, too."

"Well, I have yet to meet a man who will do as much for me as I will do for him," I said.

"Maybe you are doing too much and therefore expecting too much back?" he asked.

"Yes, exactly. The three-men model helps me keep a cool head."

"To me, it sounds more likely that your heart remains cold."

"What do you mean?"

"It may well be that you can have your way with the men, but I don't think you can experience a deep, loving relationship with several men at once. It requires a lot of effort just to have a deep loving relationship with one person," he said and looked directly at me.

I found myself looking into his eyes, and felt that he had struck a chord deep within me. Maybe this is not so surprising given the fact that we have been attracted to each other since childhood. But all of a sudden, it felt like my model was actually too small, too limiting. It suddenly struck me as a way for me to get *my* will, but it was a 'me' that would always be alone.

Nevertheless, I decided that he was wrong and told him so . . . but a little doubt began to nibble away inside me.

He said that many men would respond to me and accept my model in order to get sex. They were not interested in the other two areas. I disagreed with him, but he insisted, saying that men don't need women for such specific areas like chatting and handiwork because either they do it themselves or they call a friend to talk to and a handyman to fix the house. The only thing they cannot do themselves is sex, or if they do, it is not as enjoyable or fulfilling.

When I got home, I lay awake a long time thinking about our conversation. I sifted through my mind and evaluated all the experiences I'd had with men, experiences that have made me much more aware of what I longed for. And suddenly his words hit me, since I still long for deep love. The love with one person, where you understand each other and respect each other. Where you desire each other and feel a great tenderness and care for the other's best interests. Where you are pleased with your beloved when he achieves a goal he has worked on for a long time. Where you shudder when he rubs his fingers over your belly and slowly but surely approaches your lap. Such a love unites the physical, the mental and the emotions.

I'll try to test what Oscar said in the coming dates. Maybe my model is a great woman's way of getting what she wants without paying for it. Though so far, I admit I've mostly not gotten what I wanted but what my dates wanted. Wonder whether Oscar is right about men only being interested in sex and not caring about the other areas. My next date, for instance, is with Sam who is a handyman candidate. He'll come to fix the leak in my bedroom ceiling. There are also a number of other responses I have to look into.

I realize that I must be able to find out how to use my model to create one or more deep loving relationships, since that is what I long for.

30 Bucks an Hour

SAM IS IN THE midst of fixing the leak in my roof. He contacted me and said that he was willing to do one practical thing for me to see if our chemistry was right. Last time it rained, water came through the ceiling in my bedroom, so I asked if he could fix that.

Right now it seems like it, since he is hammering away upstairs.

I just went up to offer him coffee. He said yes. So I'll better make some. He also asked if I had any ceiling paint so he could make it look nice after the repair. Must check if I do.

LATER

AFTER HE WAS DONE, I went upstairs with a couple of beers. His repair looked really great and was almost invisible. He had covered the ceiling corner with paint and it was only because I knew that it had rained, that I could see a vague trace of something. He said it would disappear as soon as the paint had dried.

He opened the beers and we toasted.

"Ahhh," he said after taking a big gulp.

Then he started to take his shirt off! I looked at him quizzically. He realized that something was not right.

"Well, I thought . . . " he said and looked at my bed.

"No, I offer dinner, beer and coffee for your efforts," I said and tried to smile.

He took another slurp of the beer and then he looked at me and said, "That's not really my style."

"Fair enough," I answered.

"You are welcome to call me again," he said and continued, "But either we have sex afterwards or you pay me 30 bucks an hour."

"Alright," I said.

He finished his beer and then left.

I liked his forthright approach but I didn't really feel like having sex with him.

JULY

SUNDAY, JULY 6TH

Change of Scenery Needed

HAVEN'T MADE ANY ENTRIES in my diary for a week because I've been thinking about my model—and about Oscar. I don't want to think he is right about my model. So instead of admitting it, I am longing for a change of scenery.

I just called Rebecca because I need to clear things with her around Oscar. I told her that we had met at a party at my work and we were going to have dinner. Great, she said! I was so relieved. It turns out she and Ruben are a match made in heaven. They party most of the hours when they are not working. She sounded so happy.

So I went on to call Oscar. He was glad to hear from me. I said that I would like to have dinner with him since his comments on my three-men model had raised a number of questions in me. Fine, he said. And we arranged to meet tonight when Mille will be at Sebastian's.

I feel quite excited to be meeting him like this. Maybe it's because I've taken the initiative to meet. Other times we have met by chance or on his initiative.

LATER

OSCAR AND I HAD a great time together! He really is someone special. He claims that he will not settle for anything less than full commitment in a

205

relationship. I don't think I've ever dared actually stating it so bluntly. But I felt he rang my bell when saying it.

Oscar also rang my bell on overall terms. I felt really good around him in a quiet way. Not like with Ruben where I was never sure of where he would take us next. That was exciting in the beginning, but it made me uncomfortable after a while. With Oscar, though, I'm with somebody that I can trust fully, so I can relax and just go with the flow. We also talked at length about my job and he gave me a couple of ideas about how to improve the framework that the agency offers in order to attract growth entrepreneurs.

I feel that I may need more of him soon.

But he made it clear again that he was not interested in being one of three men for me. I did not tell him that during this evening he did qualify as a great talking date.

When I look back at my experiences, I cannot say that I have had any deep connections with men over the past months. I've had a variety of interesting, fascinating, horrible, or sexy encounters that have then stopped for various reasons.

Is Oscar right that close encounters with three men are not possible? Or must I keep insisting to myself that it is possible and that I just haven't met the right men yet? Or did I actually invent this model to rediscover my own wits about love, so I could eventually meet one man and make it last? Has it all just been my own experiment with me and love where I have used the men as guinea pigs?

SATURDAY, JULY 12TH

My Dad and Me

AGAIN I HAVEN'T WRITTEN an entry for a week, I've been so busy.

Mille and I just arrived at Uncle Theo's place. Or should I say *my* new place, since that is what it is now. In half an hour, Sam will come over. I hired him for his 30 bucks an hour to draw up a prioritized list of all the things that need fixing. We'll go over the list together and then he'll start fixing things. This afternoon my dad and his girlfriend Katherine are coming for coffee. When they leave they will take Mille with them since she is spending the rest of the weekend with them.

My dad is calmer these days, and he has not criticized me for my three-men model since that day in the café. Actually he has called me a number of times to hear how I'm feeling. Quite extraordinary for my dad to do that. Must be Katherine who is having a beneficent influence on him. Or maybe he still thinks that I'm seeing Frederic. Well, he can find that out later. I'm happy that things are working out better between us as it is important for me to have a good relationship with my dad.

Yesterday when I was trying to fall asleep, it dawned on me that there is actually a stronger resemblance between Ruben and my dad than I noticed when I was with Ruben. I now know that my fascination with Ruben and his strong will was related to the way I perceived my dad when I was a child. He was rather unpredictable because of his volatile temper, but he was never in doubt about the world and what role he should play in it. It was a controlling and dominating role. This combination frightened and fascinated me for years where I tried to escape that energy and, at the same time, I'm certain now that I went looking for it.

With Ruben, I connected to it at full speed and I had to surrender myself to him. But after the dinner party, I started seeing him more clearly and I did not appreciate what I saw since it was just the negative aspects of my father that remained—the controlling, bullying, domineering manner. I decided that I didn't have to accept the submissive role Ruben offered me. I could choose to walk away and build my own life just like I did when I moved away from home.

I want to take more steps toward creating the kind of life I dream of, and tonight I hope to take some steps towards that, since Oscar will be coming here for dinner! He and I have talked on the phone each day for a week now and I'm really excited and somewhat nervous to be alone with him tonight.

I can feel that I want to get closer to Oscar, and he doesn't want to be one of three men, so I need to respect that. Hiring Sam is one way of moving forward and it leaves only two roles for Oscar to fill. Something tells me he doesn't appreciate it when I talk about him and roles, so I guess I won't.

I've really enjoyed having three men as a model. It has made me much more aware of the trading of services that goes on between a man and a woman in a relationship. Wonder if it is the same trading that goes on when the couple is made up of two people of the same sex? Must ask the next time I meet such a couple.

Right now, I'll focus on how I can get close to one man without building a romantic castle and without losing my own priorities. I hope this one man is up for having close contact with a full-bodied version of me . . .

One Woman Two Men?

IT'S MORNING AND OSCAR is lying in bed, looking wonderful in in all his nakedness. He looks like a little boy inside a grown man. There's a vulnerability in him that makes me desire him, which is exquisite.

We had a great dinner last night. I had made a simple meal of shrimps on a bed of avocado slices, followed by steaks with oven baked potatoes and a homemade chocolate mousse for dessert.

He arrived and I told him about Sam. He smiled to me and I felt sure he understood the importance of my move.

He opened the bottle of wine, and we sat down and talked and talked. Then I served the entrée. And we talked some more. At some point, when I was taking out the dishes, he grabbed me and kissed me. I sunk into it but then he let go and we continued the dinner. When I served the main course, I kissed him briefly on the way into the room. Then I let go.

He made sure our glasses were always filled and we both made our discussion circle the room like a chain of lights in all colors. He talked, I talked, we laughed and then we reverted to a point made an hour earlier, and so on, keeping our discussion flowing so smoothly, without pause. We talked about our lives up till now, all the details that we had never shared. I told him about my experiences with The Thorn on my board of directors, and he shared having had a really annoying business partner that he finally managed to get rid of, so we could really compare notes.

At one point, he was looking all around the dining room and I couldn't figure out what he was checking out. Then he got up and walked into the next room and the next. I followed him. He stopped in a room with no furniture and looked at me and said, "I think this could be a beautiful library for all your books."

I looked at him and felt tears springing to my eyes. He was so right and I loved him for seeing that possibility. I hugged him and kissed him. He kissed me back and smiled. Then he took my hand and we walked back to the dining room for the dessert . . . and to talk about sex.

His idea about a library room for all my books added to my attraction to him. I sensed a desire to be really close and intimate with him. I told him that for me, good sex is a lot about the context. Nurturing each other's expectations, setting up an appealing framework, caring for each other, showing our desire for each other even when we cannot fulfill it right away because there is nowhere to do it. If the context is right, I'm ready to take off with a partner. He said that the context wasn't so important to him, but he needed a sensation of closeness and intimacy around the act. When I write it now, I wonder if we meant more or less the same thing?

Then again maybe not. For me, the set-up is paramount in creating a good sexual experience. For him, presence is paramount.

Around midnight we got up from the table and when I started clearing it, he said, "Let it go. We can do that tomorrow." Then he grabbed me, kissed me and our bodies pressed against one another. We mounted the stairs and by the time we entered the bedroom, I felt that the context was just right. I believe that he, too, found that we were close and intimate when we immersed ourselves in passionate lovemaking.

AROUND 4 P.M.

OSCAR IS TAKING A nap on the sofa, and I'm sitting here feeling good deep down in myself.

I believe that I've fallen in love with Oscar. I am so inexpressibly happy when he looks at me and smiles. When he says he's looking forward to seeing me, joy bubbles up inside me. I love it when he whispers in my ear, when he analyses things and tells me everything he knows. I love hearing him close to me, but still somehow out of reach when this closeness between us is so new. I want to be with him, to get to know him better in all areas of life.

Maybe that's what love means. To know myself well so I can signal clearly to a partner what is important to me, and then a man can choose to be with me if he sees that he can bring that. When I send unclear signals, it is easier for a man to read his own agenda into the relationship and for me not to get what I long for. Actually for neither of us to get it because the expectations aren't cleared or shared beforehand.

I've also become more aware of some of my own expectations about love and relationships. Who says that the only good things are the things that last? Nothing lasts forever. Why do so many people insist that things mustn't change, including how we love? As a rule, children need consistency while they're growing up; they can't handle too much change. But adults should be able to handle change. Maybe there's something wrong with the influences we get when going from childhood to adulthood. What if we gave all 18 year-olds an introductory course: *Welcome to a life full of changes!* We could tell young people that they will soon be confronted with a lot of new situations, there are experiences to be had and only one thing is certain: things will change.

Young people can be sure that they will need to meet different representatives of the opposite sex in order to find the right person with whom they can have a close relationship. When they do, there'll be a big change in how often, where, and when they meet with that person to spend time together. Later they may start building a nest. At some point maybe they'll have a child, and that will change everything again. Their education, jobs and careers will be full of changes. Things will change when their children start school, and then the children become teenagers, or they get a new boss at work, or their health isn't what it used to be and so on. Basically, it's a long line of changes, and the only thing they have to hold on to is their selves, though that's changing, too.

Because change is a key parameter in life, it's crucial to develop the ability to understand myself, my priorities, my feelings, and my expectations and to be able to communicate what role I want to play in different contexts. I needed to get my priorities straight in regards to love, and deep down I feel that I have done so.

I could not have said yes to Oscar before my symbolic marriage event with Ruben, because my romantic inclinations would have cluttered my mind and heart. Now I can say yes wholeheartedly to Oscar. Last night I could even guide him sexually in a way where I felt good about my lust and it turned him on to feel my excitement rising.

It gives me a beautiful calm sensation inside to be able to be me with Oscar as he is.

I hear movement from the sofa and I believe Oscar is waking up from his nap.

Have just updated my board since I have a feeling this is where love is taking me:

PHILOSOPHER	LOVER	HANDYMAN
• Oscar	• Oscar	• Sam—at 30 bucks/hour

Must attend to Oscar and me.

See you!

About the Author

POULINE MIDDLETON has been a Modern Love coach since 2010. Danish by birth, she holds a M. Sc. in Economics and has worked and traveled extensively around the world, having lived in Paris, Algeria, Hong Kong, and been to 36 states in the U.S. She worked for several companies in sales and marketing until she decided to become a coach.

Pouline actually lived with the three-men model for a period in her own life. She has also conducted scores of in-depth interviews with people who live in either open or polyamorous relationships.

She is 53-years old, and has an 18-year old daughter with her first husband before they divorced after six years of marriage. She then had a number of long- and short-term relationships, leading her to invent the three-men model that she used to find love. In 2013 Pouline Middleton met the Danish videographer and still photographer Steen Larsen. They fell in love and married in 2014. They live on an old farm outside of Copenhagen, Denmark.

One Woman Three Men was first published in 2010 in Denmark, and is her first book to appear on the American market. She has written two other novels and a handbook of love called *Seven Roads to Love,* available as an ebook and print on demand. Her website is modernloveandsex.com.

We hope you enjoyed this book. If so, please share it with others and write a review on Amazon or other book review websites.

If you are interested in hearing Pouline speak or attending any of her events, workshops or webinars, visit modernloveandsex.com for information about schedules and dates. Workshops include:

THE ONE WOMAN THREE MEN MODEL: Learn how by clearing expectations and defining the areas where you are not prepared to compromise in a relationship you can improve your love life. This workshop will look into the details of one's dreams and expectations of love in order to find the way to a fulfilling love life.

MODERN LOVE: Get an introduction to different models within the concept of Modern Love to find out if any of them appeal to you. The different personal and societal challenges associated with living love in other ways will be discussed.

BOOST YOUR RELATIONSHIP: This workshop will deal with a couple's expectations towards each other. By clearing out some of the 'noise' that exists between partners, couples can identify what kind of life each dreams of living.

You can also contact Pouline at coach@modernloveandsex.com to set up personal coaching sessions.

FOLLOW POULINE:
Twitter: #modernlove, #1W3M, #AskPouline
Facebook: One-Woman-Three-Men
YouTube channel: 1W3M
modernloveandsex.com